Part I

Prologue

Unbroken Law

The Ahzai Court was a blur of shadows and blinding blue light that danced maliciously from mirror to mirror reflecting echoes of both the High Oracles and the Great Counsel. None who sat beneath their own reflection were younger than seventy-mortal-years, and none looked older than forty-five. Most shielded their eyes in shadow, few glared calculative at the subject Summoned—but when Anara Starfallen entered the Court: *all* held her gaze.

The fate of her people rest in her womb and the blood that empowers her existence, Anara is the last of the true Ahzai Breeders. She has the purest of bloodlines running through her veins and has the power to select her Ahzai male to mate with. After her, no true Ahzai can be born until she produces another Breeder to take her rank. She would inherit the powers of her mother and her mentor, grandfather and great uncle should they do one of two things: take a journey to Death's Cradle or become exiled to the Nexum. If Anara could manage to stay alive, she would be the most powerful assassin of all the Daeviti Realm. She could even choose Immortality and dine amongst the Deities and Entities of all the Universes—should the inheritance fall to her and she accepted all that is given.

"The acts of today reflect the judgment for tomorrow," by Law, you must take *all* of what is passed on, not just the gifts, but the curses as well. This also meant that their missions and punishments would fall to her—such as the one given to her on this night.

"Bring his head back," the Oracle hissed, "Prove your honor and loyalty. It is but love *lorala desi*, love is forbidden to the Ahzai. Love is the fall of our planet. If you fail, Anara Starfallen, the evils of all the Daeviti Realm will be released. It is neither the past nor the present you defend, Ahzai. It is the future we have to lose."

She knew that this mission would bind her to the Ahzai and she would forever bow to their Law. She is not only the greatest of allies, but she can also be the greatest of enemies. Anara pursed her pale lips and turned on her heels, leaving the Oracle chanting of doom and prophecy. She knew the Oracle was right. A month before Salzah's and the others visions Anara had received a visit from a Prophet: the rarest breed of the Daeviti Realm.

She winced remembering the man's ancient scarred face and burns whispering of a painful journey. His name was Samuel and she knew from the moment he opened his dry mouth to speak the painful words he had to deliver that he was once a Crier before he had been given his mission as a Prophet. Anara envied the Crier people. It was as though they were the only mortals with true humanity in the Daeviti Realm. They knew sacrifice intimately.

"Abandon your heart, Ahzai," Samuel rasped catching the fire in her eyes, "Love returneth when it is no longer forbidden…all ye shall receive from thy love is betrayal. Trust not what you see and hear, child—know the illusionist for what *it* is."

Being told that her love was forbidden specifically with the Darken king, Lukan; was a slap in the face. She had loved this man since she was a little girl leaping from dream to dream. If the future was foreseen with such turmoil, they should have never let her cross paths with the Darken to begin with. It was written in the Crier's book that one must not lead one into temptation, and here, where she stands and breathes, Evolution tempts her yet.

She pulled her dark hair around her left shoulder keeping her back straight with her chin set—no thoughts escaping her mind. Even the Kiinak could not touch her steal mind. The Counsel's eyes glowed through hooded glares desperately trying to penetrate her defenses finding only a black abyss, churning in and out of existence. Whenever they got close enough to her perimeters, they found their minds absorbing into her barrier, feeding her shield with their own essence. They could not touch her or control her. She had entered absolute abandonment—a chaos of silence few are brave enough to explore.

Sacrifice love to save a universe, or let mankind defend their souls for once…

Nothing earned, nothing gained, Anara thought as she glared into an abyss of storm and tranquility she called home and entered the oasis she loved so intimately. On the other side behind the transport she had just taken was another Mirror transport which reflected only shadows and darkness.

Anara closed her eyes, and stepped through.

Icy chill seeped through her skin with a bite she had never known. She glared around taking cautious steps, melting the fresh snow on the ground. This is her home. She knew the land as well as her own reflection. The blue winter grass warmed to her touch, the Midnight Rose blossomed, seeking her heat: the land worshipped her presence—and would slumber in her absence.

Anara rested her hand over her stomach, rubbing it and caressing it. The past month had been chaotic and painful: even the scent of blood brought bile to her throat and threaten to spew from her ailing pale lips. She had given her heart to Lukan who disappeared leaving a conniving Damu to manipulate her. He even shifted so well into looking like Lukan that she had no clue it was not her King who kissed her, it wasn't the man she wanted to breed with. Another slap in the face, Anara knew this was the only way she could redeem herself. The Know-it-alls-of-the-Realm would have their way after all. The prince would need only shift one more time.

"Damu," she whispered, pouring a vile of red liquid over glistening black ice. She let the vile fall into the red liquid and stepped into the 'insta-port.'

He brushed the back of his fingers over her cheek and kissed her forehead, "You have decided."

"To sacrifice," Anara whispered as a black Irinoi blade fell from her belt and she prepared to strike, "Lukan must-"

Damu didn't hesitate.

"*Ah-mehn, Vias-el,*" the little princess hit the ground with a hard thud and was fast asleep.

"Come ye, Vessel," Damu knelt onto the raw Irinoi ground and lifted her into his arms, "*Bambai lai-het, lorala, Anara Starfallen?*"

~ 1 ~

It was a routine check, there was a flare in the sky and a shake in the ice—and then the door of a foreign solo-jettison pod fell open and a massively pregnant woman fell out. She had dark, blood-tinged hair, the kind that always seemed to have life of its own. He didn't reach out, aware that it could very well have life of its own and sever his hand from his body or poison him. That was all the Arkeon offered to its Soldiers, death and betrayal. The woman's cheeks burned red with what he assumed was fever, and her eyes glared with agony and blindness. She had yet to focus from the sedation of the journey—or she had been poisoned because she still had her general motor skills.

The Soldier didn't understand why she refused to give him her name while she begged and pleaded for passage out of the Breach. The Breach was Heaven in Hell…for murderers and control freaks. For a Soldier, born and raised in the darkness and fires of the Breach Wars, life on this planet was morbid and undesirable. Once you set foot on this planet, you became their pawns. He was born here. He was bred for only one duty—he was a Soldier. It was all he would ever be.

He would sooner die in his mid-thirties with an automatic strapped around his shoulder and an Irinoi-Blade in his hand than breathe the air of serenity or taste the shores of peace. When a Soldier is activated; they never stop until their life has ended—an end they all were born for.

…

The Freeze danced with the shadows of Anara Starfallen when the Darken's touch faded and she awoke in one of the 'solo-Pods' used for long distant transportation. She couldn't remember why she was in a 'solo-Pod,' and by the looks of it, she was in the middle of labor, she would soon be a mother. Memory evaded her as each contraction rippled through her body. She was lucky this land sent her a Soldier, Anara knew she would lose the unborn child if she birthed it now. The Freeze would consume the new life, feed off the warmth fresh from her womb, the babe still held *innocence*. The Arkeon devours innocence.

The deep voice of a familiar voice echoed her thoughts, *"Bambai lai-het, lorala, Anara Starfallen?"*

Her lips moved with each word forming in her mouth, "What have you done, beloved Anara Starfallen?"

The Ahzai blinked her eyes watching the snow drift across the vacant fields of a raging land. She had spent twelve hours in labor, dehydrated and alone while waiting for the unlucky Soldier who stumbled upon her on his night watch, to return for her. She could neither remember how she became pregnant nor recollect why her escape pod landed directly in the midst of the Breach's Arkeon polar ice cap. The Ahzai were forbidden to enter the Breach. What she did know was that her ankles were swollen and her heart beat frantically against the Freeze threatening to devour her and the unborn.

"Surely the Arkeon wasn't as deadly as the Soldier rumored," she thought aloud, fighting through the prisms that invaded her blurred vision.

She had been asleep and in space for nine frozen months. This woman was not due to wake for many years to come. Faces of her past glimmered upon the snow as her mind struggled to collect the lost pieces of her memory. Anara knew what attacked her memories, but *his* face evaded her as well, "In time you will return to my thoughts and I will hunt you and torture you for all eternity."

She prattled on in her mind forcing her agonizing bare feet to take another step in the direction of more polar void. Anara winced with each drift that sliced through her ankles, challenging her to give up, to sit and let the Freeze consume her.

It should have taken the man named Krypt three hours and not more for the journey. They could have taken the jettison pods out of the Breach if it was not for the event of her being in mid-labor, praying for the murderous snow to cease and for the warmth of the morning sun to show through the smoke of war.

"All dark things accumulate in the atmosphere of the Arkeon," the Ahzai glared at the horizon in search of movement. She was in no condition to fight a Drifter or even run from one.

This land was not her home land, but it would suffice until the matter of maternal needs had been dealt with. She was to be a mother—and was by no means ready for the task. Everything was a task for her; nothing done was ever her choice. She slept when told to, she spoke when told to; she even killed when told to—now it would appear she would give life even though she was still uncertain about being told to.

She took another step and felt the gravity pull her down, forcing her exhausted body to her knees. A position she only found herself in when holding a Silent Bow, moments away from releasing the poisonous, narrow blades.

It was time for the delivery, and she was as always, alone.

The Breach is one of the largest planets among the Daeviti Worlds. It is home to many civilizations and thought to be the center of new beginnings, from cities built with the highest technology to those who are primal and know not even the knowledge of language. The Breach shelters native and foreign refugee colonies, several belonging to fallen worlds and broken planets, sheltering those who are merely passing through but are entrapped by the politics of the land.

Around the planet are magnetic dust rings, the outer ring is the color of cerulean, the center glistens bright green in the summer and a pale periwinkle when winter has come—when the Breach is farthest from the Ursan sun. The inner-most ring burns a bloodied burgundy and the planet is split between a dry dust-bowl that burns during the day and freezes at night and in a few years time, the caps freeze over consuming half the planet with the Freeze; the natives of the Breach call this ring the gateway to Death's Cradle.

"There are many characters in the Breach, none are safe to befriend and few will offer a hand to save a stranger's life," the woman knew from a memory that tickled the back of her mind as the effects of her transport began to slowly wear off.

"Many resists, few ally...everyone plots their next move. Everyone sacrifices," Anara muttered, no longer feeling the strongest of contractions.

"Few succeed, " Anara returned to reality with the sound of another's voice echoing in her head.

...possession...

"The man must be a mental midget," she hissed while the pain from each contraction returned. Anara snapped her head back and forth, scanning the land, listening for the foreign voice she denied in her mind.

Every push made ripped the warmth from her lungs, leaving her shaking with an unshakable chill no infant should ever be born to. It was done, the child drew the same cool breath that she and her mother now shared and buried her face into her breast. Anara cradled her babe and gazed up into the starless sky...and swore she was hallucinating. She must have lost plenty of blood during the birthing.

An amber glow glistened like fire in the white of snow. It grinned at her and smiled to the newborn suckling her milkless breast.

The milk is more than likely frozen, Anara sighed at the odds of being stranded in a strange world with not but her unfit clothes and a newborn suckling at her breast.

The girl was not scared, fear was a sin she had never felt.

The glow began to solidify for a moment, long enough to show perfectly sculpted lips...lips that were oddly like her own.

"You are the Vessel I have been searching for, Anara," it sighed with mischief as it reached a hand out and placed it on the young mother's neck, *"All the others have failed me, but you...you will serve me well."*

Anara blinked her eyes in horror as the memories of this entity drowned her own and returned the ones lost.

"We are Kamenah," the voice whispered with seduction and surety, *"We will remain forever."*

"Forever is a long time," Anara remembered hissing, "I will not watch my heirs die before me."

Silence struck and flooded the mother with a searing light...

"You won't have too..." the serene voice whispered and faded to rest among the other lost memories.

...when she woke, she vaguely remembered how *time* had begun resisting.

And what do you know...the Soldier had finally returned.

...

Krypt peered down at the young woman who fell from the stars and crashed on the Arkeon territory during his second watch on the borders. It would be just his luck to happen upon a beautiful lady who was in mid-labor and refused to provide any information on who she was or where she had come from. The second watch always had something hidden in its shadows ready to rip their heads off if they let them get close enough.

Krypt knew he shouldn't have taken his friend's shift as he watched her stare frustrated and furious out into the endless snow drifts of the Northrun Breach. This young woman was leathal and would kill without remorse if she felt at all threatened...if threatened was even possible for her. She could be tricked, he summed, that was why she was entrapped on the Breach unwillingly—but was there anything on this planet that could truly threaten her?

"Thank you, Denny," he muttered as he knelt at her side and offered his black jacket, "Madam, scouts have been sent to retrieve your pod. It will be taken to base. Can you walk?"

"I just gave birth to a baby," she blinked her eyes and tilted her perfect little face up at him, "sure I can walk."

"We must keep moving. The Drifters will smell the blood and are more than likely hunting us as we converse," he nibbled his lip and sighed knowing that he would have to carry her as far as he could until Kai or Nathus got there on their last Skeet. He had managed to wreck the last four and therefore was punished with double shifts and a massive pay cut. The money didn't matter much to him or any single, childless Soldier, they lived on Supremacy supplement; it just cut into how much smokes and *dark water* he got to drink during the down time called sleep.

The woman laid her head on his shoulder while cradling the squirmy newborn and sighed at his warmth, "All I remember is that my name is Anara…Ka—men, Anara Kamen. I just turned nineteen in human years and I know that I should not have been pregnant: pregnant women are forbidden to travel by pods from…from….wherever I came from…"

He cringed, hoping she wouldn't begin to cry like all women do when they just have young and the abundance of raging hormones, but for some reason he laid his cheek against her forehead to offer comfort, "I'm Krypt Halen, a Soldier of the Breach. Is the baby a girl or a boy?"

Small talk, always use small talk to sooth a prattling woman, Krypt concluded the assessment he struggled to make on this woman-child.

He was drawn to her, any man would be, especially a Soldier of the Arkeon. They rarely see beauty and settled with the few women who are born a Soldier, and those women are as hungry as the men except they forget their birth control more frequently in hopes of a seven month furlough.

Anara sniffled and unceremoniously wiped her nose on his uniform, "A girl. With red hair and storm swept eyes…we called those of such colors, *anahl-kae-mahn*, 'storm of fire,' Ana will cleanse the land."

Krypt fell silent knowing that only one race spoke that language, it was the race of the *Ahzai*. They were a race born of ambassadors and assassins, the greatest breeders of the Daeviti realm. What he held in his arms was a plague, a death sentence that was forbidden to roam the Breach without a legitimate passport and an escort.

Krypt dipped his lips down to her ears and gently whispered, "You must never speak that language, Anara. I will explain when it is safer, but promise me, you will never speak your home language."

The Ahzai nodded with not an ounce of question in her eyes, "Of course, it is forbidden-" a memory returned, forcing her mouth to fall slack. Visions of light blurred her sight with a soft chuckle that warmed her soul, *"Silence is best when you do not know whom you accompany."*

Krypt found his arms tightening around this strange woman and he couldn't explain why he was feeling possessive over her. He needed to protect her and shelter her from the dangers around; the Freeze, the Drifters, the *Supremacy*. But he couldn't get attached, she was just another woman, and on top of that, she just had a baby and couldn't even remember who might have fathered the young.

"She is a beautiful little babe," he gritted his teeth glaring down at the infant who was staring dead up at him with wide alluring eyes and a curious milky grin of approval.

The sound of motors and the sight of the giant Skeet plowing through ash and snow vibrated all feelings away. He now needed to focus on getting them to safety without the government learning of what they really were or why they were here.

Even he didn't know what exactly they were here for…

"Yo! You were posed to watch, not collect!" A thick, solid black man leapt from the Skeet with only half a uniform on and sandals.

"Thank you, Nathus, for reminding me," Krypt snapped as they ushered the woman and babe into the Skeet. He smiled as he listened to her sigh from the warmth.

"Kai is at Half Peek with a medic crew to take care of them, what the hell happened? We only got half your message, Alton is bringing in the pod right now," the man Nathus studied Anara and the baby, "This ain't no Crier woman. This one glows, brother-man."

Krypt shrugged, challenging his comrade to contest his judgment. He had been a Soldier on the Northrun Arkeon far longer than the new crew shipped up. He might have trained with the majority of this shift, but he still had seniority when it came to Retrievals, "The pod crashed across the barrier. I went to investigate. Subject was mid-labor and begged amnesty and transport from the Breach. Subject was not coherent and still observes amnesia. The Freeze had begun taking over and Subject has begun the first stages of stasis. Infant is well and healthy," he added knowing this strange woman was listening to every word, "I believe with due rest, she and the child will be well for evaluation by moon-tide."

Nathus pressed several switches to the Skeet and the vehicle began moving a bit faster, "That makes no sense for a pregnant woman to be passenger in an escape pod. What destination did the Subject jettison from?"

Anara glared at Krypt, refusing to speak, "Subject has no recollection of boarding the pod. None of what world she comes from, and hardly remembers her name."

Subject. Subject. Subject. Anara smirked as she listened to them brief the past events, addressing her only as *Subject*. She had given a name to the first Soldier, it may have only held part truth, but it was a name none-the-less. Still, she was a 'Subject' to the unknown, a specimen to be studied. That was the way of the breach: to observe, experiment, imprison…and sometimes release to create havoc elsewhere.

Everyone has a role to play, she forced her teeth to release its clatter and focused on nurturing the infant which just peed all over her belly.

A Soldier was trained to have no connections with what they find on or near the Arkeon border. She understood this for reasons she only vaguely remembered. It was bred into their DNA and beat into their souls, they would never become more than the indestructible Soldiers they were born to be. Yet this one was different, so was the one driving the Skeet. They had an aura that separated them from the Soldiers she met long ago. They weren't robotic and drilled with duty and routine, Law wasn't twined into their ethics and code.

'Nothing good comes from the Arkeon, only mysteries and sorrows,' she could remember him muttering this as he left her to wait in the freezing cold to deliver her baby on her own.

But he did return, she winced knowing that she couldn't fault a man for *all* of his shortcomings.

He was doing his job. He could have left to never return, she thought and knew that that wouldn't be possible, not with the Supremacy. It was law to dissect and experiment on everything unknown, and what the Arkeon offers up is always unknown.

Anara shook her head to get the knowledge to discontinue its flow, now was not the time for memories. Now was the time for helplessness and forgetfulness and innocence.

'A past unknown is a future unwritten.' Those words were etched into her bones since birth; she knew this with every drop of marrow that flowed in her corporeal form.

"The Subject has a name," unable to remain silent, she needed to show ignorance for the ignorant.

Nathus peered through the mirrors and bowed his head, "Yes, Ma'am, we understand that. But by law of the Breach, anything that comes from the Arkeon cannot be trusted."

"Obviously I am not of this Arkeon. I fell from the stars," Anara hummed as she rocked her baby, "Whether I remember how or why or whence I came."

Krypt leaned forward to block her view of the mirror, "We understand that, Anara, but we still have procedures as well. The Arkeon is capable of summoning many dark and malevolent things from not only its heart but from the hearts of other worlds. It's a giant magnet that only seems to offer infinite ways to create hell for the rest of this planet and perhaps worlds."

Anara knew he was right and that she could possibly be another plague summoned to this world by the Arkeon, "My name is Anara. Please call me Anara."

The Soldier bowed his head to her and clasped her hand, a movement which shocked her, "We will call you Anara for as long as permitted."

Anara Kamenah, forever, she winced at the voice, "Anara Kamen."

The Soldiers exchanged a questioning look as she repeated her name as if trying to convince herself that what she spoke was true.

. . .

The Skeet reached Half Peek where lights blazed with warmth and life. Snow sailed across the flat of the glacier making it impossible for the conception of life to exist to those who were not familiar with the planet. The Breach was vast, but it was the polar caps that held it together. This was a planet plagued with life, and all the diseases that follow.

Nathus parked the Skeet and helped the medics secure the Subject onto a skid for transport. He listened to his friend reassure the Subject like a husband would a wife and daughter. His entire physical make-up shifted into a caring and concerned gesture. Nathus couldn't place the change in his old friend, couldn't place the man he was becoming.

"A newborn needs much love and nourishment," Krypt told her as if a mother would not know of such things.

Nathus shook his head knowing his brother in arms was growing attached if not possessive over the Subject. He would know of such things, he had done them a hundred times with offspring to answer for it. Love was a game well played with the proper women to shift around.

Krypt turned to his friend and brother in arms, "She really does not remember anything from before the crash. She couldn't even fathom how she was pregnant or why she had jettisoned. It's as if something clocked her, knocked her up and sent her on her way."

"That's messed up," a muffled voice waltz up behind them, "Of all the timing a victim could have fallen onto the Breach: Owen Dame has just arrived."

Krypt growled shoving past them, "Bastard needs to return to his *high towers* over his glass city. Damn it, Kai, this is our territory."

Kai nodded agreeing with the Soldier and pointed to the *Irinoi Queen* hovering over the compound, "Technically, he owns the Arkeon."

Nathus chuckled shaking his head as they marched into the warmth of shelter and technology, "But the border *is* Soldier-land. Without us, the Darken would invade through the Arkeon along with all the creepy crawlies."

"What's he doing up in Northrun?" Krypt muttered, marching down elaborate halls to enter a locker room.

The locker room was more like a bath house with storage capsules lining the walls, each decorated with battle scenes of Soldier history. The bath house lead to the training yard and on to the mess hall, past chow was the elaborate irioni chambers for the medical and experimental departments. Every wall held computer generated photographs and paintings of endeavors undergone and achieved by the Soldiers of the Arkeon guard. A Soldier *never* failed.

Krypt could sense that Kai had a clue of why the Dame had flown to the Northrun cap, but knew better than to ask. He dropped his gear onto the metallic floor and began stripping his blood soaked clothes off to shower and then to drown in the giant hot tub that awaited his company. It would be hours before he was allowed to visit the *Subject*, so he had no intentions on becoming sidetracked.

He waded into the steaming waters nodding his head to Nathus and Kai as they left, "Chow in forty, man. Ain't saving no buns for you."

Nathus rolled his eyes at Kai, shoving his ranking officer through the door, "I'll sample all the *buns* for you, brotha. Deck Squad returned with Third Watch," he let out a huge grin with a sarcastic moan, "Why you left Third Watch for even a second is beyond comprehension, there are some fine specimens in-"

"Yeah yeah, and they'll have your quarter raise going to their pockets before you cum," Krypt yelled back hearing them laugh while shutting the door and muttered to himself, "Third Watch is for blood sucking, irinoi grubbing whores."

"Not all of us are whores, Krypt," her voice laughed down at him with the unison gaggle she usually accompanied and shared many a cold nights in steam and sweat.

Krypt immediately grew hard at the sight that stood above him, "You're right, Leigh. Whore's don't get paid."

"Nick knew what he bargained for," Staze, her friend with the long hay hair which always stayed pulled back into a bun, cackled, or was that a cluck?

Nothing in the Breach was free, Krypt knew this all too well, "Ladies, I've just returned from watch. If you don't mind, I would like to have just a few moments of peace before I report for debrief."

Leigh winked at him glancing down to his man-brains that threatened to jump out of the water, "Are you sure you want us to leave?"

"Oh yes," Krypt wanted them to stay, "I want some alone time."

"A hand can achieve only so much," muttered the Dianan-born chick with a red scar down her cheek, "You know where to find us."

He refused to watch them leave and focused on the ripples vibrating in the water. There was always movement in the Arkeon, no matter how desolate and motionless it seemed there is always something on the move. Silence was bliss even if he just spent twelve hours in the freezing chill of Hell's testicles with only his thoughts to comfort and torture him. Now, all he could think of was the woman with the baby: the *Ahzai.* He shook his head forcing the thought from his mind hoping the Harvesters wouldn't pick up on his thoughts.

…

Her room was filled with the tinkering of electronics and beeping. The physicians who visited regularly finally discontinued addressing her as 'Subject' and acknowledged her as Miss Kamen. They also provided her with uniform, and swaddles for the babe.

She stood before the window glaring at her reflection. Her hair had grown past her shoulders and down her back like long blades of obsidian daggers that had been dipped into blood and dried. She blinked her eyes at the image and noticed her eyes had a glow to them. They were once an orange-walnut brown, but now they glistened with the deep burning amber that she could neither explain nor hide. Her flesh had healed within moments of being in the compound and her tummy retracted back into a tight, firm flesh of armor. Her exhaustion had completely faded. Anara Starfallen was reborn.

Anara turned in her new boots and watched her daughter's chest rise and fall with each breath…she had fallen completely in love with the little life she gave breath and existence to. In many ways she felt like a god—in many ways, she was.

The door clicked and entered another physician and a peculiar man wearing the glimmering black suit only those with great wealth and influence wore. She watched their reflection in the parallel mirror as they approached her with eyes filled with questions and doubt. When they stood directly behind her, she turned with a faint smile that was easily forced to her face.

Anara studied the man in the suit. He was tall, cunning and with complete control stirring in his eyes. He thirsted for power and knew how to obtain it, "Thank you for rescuing us. I understand that your border Laws forbid such hospitality when it comes to outsiders and anything that happens upon the Arkeon."

The man in the black suit smiled with welcome and mischief, "Outsider perhaps, but you did not come from the Arkeon. You fell from the stars as the men seem to describe your arrival."

Anara pursed her lips and returned to her little girl to puzzle some more, "You are not a physician."

"I am not a physician," the man replied still smiling but now held appraisal in his eyes, heat in his flesh.

Anara struggled not to gasp from the lust she sensed from him, "Only scientist and Soldiers patrol the border."

He shrugged, reaching a hand out to stroke the baby's rusty red hair but Anara stepped back to keep her child out of his reach. He smirked at the woman's response, "My name is Owen Dame. I own the majority of the Northrun border. I was informed upon your arrival; your pod left quite a beacon trace on its way entering the atmosphere. I understand you remember little of who you are or where you came from. We have analyzed your pod to *no* avail. Everything has been fried due to the magnetic pulse from the Arkeon. There were no symbols or markings on the ship or in the ship to clarify language or origin which leads us to believe that you were forced into the pod unconscious and in the beginning stages of a pregnancy. We ran a trace on your blood and found the high kryo-nanyte count in your system, as well as with the baby. It is a true miracle that the fetus matured during the frozen slumber just in time to be born upon landing. Leads us to assume the pod was set to land on the nearest livable planet or moon once the fetus reached maturity. Hence: you falling to the Arkeon."

Hence, I come from an intelligent species. Hence, whoever sent me knew I was pregnant. Hence, they will be able to track nine months of travel to locate point of origin if they haven't already. Anara summed up from his analysis and frowned, "And what will come of my baby and me?"

Owen Dame studied her for a moment and motioned for the physician to exit the room, "That is up to you," he turned her to face him, "I'm a sore loser when it comes to mysteries. I have a project underway and have need of Soldiers and I am thinking those who were involved in the rescuing of your child and yourself, would suit perfectly. From your cranial scans, your brain is functioning just fine if not above normal which means your memory loss is more due to an unbearable if not tragic event, which means you will slowly gain the memories of your past back. I ask that you collaborate, if it is not obvious that you come from an extremely intelligent civilization. You have much to offer *me*. I *am* a selfish man. I have no intentions on turning you over to the Supremacy to be gutted and laid to waste."

Anara peered deep into his eyes finding the burning abyss of ambition and pride, "Under what circumstances?"

"You *marry* the Soldier who found you, and collaborate with me," Owen watched her choke on the word: 'marry.'

"Marry," she whispered at the conception, "No. I will not mate a man I do not know."

19

Owen grinned with the abundance of mischief he seemed to possess, "Well, just pretend," he assured, "You won't be the only one. I will have to couple the Soldiers with the physicians who have been in contact with you and know of your existence. The details of this project will be briefed once you all are off and far away from the Arkeon. Now I have an entire shift to reassign, your part is easiest."

She nodded, not agreeing with the simplicity he claimed for her, and took his hand to seal the contract, "I will cooperate so long as my daughter is safe."

Reluctant to release her firm grip, "I will do what must be done to keep you in my fold."

Doesn't he put it bluntly, Anara grit her teeth as he bowed from the waist like a courtly gentleman of some civilization lost in time.

The haunting voice chuckled once again in her mind, *Anara Kamenah, together forever.*

...

Chow was hot, moist and abundantly supplied. The Soldiers of Second Watch inhaled their meal as if they sat on their death bed ready to fall into Death's Cradle with their Final breath. Nathus returned with another tray of barbeque chicken and red potatoes drowned in brown gravy, his expression slightly disturbed. Krypt studied him with his mouth working overtime on his steak and pepper salad, extra dressing and cheddar.

"What?" Kai peered up from his tray with a mouth full of hot rolls.

Nathus shook his head with dismay, "Mack didn't return from watch."

Krypt traced a snaking line across the table above his tray, "Drifters."

They all bowed their head, placing their right hand over their heart in a Soldier's salute to the dead...and returned to devouring their meal knowing that their next watch could be their last.

A short feast interrupted by a Crier boy with orders for them to meet in the Half Peek south tower. They took a last bite and Skeeted to the great tower overlooking the void that would eventually lead to land and life. The snow continued to fall and now carried with it ice frozen onto ash, any larger and the combination would fall like bullets raining down on the next watch.

Denny met up with them at the base with the rest of Second Watch. He rolled the icy ash in his hands like marbles, shrugging at the men as they approached with question in their eyes, "What the fuck you do now, Krypt?"

Krypt grinned at the question having the same feeling as the others. If something ever happened, he was sure to be involved with the hell that came from it. Denny was one of his greatest friends. They endured a lifetime of training together. Covered up Denny's marriage and supplied him reason to leave the Watch to tend the wife and children. Dealt with every 'baby-daddy' predicament Krypt found himself in on a regular basis when he was working the Third Watch. Thankfully, none were his...that he knew of. Thick and thin, most of the guys on Second Watch had been through thick and thin and most of them were due to return to Third on a routine swing shift. Even though the guard detail was switched up on occasion due to mysterious disappearances or a visit to Death's Cradle.

"Let's get this over with," Kai muttered as they made their way up the tower's frozen steps.

With all the technology, they refused to put anything electronic in the watch towers. It wouldn't make a difference, if they were attacked, power would be shut off and they would be forced to combat with their own two hands and feet. That was the way of the Soldier; they didn't rely on invention or evolution to fight their battles. They killed and conquered with their own flesh and blood. The people of the Cities call the Soldiers the *Irinoi Men*: men who have the great metal flowing through their veins. A Soldier healed faster than the average mortal and they were stronger than the average man. Even the women who were born of the Soldier's fate, few as that is, could be as powerful as the men in the ranks.

The door crept open and the men froze when they saw who stood waiting for them.

Owen Dame motioned for his lap dog to hand out black envelopes and waited for each of them to open and read what was printed within.

"This is bull shit," Nathus cursed as his blood vessels pumped and grew with each pulse.

"What the fuck, Dame? How'd you pull this off? An entire watch has been discharged of their duty to the Breach and Arkeon without so much as an accommodation?" Krypt growled balling his fist with a fury like none other. His temper was greater than the rest of the men and women in the room and everyone knew to stay out of his path when he sees red.

...

Anara watched from her shadowy corner behind the scientist and physicians who also had been relieved of their employment in the Arkeon. She smiled at the Soldier who had rescued her, for he had no fear for the man in the black suit; not caring what he had to offer, if there was anything to offer at all.

Owen had no fear of the man who was obviously ready to pounce on him at any moment. This, too, amused her as well. It seemed that they had feuded for much longer then just these tender moments and it intrigued her that the suit held so much control over the Soldier. Krypt would be powerless to wage war with Owen because he was a Soldier and it was embedded in his DNA to never rise up against the Supremacy or the tools of the Government. He would be severely punished along with everyone in this room, because she knew they wouldn't stop Krypt's rage, some would even help in the destruction of this dark knight.

"New orders," Owen smirked at the man, "You will be briefed at the Dame Tower in Eere View and immediately deployed to the Wastelands."

She didn't like the silence anymore than her little girl did. Ana began to wail at the stillness in the room, bringing the Soldier's attention directly to her. Anara shushed her baby and then whipped out her breast for her to suckle on. If you can't comfort an infant with voice, you shove food in their mouth and silence it with natural endorphins.

"Woe, there, just bring it out for the world to watch," a balding man with piercing blue eyes coughed and looked away.

"For all the god's sakes and every Celestial in existance, she's feeding her babe, Austin," the younger of the two female physicians snapped. She had long black hair with tender light auburn curls at the end, "Soldiers aren't the brightest. I'm Bioni."

Anara only smiled at her while she patted her baby's bottom while she fed and the other physician with short dishwater blond hair chuckled, "It's just a booooob."

"And that's Cara," Denny grinned at the woman named Cara who blushed looking away.

Krypt's eyes fixed on the strange woman and knew then that this whole discharge had everything to do with that particular woman, and if it didn't have anything to do with her, he was still going to pin the blame on her. He was half annoyed and mostly relieved. If he knew what was to come in the latter of his orders, he wouldn't be so content with the journey ahead. Marriage was one hell of a ride, even if it was just another role to play.

Dame Towers, Eere View

The flight out of the Arkeon had been sardonically quiet. Everything and everyone had their place on this journey and it appeared that anything Owen Dame offered was not in the least welcomed. For some reason she knew that each person on this flight would be linked with her future and many would find the Cradle because of her. They would infect those they contacted with her link so she could better infiltrate the intricate webbing of the Breach. Anara might not be able to Summon the second hand touched, but she would whisper to them and encourage them to act on her influence. It was an ability only the royalty of the Ahzai possessed. Her first touch, the men and women aboard this flight, would allow her to lure them into finding her no matter where they were if she needed them.

They had become pawns added to a far from vacant game board in existence. Anara hadn't figured in that her link was far stronger now that she had the essence of a goddess entwined with her soul and that when she Summons a soul they would answer to her like a Prophet on a mission, not just a calling.

Anara studied each passenger as they exited the craft. All unaware of the connection they now shared with her as she made a point of brushing up against each of their shoulders…or rather their arms because being a Soldier left them towering over her with biceps larger than her thighs. A few stood out more than the others. She would link with them on a higher level known as: *Aprati-imahs*. It meant they weren't just mere pawns, but they held more position in her strategy than a simple link held.

Kai, who is their ranking officer, had a charisma about him that Anara could not explain. There was just something about this Soldier that she felt comforted by. She grinned at the art of evolution and the ability to seep into controlled atmospheres. Kai would be the one who could get away with murder because his smile and words would ease any doubts that the action was indeed called for. He spoke with muddled voices to Alton who was the same rank as Krypt and it was obvious that Kai and Alton were the equivalent in companionship as Krypt and Denny. Alton was a tall dark man with huge hands, a giant scar running down the palm of his right hand. It had obviously been hacked off at some point in his life. He shared the same warm smiles and same silly words as Kai; so unlike the Krypt who was cold in his charm yet accurate in his ability to manipulate.

Nathus was a mental midget like Krypt when it came to common sense, but friendlier still. He had a flirtatious glow in his eyes like many of the younger Soldiers, yet still offered a stern 'in-crowd' attitude. Denny was all work and no play, his only concern was protecting his wife without exposing their marriage and family and still be able to carry out his duty because deep down he knew that his job was the root to their safety. And Cara understood this with her shy blushes and occasional glances towards Denny as though the next time she looked at him, he would not be there.

Bioni was another matter. She was blunt with her thoughts and held nothing back whether she was wrong or merely restating the facts. Yet, she had a need to protect like nothing Anara would have expected of anyone, especially a stranger. Bioni would whisper hints and suggestions on how to better take care of her daughter which lead her to believe that Bioni too hid a child and perhaps a marriage if not a relationship like Cara and Denny. Anara felt comforted by her words and considerations, and enjoyed every time Bioni rose in defense of those she kept close to her.

A circle is only a circle if all the pieces are linked and it only grows strong when you link the right parts.

Zende Dajan, the foreign ambassador of such and such, Anara came to address him even if he was a scientist. She didn't truly understand his purpose of employment with the physicians. She continued to draw a huge blank when it came to dealing with him. He wanted to befriend her more than the others, yet knew that too much too quick would ruin his passage into trust: Which disturbed her even more so...

This brought her back to Lance Haeden who was the perfect Soldier who asked for forgiveness for so much as a sneeze in the wind. Could killing be forgiven? Would his prayers be heard? Anara focused on how the light fell on his hair like a crown of silver Irinoi, freshly drained from the core and still in its liquid and lucid state: Strong yet malleable.

Lyle was Owen's lap dog. He would blend where he must and roll over when commanded; a foot Soldier, the one who kneels mindlessly. Anara often wondered if there was a brain missing from his head, or if he had been programmed rather than trained. She could admit that it was hard to tell, but then she would be lying. He was a puppet and cabable of being nothing more.

She pulled the cover from Ana as they entered the building. It was warmer in the Eere View towers that stood on the other side of the great ocean they had crossed. They turned what would have been a several days journey into several hours. The Breach was a large planet; transportation was created in *many* ways and Time was made irrelevant…infinitely resisting.

Attendants immediately separated them into pairs and groups. Denny looked hesitant as Cara was ushered off with Lance while he was accompanied by Alton and Kai. Nathus left with Bioni; Nick, Ron and Austin left with Lyle. Zende put on a lab coat and bid the other's farewell, he was an employee of Dame Industries—not a Soldier of the Arkeon.

Anara hung her head observing Krypt who obviously did not like the situation or the pairing he was observing. She offered a smile and then frowned, finally unable to keep in the information she knew, "He wants us to pretend we are married," she whispered as she moved closer to him as a lover would, "He has developed a new section. It has much to do with Project Control."

Krypt placed his hand on her back to comfort her, "That half-consort has been working on Control with the Supremacy since he drew *First Breath* and he won't stop until someone is able to deliver his *Last Breath* and send him to Death's Cradle for re-evaluation."

Krypt puzzled at her shock not expecting her to be so naïve. Owen was a snake in a human's body, and that was known by the universe. Her eyes glittered in thought and he knew that she would slowly regain all of her lost memories with time. He could see a universe in creation when he looked in her eyes. She was more than just an Ahzai.

They were escorted to an elevator where a man entered a code and exited the elevator before it took lift. Why would he do that? She didn't like the action any more than he did.

Anara began bouncing in rhythm with her infant to comfort the babe, "You know, I wish I would have remembered whether I planned this child or not. I can't even get frustrated when she cries because I know it can't be her fault she is in existence."

Krypt only smiled at her unable to speak. He was too tense to so much as loosen his jaw enough to lick his lips.

"Would it be so bad?"

He heard her whisper.

"Hm?" Krypt blinked his eyes staring at the digits that flipped onto the monitor delivering a 'bing bing' with every floor they passed.

"Would being married be so bad to you?" She said, never taking her eyes off the little girl. It was hard for Anara to admit that she was being insecure at the moment. That he would refuse her, and she, for some reason, couldn't explain the feeling. She hadn't even wanted his attention, before. He was a Soldier...the Supremacy's puppets.

He turned his head slowly to look at her, "No, I just know that I won't be a great husband. I am a Soldier, and duty comes first."

Duty comes first, she thought she would die.

Her life had turned around and caught up to her: *Duty. Comes. First.*

Isn't that why she ran a—Anara gasped at the memory that blurred her vision. She had been running away from her obligations, and in the process, the *It* situation she ran from gave her a parting gift and she had a feeling he did not know about the conception. She was bemused that she had accepted the link.

"Son of a bitch!" She shouted at the memory, the image of a man with power unimaginable: a shadowy figure with dark hair and ever-changing eyes with a black abysmal pool churning in the center.

Anara had only herself to blame.

"At least I'm being honest," Krypt snapped back at her.

"Excellent, we have this married crap down," Anara hissed, not explaining her outburst.

Krypt laughed, hysterically, "We'll make it work. If all else, we can prevent *him* from destroying the world."

The man in the black suit is planning war against the Supremacy, and doesn't even know he is a puppet himself. No human or mortal could rise up against the Supremacy of Governments, on their own, and succeed at full succession without the help of *greater* Power.

Anara froze at his accusation, "Can he do it? Would he?"

Krypt shrugged, lifting his hand to tuck her hair behind her ear, "He's evil with ambition. There are those who help others because it is right, and there are those who help others because they expect their loyalty afterwards. There is not a species out there that does not owe men like Owen Dame."

"Gods, there's more men like him? Do you owe him?" Anara glared up at him with wide eyes.

He felt as if he stared down at a child of pure innocence knowing that she was far from innocent and that her hands had more than likely dealt Death to more victims than he himself had, "I am a Soldier, Anara Kamen. I work for whoever the Superiors tell me to work for; even if it's a *Consort.*"

Krypt frowned just as their stop came. They exited the elevator and entered the long hallway of the thirty-sixth floor. The walls were painted a crimson red with long vertical transportation-mirrors hung every three feet. Anara grit her teeth feeling danger surround her. She peered into the mirror to her right and stopped as she stared into it. An island with nothing but ocean surrounding a great castle which cascaded with waterfalls that fell into pools of more water, rippled in the center of the mirror. When Anara took a step closer for a better view, Krypt gripped her arm and yanked her away.

"Don't touch it," he hissed, "it's a mirror transport to only Owen knows where. You touch it and you're going there whether you know how to swim or not. You take what you wear, even your child would be sucked in with you. If it is overlooking the castle, the receiving transport is in the sky, so you would fall to the water and die or eventually drown from impact unless you're entrance was expected."

Anara took a quick step away gripping her baby tighter to her breast, "Let's get this over with."

They hurried to the end of the hallway where the only room on the floor resided. She looked to the mirror next to this doorway and noticed a man peering through it at her. He had bandage wrapped around his mid-section with notable blackish-blood trickling through his shoulder blades. She saw sorrow in his eyes and knew exactly what he felt. He was trapped, he was a prisoner…and he had been there for a very, very long time.

Krypt tugged her into the room and closed the door behind them. Owen sat at a desk reading over a portfolio with earnest approval. He lifted a hand without looking up and motioned for them to take a seat. She could see Krypt's jaw tighten and stay that way.

Owen lifted his head up and handed Krypt the portfolio, "Do you, Krypt Halen take Anara Kamen to be your native wife? To serve and protect, till death do you-"

"Shut it and get on with my orders," Krypt snapped at the Dame's humor.

"It's all in there. I've already briefed the lovely Mrs. *Halen* on her new job. Incinerate it when you're done," Owen glanced at Anara for a moment and immediately looked away, finding a stack of portfolios to shuffle through.

He knew something and she could feel her gut clench at the thought, "Mr. Dame, where will we live?"

"Wastelands," Owen bowed his head, "Krypt will take care of everything, my dear. I'll visit bi-monthly for debriefing on the Wastelands, as *you* will do the same at the Tower."

That wasn't good enough for her, "What about the others?"

"Same-oh-same-oh, you'll keep in touch with them. They're okay. There is an address list in there as well," Owen stood and came around the huge cherry lacquered desk and lifted Anara's hand to his lips, "I promise."

Krypt bolted from his chair and shoved Owen away from his new *wife*. Anara smirked at the growl in his voice, "If she's to act my wife, I would appreciate it if you kept your slimy paws off her."

Owen grinned stepping away and straightening his suit, "Indeed, so how many more little tykes will you be kicking out, Soldier? The Breach is always in need of well-bred Soldiers."

Krypt winced while Anara stood up from her chair, resting a warm and steady hand on his shoulder and handing him her daughter, "Come, love, let's get *home*."

He blinked at the sincerity in her voice, for heaven's sakes, she sounded true, "As you command, *dear*."

Anara smiled at the endearment and nodded her head to Owen, "Thank you for these arrangements, Mr. Dame. I'll get right on top of it," she winked pinching Krypt's thigh.

Krypt wasn't the only man standing shocked.

Owen was now blinking with confusion and frustration as he watched her exit the room with the Soldier wrapped around her slender little fingers. He puzzled as the door clicked shut, wondering if she had planned this arrangement, the landing, everything. He watched them enter the elevator on the monitor that hung from the door, and rose once they had began down the tower. His business was never done, events needed to be set into motion for the Supremacy to bend and break.

The mirror next to the office door in the hallway glared at him. The bleeding man captive within, glared at him as still has the mirror, unmoving and unafraid. He crossed his arms to keep from clenching his fist as Owen stepped through and pulled a syringe from his coat pocket.

"Now, my little plague, I need some of the good blood to raise a few little demons of my own," Owen chirped as the man held his arm out, "Fallen and forgotten, such a travesty for the Guardians of the Criers. The other's had sense enough to flee; you should have fled with them back to the fading world of yours."

The man didn't wince as Owen drove the needle with precision into his flesh, "Ah, but then my work would never get done. You only delay my mission, little halfling."

Owen shrugged and tucked the syringe back into his coat pocket, "You will have your freedom, when my deeds are complete."

The man chuckled hysterically, "Never trust a Darken."

Dame chuckled back at the Entity that stood surely before him, "Who said anything about trust?"

The Entity purred as he stepped away from the half-consort, "Do you really think you can control *Her?*"

Owen stepped out of the transport and didn't look back. You couldn't believe half of what the Fallen spoke. They were the undoing of the Criers and the poison of mortality. They were the uprising of The Score. The Breach even now struggled to regain purity after the Fallen began to poison it with their thoughts and doubts. Control should have taken over the entire planet by now, if not for the Crier's devils. The Arkeon was to thank for that…it allowed the Fallen passage into the Breach's realm even though it was the Crier's mission to colonize away from their home planet to retreat the wrath of their God's demons.

Sacrifice the majority to scare the minority into flocking to the cities below. That was where the Darken came into play, they would inhabit the territory until the will of the people had been broken and Eere View, Traverna, Woke Free Base, and the Wastelands begged for protection. It was science that Owen knew best. He had no special powers or gifts like many he has captured, but his influence over the Supremacy secured his suit of armor. He knew the art of war and specialized in crumbling civilizations.

"And so they shall kneel," Owen glared down at the little brown ledger taunting him to dig deeper for the knowledge and power he sought within its plaguing pages.

4

"I am not going to put up with you more than I have to already!"

Nathus massaged his temples as Bioni screamed at him in her usually fits. Even before they were forced to assume the married life, child support had been hell on wheels with dry meals. He watched her run her fingers through her hair and lip complaints in silence while their daughter slept in the crib behind a closed door. Owen not only destroyed his hopes of transferring to Third Watch, but managed to exterminate his sex life. They had been the only Soldiers assigned to the Old Worlds. It was a shock that none had suffered any fatalities yet.

"You need to go."

He had heard this one too. But he knew that she would call on Anara and everything would smooth out, they would have great make up sex and she would be down his throat within thirty-eight hours after the rough sex and possible pregnancy scare. It had been six months after their deployment and he begged every god there may be to send him back to the black frozen hell of the Arkeon. He would rather his nuts freeze off to save listening to Bioni rip his cock every time their credit zeroed with every taxation due-period. Civilian life was murder for a born and bred Soldier. Nathus had only one positive and definite position in his existence: Duty.

"Hello? Get off your ass, start packing your shit, and go."

Five. Four. Three. Two. One.

Ring. Ring.

Nathus handed Bioni the phone, knowing who it was: *It was like ESP*, the woman knew when Bioni was in stress.

"Yes," it would start, "I know," and again, "I know," and again, "But she's still young, Anara, she won't miss him," pause, "I know," a frown, "okay," another pause, "Yea, I guess we can do that. Do I need to bring anything?"

Thank you Anara Halen for calming the storm before the war, "Who that?"

Bioni gave him the evil eye and rolled them to the sky knowing that 'who that' was a stupid question because there had always been one person who managed to call her when she was in the middle of kicking his Adonis tail out. Where she expected him to go, was beyond him. His orders were to maintain this marriage, and live in this dwelling...the barn?

"Okay, what we doing?" Nathus got up and began readying the diaper bag waiting for Bioni to give the pouty lips and go to the bathroom to shower and get ready to go to Krypt's place in the Wastelands.

...Pouty lip, bathroom, shower, pregnancy test, and car keys.

Nathus had their daughter bouncing in his muscular arms waiting for Bioni to latch her shoes and drive them to his saving grace. She said not a word to him but spoke only to their daughter.

"Yes, Mercy, daddy is a meanie," Bioni chirped, reaching back to offer a pacifier, "But he is still an okay daddy."

Nathus knew that was her way of making mends to a sour fight that would have not happened if not for the work of Dame Industries shoving them into the same household. Relationships work better from a distance, when you were a Soldier.

"Let's go see little Ana," Bioni smiled sweetly at her little one, "I think Auntie Nari is gonna have another baby."

...

Anara glared down at the test tube and sighed, trying to control Kamenah and keep her tucked tightly away in the confinements of her soul was exhausting enough as it was. The goddess slept snuggly in her body and mind. It was like taking two ten thousand piece puzzles and pouring them into a bag, shaking, and then dumping it onto a table for some poor soul to piece back together: the poor soul being the Vessel, Anara. She still felt the need to give Krypt the only gift that would save him from his future, a son.

She hadn't aged. She knew she wouldn't so much as suffer a gray hair like the others will. Anara knew it had little to do with the goddess, but everything to do with her heritage, her home world. The Ahzai was capable of collecting time, much like born Collectors collected all that exist. Her body would do it naturally, without her needing to Summon Time to lend her a few moments to breathe on. Her people were born survivors, they could adapt to *anything*.

She watched Krypt as he worked on his weapons, shining, buffing, sharpening, oiling and testing effectiveness. He could be wonderful at times, but others; he was a complete stranger; especially when he was called away for weeks to work with the other Soldiers on locating what they called the Eyes of Prophets.

A Prophet was a Seer who couldn't be swayed from enlightenment, unlike the Seer who can turn on a watcher without moments warning. Prophets were all linked as one. They know the visions of their brothers and sisters and even know the thoughts that traveled within their connected minds. A Seer was one individual and could be extremely powerful and useful to their own cause or they could create their own demise without a second thought. A Seer was unstable when working a vision to its full affects. Anara knew more than they did on this matter and had no desire in sharing her knowledge on the matters involving evolved species. They shouldn't know why or how a species was created. The Breach was after all, not her world but the world in which the goddess held interest in.

Mercy let out a squeal and ran to Anara's side. Anara knew her belly would show, and knew they would know: and made it clear that Owen was not allowed to know. It was bad enough that he knew of Ana. The suit watched the girl as if waiting for a miracle to happen.

Insisting on schooling her and teaching her politics to become a tool the Dame Industry desired. Anara had other plans for her children, Ahsai children had to earn Blood Rights to wield the power of their people. Unfortunately for Anara, her first Blood Rights consumed her life at an early age. Thankfully, Ana wouldn't receive any of such magnitude unless Anara died. Anara was currently immortal.

Bioni had become a sister to her, that was apparent as Anara told her the secrets she hadn't even told Krypt. Bioni was the mortal only soul who knew that she was a Vessel. Bioni still couldn't believe that she had given in and mated with Krypt. That was the mortal's only concern. She had suspicions about Dame but knew that was a dead end. Anara despised the man too much and he held more than enough influence in the Breach making him untouchable with a target on his broad back.

Beep, beep…Beep, beep. The sound of Nathus and Krypt's pager went off in unison like a heartbeat they wished they could murder.

Anara looked up and knew that this would be the last time she saw either one of them for a very long time. She ran out the door and grabbed his wrist. A kiss was obviously too much to ask for because he just looked away and walked out. Her heart sank and shrank, and felt much like something was ripping at it. A feeling she had felt before with the man who shoved her into the escape pod months ago taking her memory and supplying the seed that had grown within her. It wasn't love that caused her heart to beat rapidly to a stop…it was the replacement of one of her pawns to someone elses battle field. In her current state, she couldn't enter the game offensively without risking the lives of her young children. Though they were not unprotected, they would still suffer the aftermath of any event that took place. Their molding began now, at this delicate age.

Anara loved only one man, the one she had been sent to assassinate, but failed. They, like *him*, only wanted possession over her, discarding her like leftovers of a banquet.

"They will never know their fathers," she muttered, feeling the mortality go cold in her.

Life had been tolerable since she arrived on the Breach—she knew it would be naught but war. Owen was one of the evil men Krypt warned of, and he was working with something even darker. Anara would need to find out to whom and what he consorted with before this planet fell with the others *they* had lost. Anara understood that in this moment the power of Kamenah was her most treasured weapon and the goddess gave to her infinitely.

Together forever, Anara closed her eyes listening to the echoes of Kamenah singing into her mind like a replayed song that stuck on the tip of her tongue with a hum and never to be spoken aloud.

... the past will always speak for the future...

Anara watched the tears roll gently down the face of a child resembling much that of a cherub fluttering in a darkened chapel. Her weeping became the tender bells in a high summoning steeple. The cool breeze from a cracked window carried her sad song through the air coaxing her rusty-red hair to smear the glistening tears from her pale angel kissed cheeks. Ana's stormy eyes blinked the sorrow away from her hurt and suffering within the caves of a distant battle. It was as though winter shimmered from her skin.

Her mother's familiar voice of comfort sailed methodically through the air with a chime of lull-a-bye dancing across the moonlit room, "Why do you cry, my little song bird?"

The child whispered timidly not wanting to wake her slumbering sibling from his pleasant dreams, "Mr. Dame said daddy is lost."

The voice of comfort became a shadow in the night that sighed at the emotions her young daughter felt from what might have been an overheard and less-than-worthy argument with Owen Dame. She replied with the typical comfort offered a child after the unfortunate eavesdropping children tend to trip into, "He was just angry, Ana. Being lost does not last

37

forever, my love. Let me tell you a story about a world far from here. To some, Death is but a *Game* and those who play resist *Time's* hungry sister."

From the moment Owen had discovered she was pregnant with her son, he had been adamant about convincing her to move on so he could father both children—to *protect* them, as he graciously put it. Anara laughed in his face and told him he should leave, it hadn't occurred how much her daughter was like her *mala*, Ana had obviously snuck outside to question the man who upset her mother in hopes of avenging her mother's hurt feelings.

Ana sat up on her delicate little elbows, anticipating her mother's fabled bedtime legends of past lives. She was still too young to understand that these stories where memories shared with a soul that hid deep in the depths of her beloved mother, "Another planet?"

Her mother paused to study her daughter's expression to assure that she was listening to every word, "The planet of a red sun: a world which has begun to resist time. It was once a planet lush with life and color. Warm with hope and love—now it weeps; frozen and starved, always yearning for the kiss from *Life*. Some of this planet's species have travelled to the Breach, you know."

Ana blinked confused as she was expecting a fairy tale like all the other nights when her mother would mend her broken heart. She shook her head refusing to acknowledge the origin of this story that was unlike the others. Ana suddenly felt that deep within her mother was the voice of *someone* else clawing *her* way to the surface.

The innocent child spoke timidly below a whisper, "Did it die?"

Her mother's angelic face came into the light of the glassy Isosalan moon with a tender grin of secrets and power, "No. I like to think it slumbers beneath deserts of cerulean blue and remains trapped in a resistance of time like all imprisoned worlds beyond the Daeviti Bond."

Her daughter wrapped her arms around her forth-drawn knees resting her peaceful chin in thought, "Momma, I don't want to know this story. It sounds sad. Tell me a story that will make me laugh – a story about the Wise Men of Celeston."

Anara conceded with a charming grin. The story of the 'Wise Men of Celeston' had originally derived from her time spent with several important and interesting characters she interacted with in the mirror halls of the Dame Tower in Traverna. It amused her that Ana would find their life-evolving games humorous, "Ah. The three Wise Men," she began her story.

"Three men sit in white muttering through mirrored light. The first man with fat, obese hands chuckles a chuckle so raw. Roll after roll, his body so wide it would make a child cry, he saw no evil at all. The second man sat torn and tall with flesh so scorned the flight of morn would eat the sight if not for such dim light, he saw that which would come. The third young man hid his hands for fear of what they held. Through blood shot eyes, he cast his dice and gambled with life which was never his own.

"For every dream there is a reality and for every thought there is a truth. A wise man knows that if he may think it then it can become true—if it has not already. In all the heavens there is a light hidden within the *Light* and this room shields the contenders of fate. All may see, but none may enter, unless they are invited to *be*. They pry and divide, conquer and smite, but never yield. To yield in the misted white rooms of *Celeston* is to quit the game, and to quit this game of fate is to forfeit your turn, and to discontinue resistance leaving only a roll with *Death*; sister of *Time* and *Life*.

"The characters of *Heaven's Cradle* are far from usual...

"Celeston is *like* a chamber of pure white and forever filled with light. Smoke and clouds shuffle around with fog and mist its window panes. The one thing truly solid is the mirror which comes and goes bringing travelers of worlds forgotten. Some may leave others are forced to stay, it all depends on what *role* they play."

"You make the bed you sleep in," Saul the Blunt
taunted as he tipped his cup pointing at a shadowy
figure on the board.

"Saul was a creature of secrets and deception. Words flow easily from his fat lips and
it would be foolish to trust anything he has to say. Though there are times his words do hold a
mockingly twisted truth. The Blunt was the oldest of the game and has occupied the table for an
eternity it would seem. He was not of this *dominion.* He is not Daeviti."

"Shame on you once, shame on me twice," Sams the
Silent rasped in searing observation as he stood
peering over the light within the shadow.

"Sams found his seat at this table from constellations unknown. It was unfortunate
calculation that trapped this unknown Celestial in the clouded chambers of Celeston."

"Vengeance is mine, says *One* lord," Malice the
Trump said as he tucked his nervous pale hands
between his legs, forcing away the urge to bite his
glassy false nails to rubble.

"Now the Trump is an entity who always knows a way out, except when the walls are
made of smoke and his existence is being viewed through great scopes with unknown faces; he
can only *whisper* in hopes of a blurry exit to crash in his favor."

"Innocent until proven guilty," Saul chuckled,
rubbing his fat chin with his fat fingers.

Malice shrugged to his opponent, "What does not
kill you makes you wiser."

"Your move, Mal, and all you have left on the table
are two pawns, one *rook,* one bishop, a queen and

two more nights before a great flood," Saul knocked

over a rook grinning with his bishop in place.

"Saul has brought many tricks and a variety of new games from his dominion to Celeston, challenging the contenders of Celeston with the souls of Daeviti as their pawns."

"He always has a trump card, and by the looks of it, I believe he has a dark queen," Sams the Silent smirked at his mischievous partner.

Saul began walking his obese fingers into the air mimicking a pair of stubby fat legs climbing an imaginary height, "Up the ladder, you know, I just conquered *Hell* a while ago."

"Which one?" Sams rubbed his temples, confused as he flipped an invalid card, leaving ash flaking from his hand with the swift motion.

"There is always a new hell in the making," Malice rolled his rheumy eyes at the card, "He rummied a bluff twenty one centuries ago."

"A phase ago—wait a minute, you can't build a dome *there*," Saul forced his bare fat belly forward, "I have Diggers there—what a *Travesty*."

A hard chuckle mocked the protest as shadowed hands moved a transparent piece, "I need somewhere to keep my queen."

"Told you he always has a trump buried somewhere," Saul accused trying to cross his fat arms over and over, "Queen me!"

"One! One! One!" Sams squealed, wrinkling his charred expression.

"Cheater, you cheat! No threezies!" Shaking his fat fingers, Saul growled, whimpering at the huge loss just made.

"But there are three queens, as there has always been," Sams corrected through pouted, blistering lips.

"Four, where's the forth?" Saul gripped the black star swept table leaving moisture to evaporate into cloud.

"Which do you have?" Sams began counting what had been dealt.

"Two blood, one shadow," the fat man cordially lied.

Sams whistled at the wise men, "It's a sleeper."

"She's the trump—my trump," Malice assured with pride at the turn of tables.

"Is that Death in your hand?" Saul narrowed black eyes beneath thick eyelids.

"No, Wise man, it is the next play," Malice mocked accomplished with already reddened, seemingly drunk eyes.

"There is a *charge* to every game, and her name was Akisma. It would not be wise to share this with the other players, they would devour her tactics with but moments of entrance, for she is the only one who can leave the room, leave Celeston—and what is not within Celeston, is a part of the game board."

Akisma the Folly stepped out of the shadows and into their light with a smirk of utter delight. She revealed white teeth and gently chuckled underneath a withdrawn breath, "I see Malice is cheating once again."

"Folly! Told you the dark queen is the trump," Sams clapped his hand at his favorite opponent.

Saul growled at her presence, "Death, wise man, roll those dice thrice."

"Another six of sticks," Sams hung his head studying the layout.

"Bad luck, you old maid," Saul grinned at another triumph.

"Bad luck old maid? Wha-" Sams began but fell silent to Malice's dreaded fury.

Malice narrowed his bibulous glare, "Folly, blasted, cursed Folly. You tamper; Saul the Blunt, black queen is the thirteenth trump."

"Tossel-Bossel. You called red on that wild," Saul denied pointing a finger to a different piece.

"I called the Reaper, not the wild!" Malice corrected knowing Saul needn't correction…only a bit of honesty.

Saul refused to give him his win, "Death is the queen."

"No, the black queen is the trump," Malice demanded his recognition.

"She can't trump in a hotel," Sams stared his usual confused burnt gaze.

"He would have been truly handsome if he hadn't the scars that still seemed to flake ancient ash with ember. Imagine our great star trapped in the form of a human; that is the life of a Celestial. Only he could tell you what universe he kept warm."

Saul shrugged with his fat pig-pink hand lifted high in the false air, "I demand a luxury tax on Malice the Trump."

"Don't be tempted because you're stuck in jail," Malice chuckled charmingly beneath a measured breath.

"The Colonel is guilty," Akisma reminded, pointing out the forgotten piece hidden by Saul's blackmail.

"Take the risk," Malice challenged his partner.

"They are already invested," Saul reminded as he focused his attention into the white mist around them.

"If you have nothing nice to say then say nothing at all. Why take the Risk?" Sams crossed his thin, charred arms with not so much as a wince of pain.

Saul defied, as always, "I've said nothing but the truth."

"Truth is not kind," Sams reminded the wise man.

"Shall I speak never?" Saul snapped, nibbling on a nailess fingertip.

Malice snickered making several moves while they fussed, "Suits you, bluntly."

Akisma precariously noted every play made.

"But I can't be anything less than my calling!" Saul whined lifting a dark cherry to his missing lips. The fat upon his face so thick that what should have been there hid beneath every sluggish layer.

"Says the Wise man," Sams only stared at Saul with spite.

Saul bellowed with a false laughter, "Perhaps you should have named me Saul the Silent and made Sams the Blunt!"

"Shush, its Sams' spin. Roll them Silent," Malice interrupted their feud to wait on the results of his moves.

"Folly, Folly," Sams bowed his head to salute his favorite beginner, "slide to Sorry!"

"Uno!" Folly laid out a wild card, "Blue."

"Ha, slap jack," Saul snorted with humor and amusement reddening his cheeks, "A Sultan's salute after all."

"The Hermit flipped with Love at his side," Sams grinned at his own personal game, "Folly, delicate Folly," Sams whispered passionately with a feint of charm.

Akisma giggled like that of a school girl, "I fear Folly would not know Love save the wisdom of a Hermit."

"A moment passed leaving them in an unusual silence, so unusual that the presence of an intruder stepped forth out of the mirror into the circle. His darkness a riddle and his origin lost. The man with solid black eyes gave no welcome at all."

"Another player!" The Wise Men chimed with no clue of what had truly entered the game.

"The three wise men cheered, always welcoming another challenge, a new defeat. Being at their table for so long, fear of shadow and strangers was unknown to them. Their only desire was to conquer and control the game at their manifested hands. It didn't even matter whether the intent was good or evil. This was the closest to humanity they would ever know and the only freedom they could ever have.

"Akisma's heart raced knowing that this new player would prove the others to be sore losers. She knew that this opponent was heartless and what she had been waiting for—for she too had a role to play."

"What does this new player bring to the table?" She requested, already knowing the wager to come.

"I spy with my black eyes, exiled queens and the Devourer of lives," he let the words roll seductively from his lips.

"Akisma could already see the hate in the blood shot eyes of Malice and the meditation in Sams' lowered gaze. Calculating, always calculating. Saul only motioned for him to take a seat, over confident to the core. Snakes do tend to share the shade, hibernate till they hunger and strike. They will even turn on their own kind when nothing remains in the den to devour.

"Reflections hold shadows. A mirror tells little lies and never completed truths, for you see only what reflects. A new player was never refused. Celeston was created by Time to occupy her days and nights. She trapped whoever resisted the natural flow of Evolution, each player her prisoners, to pass the time away."

All are welcome, because all are damned and yet trapped indefinitely, Akisma thought annoyingly, *everyone has a role to play.*

"Akisma knew this man who took his place among the great manipulators, but did not know what sat arrogantly snug in his body peeking hungrily through his eyes, hunting. She had been warned of this player long before Time had Summoned her to weed out the losers. She could feel the cold hatred that seeped treacherously from his extraordinary demeanor. He was perfect, that of stone with the color of eminent life within shadow. He was the embodiment of an angel but the soul of—darkness, a black hole that hungered, that starved."

Had that cold planet awaken in all the turmoil? Akisma calculated.

"Honor us with a name?" Saul begged throwing a set of black cards in his direction, accepting his challenge.

The man smiled at the Wise Men, never glancing towards Akisma, "I am Lukan, Lukan the Bluff."

"Akisma snickered under her breath knowing it fit him well; for no truth shall ever come from him, *now.*"

5

Owen waited in the Hall of Mirrors of the Eere View Tower for the Darken's return. Waiting on the Darken had become habitual. The man was never on time. It was much like dealing with his Soldiers after each mission they completed, late. Always too late, so much so that Owen would rather them not return. He only needed them to locate and give coordinates, not retrieve and return in one piece.

The retrieval of the Prophet's Eyes had so far been successful…but exterminating the Soldiers assigned to this mission…a complete failure. They were like cockroaches, he could drop a bomb on them, destroy all that is around them, and they would still walk out of their dirty little shit holes and laugh in his face.

The power to know the complete future, and to be able to manipulate it, was a breath away. He knew that capturing a living, breathing Prophet would be impossible, honestly, how do you catch an Entity that predicts its future from first breath to Death? Even if he came upon a Prophet, it would sacrifice itself before letting a Consort use it.

He couldn't afford the risks of employing a Seer, they saw only for themselves.

When his Darken partner stepped out of the mirror, dusting his black suit off (a suit which seemed to absorb whatever light that bounced around in the Hall of Mirrors) with pale hands that had obviously rarely felt the heat of the Ursan sunlight, he smirked at the half-Consort who strained to acknowledge his Darken bloodline. Lukan knew that Owen's mother was a Drifter slave and the mortal's father had been a Darken General, information Owen slowly gathered over the years.

The man raised his eyebrows, "Have you nothing better to do, my friend?"

Owen walked a step behind and to the side of the malevolently charming man, "Well, Lukan, you can't remain in my towers without the Supremacy becoming agitated at your presences. I only wish to bid you safe travel back to the Southrun Breach, the Arkeon is where

your home is."

Lukan narrowed his eyes at the little human's arrogance, "Pride in your mortal

existence? That is truly a flaw in half-Consorts. Willem should never have seduced that Drifter

slave woman, and then what does he do? Returns her to the border Soldier with child and

hypnotizes the master of that shameful tower to claim the breed."

It was moments like these that made him grin at the knowledge of having his friend's

most prized possession in possession. Lukan would topple mountains to regain what he cast out

all those years ago, "You should thank Willem for begetting a useful spawn such as me. How

else would you escape the confinements of the Arkeon and break the gates of the Nexum?"

"I should like to, if he would dare to visit the Arkeon once again. This time, I will

chain him to the dark moon and beat him to pulp with the nearest Drifter slave still breathing,"

Lukan mused at Owen knowing the mortal knew not what he consorted with.

"When will Damu return?" Owen slid his finger down the mirror activating the

transport device that would take Lukan back to his frozen hell above the Southrun Arkeon.

If Owen had any sense about the moon above Southrun, he would know that paradise

hid behind shadows. The Darken had inhabited the planet long before human's ever settled. The

Score forced them to retreat from the battlefields and play a bigger game with greater odds to

lose. Why walk the board when you could control the pieces?

Lukan frowned, clicking his pointed tongue at mention of his brother's name, "He will

return when he has finished with that which he has begun. He has his orders to carry out before

he shall tend your needs."

Owen smirked as Lukan stepped through another mirror and pulled a sheet over to

block out any and all nosey onlookers, "Yes, planting a plague is only second to whatever Damu

has strung up his sleeve."

You can only begin true Control by tearing down the empire first, Owen thought to himself.

He paused at the thought that whispered in his mind with a sadistic voice, "I *am* the Supremacy."

... Time flies...

Years had passed and Krypt Halen had not returned home to his family, to his children, to his son whom he had never met. This was not acceptable by the standards of Anara Kamen because she was the one who had to collaborate with the Dame on matters involving evolution and ancient species. She had completely recovered her memories along with that of the goddess she fought with daily to control. Kamenah firmly believed that Time was wasting and they were letting too many events slip through their fingers. Anara knew she was right, it was time for her to play a more active role in the Breach, but total annihilation seemed completely outrageous. The innocence would have to live here once darkness fell, if there was nothing left, what was the point of existing and dwelling in a frozen hell?

It had fallen down to her creating a collar that would bind the goddess within her, unless Summoned.

Had things become so desperate?

If it was not for the existence of her children, she would have yielded to the *goddess* and allow the woman to devour this planet with little to no remorse. Anara's time spent on the Breach made it difficult to not desire devastation and extinction of this particular Daeviti planet. Every man in existence is power hungry and starved for worship. Greed flows in their veins and lies spill out from their mouth. She had no desire to let her children become as the people of the Breach. They needed a good Ahzai colony, but the old Ahzai no longer exist.

She had just dropped off Ana and little Jon with Bioni and Mercy when the urgency to enter the game of power consumed her and she begged Bioni to watch her children while she took an Insta-port to the Dame Tower in Travena. When she arrived the receptionist made it clear that Owen was not on the premises.

Anara thanked her and silently thought; *it didn't take long to befriend this mortal.*

"Where is the Dame this Evens-fall, Starla?" Anara question as Starla rolled her eyes at the inquiry.

She tilted the computer screen and tapped a file with her finger, "He has an appointment in the Southrun and won't be back for a week or so. Technically I wasn't suppose to inform you and definitely was not suppose to permit you access to the sixty-fifth floor," Starla smiled pushing a card to the edge of the blood-red Karonan marble desk and lowered her voice, "I fear for my life like everyone should, Mrs. Halen."

"Good day, Starla," Anara slid the card off the edge and held it at her side, "You should take a vacation."

Before she entered the dim elevator the receptionist stopped her and stood directly behind her, "Lance returned from their last mission and will leave in two hours."

Anara's jaw tightened as she stepped into the elevator and watched the doors slide close. Lance returned but not Krypt, Lance was a Runner, the best one they had, which meant they not only found what they were looking for but they had proof that there was more to be found. She shook her head and began grinding her teeth in frustration. The thought of having more than one Eye in a single room was nerve racking and the idea of Owen controlling the future with them was even worse.

Twenty-eight, bing. Thirty-two, bing.

She wanted to close her eyes but truth and answers were only several floors away.

Fourty-seven, bing. Fifty-three, bing.

Krypt had not even so much as attempted to make contact. Bioni had at least spoken to Nathus. Anara had not seen a helpful piece of dust come near her home. It was as if Krypt Halen had died.

Sixty-four, bing. Sixty-five, "You have reached your destination."

Anara rolled her eyes at the reminder to grab your bags and get off the ride. You were permitted one floor and the Receptionist had sent her to the sixty-fifth. She stepped out of the elevator and froze stiff at the archive that stretched before her. Every bit of information on the Breach and the greatest of collections in artifacts and Supremacy knowledge; was located in this room and she had a hunch that the Collector who owned the archive was nowhere to be found.

The light remained dim and many of the items in the archives had been sealed away in transparent cases to maintain quality and perfection. The room's shutters had been closed and locked for the night, only a single window peered out over the city of Traverna. Traverna wasn't as big as Eere View, but it still shimmered in the night like a beacon inviting parasites to pounce on the unaware. She detested cities. She grew up in a palace which was worse than a city. Both boiled down to too many people, everyone wishing they knew your business, and everyone being jealous that she was the last Breeder. She never asked for the deed, it was Evolution's way of telling the other's they were obsolete.

Her gaze fell on a giant cross with several engravings etched up and down the center of the metal, "The first settlers of the Criers."

The Criers were people of ancient yet foreign blood. They had settled in this world near its beginnings of civilization. They had suffered more than most species in the Breach, and they knew more about the One God than the rest of the worshipping souls on the planet and moons surrounding. They were exceptional breeders when it came to the mix of blood and brood. They believed in hope and that there was a single God, and He was their savior. They are nearly extinct, now that their Guardians have abandoned them.

Anara held her hand out and ran her finger down the engravings. Heat seared through her fingertips and traveled up her arm forcing her to rip her hand away. The Ahzai was forbidden many things for the deeds they carry out. They were in many ways the Anti-Christ of the Criers. This was a fault she couldn't even lay at the feet of the goddess Kamenah. The Ahzai were born from a vengeful darkness who sought peace through ultimate control of existence—a truth she hated the most about herself: Deep down in her soul, she too desired absolute and complete control over the universe.

She whirled around and fell back staring into the sunken eyes of Lance Haeden, "Where is Krypt and the others?"

He shook his head with thin, delicately pursed lips, "I cannot tell you."

She had always thought of Lance as beautiful and deadly. To see him so weakened and defeated gave her pause and alarm. There was still strength behind his eyes, an unbreakable will that was born through his Crier blood. Faith that no Soldier of the Breach could summon: the Crier were a strong people.

"That is not the answer I look for," Anara stepped forward and was found speechless once again. Lance was bone thin and battered beyond immediate repair. If he looked like this, what did Krypt look like? She tapped into the gifts of her Ahzai blood and demanded his cooperation, "What happened?"

Lance hung his head and frowned feeling the tinge of energy surge through his blood. His body ignoring his brain because it needed the energy, it needed the power and nutrients her seductions could supply, "The Arkeon."

"The Drifters?" she wrapped her arm around his waist and helped him sit on the mount the great cross was set on. Her physical contact creating a link he knew nothing of, a link that would connect him to her permanently.

"No," he closed his eyes with a smirk, "If it were so easy."

He was right. A Soldier of the Arkeon could handle the Drifters, especially with the amount of Soldiers in his squad.

Anara knew he would be the last man she would ever squeeze information out of, Ahzai or no. She didn't have time to do an in-depth soul confrontation. Lance wasn't a full Soldier, he had the mixed blood of a Crier and the Crier had divine shields wrapped tightly around their mind unlike all other souls, "Just, please, is he alive?"

Lance's eyes blanked and he shrugged, "I was cut off. Last I heard, yes, Krypt still lives. The others still live."

"You were cut off," she pushed like a mother demanding answers from a naughty child who had just returned home with a black eye, bribing him with sweet cookies and candies.

"The Arkeon," he answered with no intentions on elaborating.

"I understand this," she hissed as she knelt before him, "How did you get out?"

Anara sighed offering energy to flow to him, comforting his body with promise of healing. In many ways, she seduced his willingness through healing. His cheeks were already rosy with the affects of the new energy in his blood, warmth pushing out the Freeze of the Arkeon.

Lance grimaced shaking his head to and fro, "His Collector met with me to gather the Eyes. That was when we were attacked by waves and waves of energy, a continuous pulse of malevolent energy. The Arkeon didn't want to let the Eyes leave. The Collector escaped using a Waterhole Insta-port. Not all of Southrun is frozen in the shadows. Not all. She stepped into the chilling indigo blue puddle and was gone. The puddle froze but I still I tried to go in and escape with her, hoping there was a drop of moisture left, but it had already closed. After the Arkeon pulse had faded, Damu arrived and he was far from happy. I guess he lost a Collector and went chasing after her. He handed me a port and I used it…"

"Who is the Collector?" Anara began clueing in pieces that Lance wanted her too, whether they were completely true or not.

She knew he had been swayed by Damu...she herself had once been under his web of spells.

Lance glared at her now grinning with insanity, "She is Ahzai."

Anara stood up and stepped away from him unsure of how much he knew about her, about what she was, "Ahzai are forbidden."

"Ah, yes, yet here one stands before me," Lance puzzled, watching as her eyes began to glow. He blinked with shock and delirium, "Now, *Ahzai* don't glow like that."

"What is her name, Lance?" Anara's eyes now burned and boar into him.

Lance still defied her.

She felt her necklace crack around her neck, sighing, "A name, the name of the Ahzai Collector," she watched his eyes mist over as the Vessel began tapping into his mind and linking with his thoughts.

He wouldn't need to speak now, "Sera Demeska."

Anara pulled back out of his mind and watched his eyes glare at her with a blurred expression vibrating out of his lids. He smirked up at her, fury burning in his eyes knowing what she had just did. The Crier in his blood screaming at her...she turned away from him and returned to the elevator. It was time for her to leave.

The daughter of Onett and student of Scarlet, Anara hissed at the complication that sat at her feet, *the greatest Ahzai Seer and Ahzai Collector of all realms.*

There were ranks in the Ahzai division. Anara was labeled as Warrior, even with her royal blood that supplied her with infinite power. Onett was a Seer and Scarlet was a Collector.

Sera wouldn't be allowed to claim rank until her mother *and* mentor died. Considering a Collector has the ability to collect time and health and life and death, the chances of Scarlet killing over would be next to never. Sera's only hopes of rising to rank would be to cast her mother and the Collector into the Nexum.

They may already be there if Sera roam's freely from her missions.

The elevator seemed to shrink with the players who had entered the game. Anara hated complication, and she hated dealing with her own kind. The Ahzai were masters of the game, they have sought control for longer than the existence of many Daeviti civilizations.

She returned to the Wastelands and sat silently watching her children play with no worries of the future's turmoil. Her daughter's hair caught the rays of the Ursan Star, capturing its glow with every strand. It was like the burning fire and Anara knew that when she gave Ana her Blood Rights, that her daughter's hair would begin to show a burning white near the roots, making her look like a nymph out of a fairytale. She puzzled over her son, he had begun showing features belonging to his father, but his wisdom was that of his mother. He would become a great Ahzai, she was yet to pin what kind of Ahzai he would be.

Bioni observed her silently until she couldn't hold her concern any longer. As always, and this made Anara love her dear friend even more, Bioni was sure to speak her mind and speak it true. Her mouth ran a league a minute, never stopping, not even for a breath of air.

"He is dead," Bioni spat out at Anara, relieved when she shook her head no.

The Vessel continued to shake her head with a grimaced grin stretched across her face, "If it were so easy."

Part II

~6~

...echoes...

Life still echoed throughout the steel halls and corridors as Krypt lead his team through a forgotten part of the Breach. Ever since he had been reassigned it was as though he faced one death after the other. There were times he absolutely knew that Owen was out to get him and his fellow Soldiers, and other times, more so. The Breach had not been fully charted, the planet was so large that much of the land had no name or settlement or worlds that had died in one tragedy or the other. People who had been forgotten or lost in Time surfaced during their travels and it usually lead to their own detriment as if these ancient civilizations had awaited their arrival.

It was in these dead worlds that they were searching for the Eyes of Prophets.

You would think that there was a reason that those cities were dead along with the accursed Eye of a fallen Prophet.

Krypt wiped sweat from his forehead and signaled a halt.

The scent of ancient decay alerted them that they were near the center of the tomb. This was the place the deceased people of Hedruin had stored their dead kings and queens, the dry chill preserving the corpses of their leaders. The center of the pyramid held the entrance to the other world, the world that Owen sought, the world that kept its very own Eye that was still in use: a world within a world. Not all the dead truly remain as such. Not all.

"Ye who walketh the flaming waters seeketh the shores thine shadows," Alton translated the hieroglyphs carved into the totem of a great bird they neither seen before nor cared for what it might have been. It speared out of the still waters of a massive black pool in the center

of the tomb. Around the sand stone walls were statues of what had been their rulers, many lined this tomb.

"They had to have been here long before the Score," Kai pointed out a 'dot-dash' time record beneath their soles and under layers of sand and dust, "The Score probably was what destroyed them."

The Score had set the beginnings of the current Supremacy of Government. When the Counsel of the Supremacy enacted the entrapment of all that was Immortal, Entity and of Unknown descent the first wave of Control had began and set the Score. It was the Score that gave birth to the first Breed of Soldiers to reinforce the orders of Supremacy. The truth of what exactly 'The Score' is has remained unmentioned and hidden from the reality of mortal existence. Some believe it is a God that reaped the ancient civilizations and Summoned the gate to release the power of the Arkeons. It was also theorized that the Arkeon could be controlled, which was Owen Dame's sole interest in the polar caps.

Krypt lifted his hand up to a wall and aimed some light for them to observe the pictograph, "The canals and the construction depleted their water supply. That river over there, it wasn't the Score that killed them it was the arrival of those things right there."

A glyph showing a hoard of beast with wings, (once blackened with evani mineral but now faded) was shown flying over the line of pyramids, snatching the humans and slave beasts up as they went. Below that was a glyph of a dominion in the beginning of creation, a land the missing civilization was creating. For this glyph the ancient people used elaborate color and engraved it into the stone so that it wouldn't fade over time. Great tropical trees and flat cerulean pastures stretched clear across the wall to reveal a drop into an ocean of emerald and lime green. A huge bell set in the center of the pastures facing a high wall that should have spewed out a waterfall. Beyond the wall was a pyramid, perhaps the pyramid they were trapped in, or perhaps one that would receive the travelers from this pyramid. On it was a single door and at the top looked a large red eye—a Prophet's Eye.

Denny let out a whistle, "Those are Arkeon Hybra. This means that the Arkeon succeeded in destroying civilizations in the past."

"Southrun Hybra at that," Nathus grunted with a frown. The Northrun Drifters had extinguished the Hybra long before the Barrier was placed—before the Score, "They could still be roaming this death-trap of a desert."

Krypt only shrugged staring into the black waters they would need to wade through to get to the totem in the center that would transport them to another hell Owen wanted them to conquer. It wasn't just Owen giving orders; it was Damu, a whatever-the-hell-it-is that seems to have more power than Owen. A warrior—body and soul with an agenda that did not involve the power crazed Owen Dame. Damu had been the one who saved their tails when Lance got cut off and couldn't get to them.

Krypt still struggled to replay the event, and continued to fail recalling every detail and trap that had taken place.

If all the good in life has died, only darkness will reign, Krypt could hear Anara's words echoing precautions in the back of his mind, *hope is all the innocents will have left and when it fades, shadow remains.*

"Let's get to it," Krypt muttered dropping sand into the water.

Before he could step in, Kai grabbed his arm. His equal in rank, Kai pulled him back shaking his head. Krypt looked down and realized that the sand had disintegrated and smoke rose from the liquid acid. He grit his teeth fighting the urge to stomp his feet and ball his fist like a little girl throwing a tantrum.

"Great," Krypt growled.

Kai rolled his eyes fighting his own urge to tell him '*I told you so,*' instead, "There's no way in hell we are supplied to get across. We don't have the gear. We need to find a way back."

60

The hall they came through to get into the tomb had collapsed. The only exit was the one in the center of the acid pool. There had to be a way in, the surviving Hedruin people escaped through the transport before them. That much was written on the walls of the tomb. They left a few people behind to pour the pool of acid, preventing any intruders from entering their new home.

Nick smirked at the irony they faced, "Is there nothing easy to these missions?"

"Lance, we need Lance," Nathus muttered, kicking some more dirt into the acid, "Dis bullshit."

Krypt eyed the mocking bird, wondering how the totem standing in the water stood without dissolving, "Wings."

"What," Kai stared at Krypt as if he had lost his mind.

It wouldn't have been the first time a Soldier 'took a walk.'

"Get your rope, drill gun and cliff bolts. I'm building a sky bridge," Krypt grinned already making for the nearest wall, "We can't go through it, so we'll go over it."

...

It was a severe annoyance when Owen received the transmission that the team had reached their destination and acquired the Black Eye that existed in another realm. They sent the beacon readings and now waited for a pick up. Owen, begrudgingly, sent Damu to yet another pick up and the favor was sourly received. Damu made it clear to him that this was the last time he would answer one of his calls. The Darken had better things to do than to answer the beckons of a half human. As far as Damu was concerned, Owen was *only* human. The Darken was a classification that needed to be earned, not born to. They were, after all, here long before the homo-sapiens arrived and caused another phase in evolution.

61

"Show yourself, goddess," Owen whispered as he flipped through the thick journal he stole from his Collector. It was a Traveler's journal, a log of everything that has ever happened and what has been foreseen by the owner of the book.

He had been so caught up in his brooding that he hadn't realized the shadow that stood over his desk smirking down at him with humor, "Little friend, you are chasing fire and ice."

Owen didn't bother raising his head. There was no point. His secret was no longer a secret, "Yes, Lukan, she is ice and fire: now if I could only find exactly where the ice and fire is."

Lukan took silent steps back towards the shadows he arrived through. His face was a mask of thought and dark emotion, his eyes a shifting of silent fury, "Damu will tend to your human team and after that, our contract is void."

Owen watched as the Darken faded into the shadows and heard the mirror transportation on the other side of the wall shatter, the burning itch of knowing that he had just made a great enemy set in as he massaged his temples hoping to ward away his oncoming migraine.

...eye of the storm...

Priman Metropolis, Antila Underground.

Antila would not be the first to have succumbed to Control, and it would not be the last. Confusion struck the reality of the first who had arrived in what was now the new home to the underclassmen: Priman Metropolis, Antila Underground. This new home with a constant flow of dim light and new neighbors seemed more like a prison the longer they settled into their quarters. What sealed the fate of their future was when Evan Priman tried to resurface to continue with the move and was not allowed to so much as see the light of day—or was it night? Evan returned to his family with a shadow glooming in his persona. Silent in thought and annoyed with the decision to vote for the great president that cast them down beneath the earth in the name of

Environmental Conservation. Yet his brother and his brother's family lingered above the surface in military headquarters with the rest of the politicians.

Evan had signed on for the great move as an agreement with Xander, his eldest brother who was born a Soldier, since he willingly chose to live in the new city he would receive a respectable position in the new society that was being created. One-hundred-thousand Antilan citizens have moved below and word that more has yet to come from surrounding territories. They were the first and they would be invincible to the plans the government had set. Somehow, Evan felt as though he had sold his soul to a devil in a presidential suit with his brother holding the pitchfork in his face, *some brother.* This was proof that blood was indeed not thicker than wine.

Sacrifice his sanity for the safety of his family in a world that may only know struggle.

How true was the promise of immunity from the Experiment? If they couldn't control the rest of the population once it has arrived, what will be left for them? No single man has the power to control millions. With the aid of Dame Industries, President Don McCoyan has successfully fulfilled such a dominate fantasy, leaving Evan with no choice but to be the ambassador between what seemed to be purgatory and hell. McCoyan had secured documents for Evan to review once the move was completed, vital information that would keep his family safe from the population.

Guess I was suppose to keep myself and my family locked away in a separate sector yet perform the act of governing general underground population of the underclass Antila civilians.

A tormenting ringing still haunted his ears as he walked down the hallways of their new Under-Division. The words of a Council woman continued to taunt him, *"It is a mistake, and you shouldn't follow through. Millions will die."*

He still had much to accomplish with the rest of the advocates appointed to the new cities beneath the surface. There was to be files on every person living below, mug-shots and geno-tags, (the military would implant a code on every denizen before entry). Why this was important was beyond him, it used to be a neck-tag with an individual number was good enough. Now, not only a number but chemical and biological tags would be placed in the body of each individual submerged willingly or forcefully into their homes down below and within the thick walls built and molded of irinoi core.

How the government was supposed to force the rest of society into dormancy was also beyond Evan's reasoning. The Traverna Council was against Control, was against moving all civilians beneath the Breach for Environmental Conservation. What will they do to bring them into their polluted idea of Utopia?

At some point in time, Antila was a land of the free and was at peace with their neighbors, but now it felt as though they were being punished with the government's definition of peace.

Xander still assured him that it would all work out, this Reformation. His brother had changed, as if brain washed upon the past three years of military service. He was stationed at the Southrun Arkeon and returned, changed. He once knew laughter and joy and understood jokes. Now, it was only about the Reformation and Conservation, and Control. There was nothing humorous about the man he once knew as brother, *only Duty and that damned Control.* Xander had even gone so far as isolating his family from the rest of them as if the free citizens were contagious.

"Soldiers live among Soldiers," was his belief now, and Evan for some reason believed that was now Law.

Dreams accompany the agonizing ringing in both of his ears, vibrating throughout his head and body, invading his sleep when the curfew approaches and there was nothing to do but sleep. Evan continues to dream of the woman on the Council with a glistening galaxy twinkling in her eyes. It was as though one moment she sees him and the next someone else is staring through her very eyes. She seemed to know he was watching her and tried everything to wake him. Trying to tell him he is somewhere he does not belong.

Turn around, her smile gently radiated: *turn around before it is too late.*

The first time this dream had awoken him, he tried just that, to leave the city. It only got him so far as the third check point when he realized it was locked and he had no key. Soon, the woman would frown at his entrapment with tears swelling in those stony eyes as she held her hand out to show him something. Every time he looked down to see what she held: only stars swirled in the palm of her hand with something blue twinkling in the center. When he would look back up to her she would point to his family warning him.

The only words that escaped her feverish lips were, *"Survive and preserve."*

He would wake panting for breath and trying not to drown in his own perspiration, *what's that suppose to mean? Survive until it's your turn to unwillingly leap into Death's Cradle?*

His wife believed he was going mad, until she began having her own dreams of children who ran around in circles singing an old melody the Crier children would sing, "Ring around the roses, a pocket full of poison, ashes, ashes, *they* All. Fall. Down-" a melody twisted from the original version to hint something was wrong with their new reality.

"They sound so innocent. I can't help but to think that they know the woman you dream of," she gasped at her husband who rubbed his eyes trying to wake up from his own dreams, "I think we have made a huge mistake, Evan Kyle Priman. We should not have come down here."

He nodded glancing at the time that flickered on his clock, "Carla, what do they mean? 'Survive and preserve', 'poison and ashes.' Could it be death? Will everyone down here die?"

She only shook her head struggling not to sob. Her green eyes melting away with exhaustion, sleep deprivation had begun its course on the soon to be mother. Evan knew the dreams would have to come to a stop if they were to have a healthy baby—if he were to keep a healthy wife. How could he manage to keep the sanity of another when he too struggled in keeping his own marbles rolling in a row?

Carla could feel the baby move anxious and blindly in her womb. Moving, always moving.

The wind raged carelessly, whistling the approach of a coming tempest. The weather cried the secrets of the land announcing that change was coming as the Breach rotated further and further from the Ursan sun. Some say it was this detachment from the star that made the minds of men become ravenous and the women become numb. Old wise tales the ancient scientist of faded settlers had their truths. The Immortals will attest to their words, even they know when it is their time to come out and play.

Angelic storm-swept eyes stared ominously out into the dark, quavering window that fought defiantly against the wrathful beads of cool rain, gazing passionately at the unwavering reflection of the woman she found immortal comfort in. She smiled, thin pink lips, as she listened to the sound of her mother's wind chimes dance with the moist wind. She was sure to find unconscious sand wasp on the ground in the morning from being shook out of their homes.

Ana sought refuge in the warmth of her mother's study. It had been years since last she gazed into the eyes of an entity she despised, the goddess Kamenah. In this moment, her mother was the warmth in the room, vacant of all heartless *chills* the other *thing* created. The girl could still count every marking upon her mother's body that had been made by what seemed a dream or fairytale in hopes of keeping the host in control. Her mother was Ahzai, powerful, but she knew that with the ongoing success of Control in the Breach there would be little need of the mortal and more theories from the goddess.

The reflection also held the image of a teenage boy leaning over her shoulders seeking the sight she focused contently upon. He smiled through flawless pink lips and pearled white teeth with a gentle hint of mischief twinkling in his eyes. They both focused on their mother who read intensely under a small candlelit lantern. As they watched, they noted the way her long bronze hair fell lock by lock down to her knitted shoulders wrapping around the nape of a long, unscathed neck with only a dull black necklace fitted tightly in place with numerous engravings and infinite cracks. This item was the most important of all artifacts in possession of their mother: the binding that kept the goddess at bay.

Their mother hadn't aged in all their years. In fact, she still appeared to be in her early twenties with an ancient wisdom brewing in her shielded eyes. Such mortal beauty should be sin for any soul to possess. There was a flicker in their mother's expression, an electric light that illuminated otherwise dull chestnut and amber eyes.

Paint chipped from the white rocking chair as Anara rose from her seat and spoke with a voice that was strong and demanding, charming and foreign to life itself and somehow being in tune with every seed the land had birthed, "The storm will pass quickly, Ana. Class will continue tomorrow, Jon. So quit counting your marbles and finish your essay."

"What if tomorrow never came?" Ana muttered absently as she flipped a page from the hidden book in her lap, she always had something hidden away from her mother assuming she passed unnoticed, "That there was no lesson to be learned?"

"*There is always a lesson to be learned*, Ana. I will find something for you to keep busy with. Day-dream all you want, but there will be a shuttle waiting for you at the Safrai Gardens. We brainwash our children now days," their mother reassured her with a slight snap in her voice.

A sly curve in their mother's lip eased their tension letting room for the remainder of the storm to finish with a loud bang and drum of thunder on its way to the East. Their mother stretched her arms out and yawned behind strong slender fingers. She closed the book in her hands motioning them over to the table with her other.

"When you fall asleep and dream of all the things you dream: remember that you are loved," she chanted with not a hint of smile or the invitation that would normally invoke excitement.

A child never understands the sacrifice a mother makes for their safety and happiness.

Ana's smile faded as she kissed her mother on a cool, tanned forehead. This meant their mother had a meeting with the greatest villain known in their existence. It wouldn't be before long that they learned there were bigger sharks in the sea…many of which had wings and halos with horns hidden on the other side of each shadow.

There was nothing to say for fear of losing the tender images their mother's love. Ever since their father had vanished, life seemed to turn into a blunder of torment and struggle. Ana could remember the emotions that would leak from her mother during those dark nights where fighting was a ritual to pry information out of Owen Dame and her mother would comfort her by reciting a story of some long lost world. By morning, all things said would have been forgotten and love would fill the essence of life once more. To this day she can't remember what exactly the fights were about, or even why her dad had chose to leave them behind. Comprehending the duties of a Soldier was beyond the will of a young, sensitive empathic Seer who still didn't understand the visions that invaded her sleep.

Ana, Jon and several others of their youth had already meddled far too deep in the locating of the missing Soldiers that it was too late for them to turn back. When morning-rise blessed the new day of the Breach, the children of the Soldiers were beginning their search at the first mission site their fathers had been given orders to recon.

…

Anara Kamen had discovered long ago that you couldn't save a world that did not want to be saved—not outright anyways. The past held the pieces as the present became the game board and the future was a level the player wished to reach. The universe offered a number of tyrants and victors, plenty of sacrificial lambs rise to the cradle to become the pawn of the next play. A part of Anara agreed that humans were like cockroaches and that a few hundred souls could be spared for such sacrifices, but the Ahzai that ran through her veins disagreed and desperately tried to save itself from eternal damnation. That part of her knew that deep down only the one can save the many.

Some say that it is in the darkest hour, when not even a star twinkles in a child's eyes, the future will unfold with riddles of twisted vision forgotten with the waking cry of day. Indigo *skies can play tricks on strong minds which travel through night's shades,* Anara thought as the sound of a songbird struck through the water like a knife slicing deep into the heart of its possessor.

She didn't open her eyes as she listened to her children fight for a cold shower and waited for a hug and kiss to be delivered to her before they made their escape out through a thick and splintered door. She waited and waited for them to creep through her bedroom, as quiet as they could to lightly kiss her on her forehead and tell her they loved her. None came. She lifted her hand to her neck and froze with panic pulsing through her nerves. The binding cuff that belonged there was no longer in its place and realized her words were not her own.

Silence...

> *In another world the great star of a long forgotten*
> *galaxy became of such heat that every rock in its*
> *orbit became a pale gray dust in an event time-log*
> *only few have witnessed to record. This* He *could*
> *have stopped, but abuse was not acceptable amongst*
> *siblings; all the children must be punished—for it is*
> *not the one but the many that keeps a circle*
> *connected. The goddess shook her head at the man*
> *who thought her into existence and defied him*
> *further. It is not her fault that 'They' tamper with*
> *the evolution of this realm... it is not her fault 'They'*
> *serve the dark matter that pollutes the universe.*

...

Ring, ring—ring, ring.

Anara tumbled out of her bed with no air in her lungs and recklessly stumbled out of her room in search for the wailing phone, her vision still trapping her in a dream like state. The walls of her hallway wavered and shifted between reality and memory around her and the floor washed her feet away from each clammy step she struggled to take. In her heart, she knew it was too late to warn her children and get them to safety. What was safety and where would a mother find such a thing in the Breach, in the Daeviti Sector?

Forecasting a future was complicated and twisted behind the truth and lies of mortal life. Mortality was the only stable truth that yielded her the ability to give her dreams and nightmares some sort of meaning. It was only when the higher Entities manipulated the present and the past that the future becomes unreadable, making true Visions unreliable.

"Hello?" she exhaled grabbing her chest forcing aside her panicked feelings. There was something she was supposed to remember, but her mind could not grasp its truth.

"Miss Kamen?" the voice of a man with a Karonan accent questioned with the sound of urgency.

"Yes, who is this?" Anara snarled with subtle irritation unable to recognize the voice that addressed her.

The man paused with hesitation, "Your children are in danger, Miss Kamen."

Anara glared through the front window, numb and ready to pounce on the nearest threat.

"Miss Kamen," The man addressed in that deep Karonan accent.

Anara turned the phone off and let it fall from her hand to crash into the dark floor. She knew that the children were skipping school to dig up information on their fathers...of all the times for her children to skip school in pursuit for their father, this was the worst. Ana of all people should have felt the disturbance in the air. Anara cursed her daughter in the back of her mind. The thought of something happening to her children began to awaken the darkness in her that she kept buried and hidden from the entire existence of the Breach. The Ahzai were a territorial species.

The children could have easily been abducted in these dark times when the Game seeped unannounced throughout their realm. Their blood was wild and filled with an abundance of energy waiting for someone powerful enough to manipulate.

"What have they done?" Anara ran out the door in the direction of the barn with the mirror hiding below it only to freeze at the figure limping in the middle of her driveway.

A tortured voice escaped a wounded mouth dripping tainted blood, "Ahzai."

She ran to his side not catching the name he addressed her with and caught him as his knees gave way, "Denny? What happened, where's Krypt?"

He shook his head with hate and anger seeping from every cut on his body, "Control has now been activated."

She helped him back into the house examining him with furious narrow eyes. Her children were missing—of all the times for her past to creep into her graveled driveway, broken and bleeding as it was when she first left it behind.

Denny shook his head letting beaded sweat trickle down his face, "The children went looking for Krypt. They *know* what you've been doing in the shadows, Ahzai. They thought you had stopped looking for him."

There was no way they could have known about the Protocol or the Solarun or the Project or even that she was Ahzai. The Soldiers had been out of contact for years, Owen Dame would never share vital information with the best friend of Krypt, and Bioni was the only soul aware of her Ahzai heritage other than Lance. Some suspected her heritage but remained silent and loyal to the woman who always offered a safe haven from reality.

Wonder what they would do if they knew I was a Vessel, Anara tilted her head at the thing that mimicked an old friend in need. She could only stare amazed that her nightmare had indeed come knocking on her door, only one race used technology such as the creature hunched before her. She wrapped her arms around his waist and carefully set him back down on the floor breathing heavily from the move.

"Whom are they working with?" Her hair fell delicately over shielded eyes as she decided to humor the imposter slumped before her, "How did-"

Ring, ring.

Anara stared at the phone sitting on the floor next to the man she called Denny. She lifted it to her ear slowly and measured, observing the '*transbot*' that glared down at her feet, peeking occasionally to study her face.

The terrified voice of a man who had just recently surfaced back into her wavelength now growled into her frequency, "They killed them all, Miss Kamen, you need to get here now!"

Why is everyone calling me Miss? Anara thought absently, insanity already seeping into her mind as she closed her eyes at the assumption that her children may be knocking at Death's Cradle.

Throwing the phone across the room, Anara glared down at the transbot before her, "How would *you* know what I've been doing? Where is he?"

"Ahzai, what will you do?" The duplicate of Denny Eneek looked away refusing to comply. Denny took a struggled breath, "They'll take you down the same hallway and leave you to rot in Death's Cradle with the rest of the mortals."

Anara stood up and away from the man who looked like a tortured Denny. He was made in the image of the Soldier who was married to Cara Castas, a woman with powerful blood flowing through her veins and did not know of it. He was a father of children who were more than likely missing with her own and endangered along with her own—children who sought the truth about their fathers and mothers. *Everyone had a Role,* the men in their lives were Soldiers to this Realm.

Emotions couldn't blind her, not now, not when Death was so near and starved, "Mortals?"

She reached down pressing her two forefingers into the imposter's neck, "Who are you?"

"Transbot," mocked the transbot Denny staring contently up at its enemy, waiting for a retort, "We have searched long for you, Ahzai."

There is always someone looking for her, hunting her and demanding she perform her universal duties to the Daeviti. Anara had only wanted to fade into existence and live like normal, primitive mortals lived. She had only wished to be free and ignorant to the politics of this world.

She growled, narrowing her eyes with rage forcing tears to lace her eyelashes, "Why do *They* seek me?"

"They-" the transbot mocked, "Use the sight you were bred with and see for yourself. You are the last in this galaxy, from what I've heard. Tell me, where is your Traveler?"

*No, s*he studied the bio-machine's false expressions. Debating the sacrifice she would risk making once she let the goddess devour her soul. To get, you must give—that was Law…but if she didn't use the Kiinak sight, her children would suffer more and it would be her fault for dealing that hand she had dealt. She only suppressed the goddess by suppressing her own Ahzai abilities.

Anara inserted her fingers into the Transbot's neck, paralyzing it while holding her bloodied hand over his face. She closed her eyes, focusing and plucking his memories from the living brain that had been planted in his alloyed skull and began the process of sorting truth from lies. A talent she had long perfected from many years of serving the Ahzai.

> *…Darkness… Walls the color of innocent blood and a never-ending hallway etched into the solid earth. They walked hastily avoiding the touch of, what? Her gaze turned to the right, along the walls hung dozens of mirrors—four-foot in width by seven-foot in length. Next to her was Krypt Halen being dragged and forced to face a mirror. Searching for the reflection she turns her head to see the parallel wall, nothing. The reflection was black, an endless darkness, coolness seeping from the mirrors glare. Krypt looked up seeing his reflection smiling back at him. A terrified word escapes his bloodied lips following a sharp, insolent smile: "She will sacrifice where you could not," he was gone.*

Anara opened her eyes hearing a voice behind her and ignoring his words. The Vision could not be true, or it has yet to come to pass, that could be an intention. Either direction taken in Vision, those halls belonged to one man, Owen Dame.

"Gas. They killed them with nerve gas," the voice was strong, deep with the Karonan accent she heard earlier on the phone, "the Tip of Antila has conformed."

"Did the President order the strike?" Anara turned staring blankly through her wide chestnut-amber eyes, fury churning with every thought as she stood to wipe the black blood of the informant from her hands: the transbot was no more.

"The Superiors are taking the steps to war by killing the greatest threat first: those who still *believed*. I fear we will be the next to undergo the beginning steps of Control," he took another step forward.

Anara could only stare at the man with a numbness ripping through her soul. Her children were not here and could be captured by the transbot abominations and she had a responsibility to save the innocence of this world. The Vessel in her screamed for the freedom that Anara had just granted. The game was over and the enemies have crossed the wrong lines. Immunity from this war was no longer written and the future would be reduced to waste if anything happened to that which was hers.

"Together forever, we are Kamenah," Anara closed her eyes at the whisper echoing in the back of her head, *"they still draw breath, sisa, you still have time."*

Her soul screamed and finally yielded to the deity awakened within, "So be it, it is done."

Fire and ice coursed through her blood as the power of Kamenah began to absorb the energy around her. She could feel her eyes dry and moisten as her body yielded and began to transform into the goddess's ultimate Vessel. It would be several months before she had complete control over the land around her, years before the planet bowed down and worshipped her name. Anara purred at the heat that consumed her and the Freeze that contented her. In this moment, everything was as it should be. Anara knew that she was born for only this purpose, to bring forth the Devourer and unleash Death into the lands of the Breach.

Anara shook her head, "No, not to rule as such," she growled, "For only but one purpose, that is the bargain in which you are freed, to resist Time and distract Death."

She clenched her fist and sighed at the assurance the goddess promised, *"We are one, we will exist together."*

"Owen sent me to gather you and your children for Protocol," the man studied her with narrowed, dark eyes and hesitated, "Do you not remember me? It is Zende Dajan. You have not seen me since our first flight to Traverna."

She frowned distantly with despair swelling at the rim of her eyes, "They sent a decoy. How did they find out about Ana and Jon? Zende, I will have my children returned to me or sent unto a safe place."

Zende hesitated as he cupped her face and whispered serenely into her ear, "I know one who can find them."

Safrai Gardens, Wastelands

The blood of the Ahzai runs so thick in their race that you need only one parent of the Ahzai for the offspring to muck around in mischief and create calamity if they are not trained to place their energies towards motives that would be less disastrous. The trouble with untrained Ahzai was that they know not the effects of their immediate actions, leaving the *masters* of the game to play clean up or improvise to make the outcome not so much of a total loss and completely to their own advantages.

"She'll find out what we've been doing," Jon stared at his sister knowing what bounced around in her head, "Mercy is right. We need to tell her."

"Owen should have met us here by now," Ana didn't respond to Jon's paranoia as she nibbled her lower lip in thought and concentration, "Fine, let's go tell *mala* that Owen has been leaking information to us for three years. That should send her into a *cold spell.*"

Ana hated her mother's *cold spells.* They were the moments of rage that brought the inner goddess out to scorn any and all who would oppose the safety of their mother's children. They weren't impenetrable after all. She was five years old when her empathic sensitivity elevated and when she got her first cycle it exploded. Ana didn't truly hate the link with the deity, but she wanted her own mother at all times. Being torn between two raging women was hell on a young teen who desperately wanted to be a woman, who desperately wanted to be strong like her mother.

Home wasn't too far from the Safrai Gardens. It was an easy hour run for a healthy young boy or girl if you went through the Dead Fields and knew the shortcuts to avoid what hid within—they were forbidden to enter without their mother with them. The Dead Fields harbored fugitives and criminals in the shadows of an ancient battlefield. You rarely crossed paths with their kind but the risk was still there, especially with the sweet and fresh temptation of an untouched child running astray. Their mother warned them many a times that great power drawls evil things and that as the children of Ahzai, there would always be something out there that wanted to control them. She had also shown them all the secret trails in case they needed to escape those 'evil' things.

The hair on Ana's arm rose as she noted the silence that boiled with chaos. The closer they got to their home a flood of *trace emotions* echoed through the air, polluting her balanced emotions with a tangible fear. The whispering breeze exhaled with torment from the impaling tips of the dry corn and wheat fields that were at one point in history, edible. There was *nothing* they could consume without growing it in a controlled shelter that had soil replaced twelve feet deep into the ground with a wall that wouldn't let the roots penetrate the poisoned soil that ruined the vegetation in the Wastelands. An expense most of the people who were of residences to the Wastelands could not afford.

Closing her eyes, Ana could hear her mother's voice whispering to her as she slept at night, asking her over and over:

> *"Where do the gods go when their worlds*
> *are destroyed? When they have none to worship*
> *them... none to offer the breath of Life and the*
> *welcome of Death? When you are Immortal, Ana,*
> *what do you suppose you would do if all that*
> *existed—existed no more?"*

This question she answered when she reached her sixteenth year and had just suffered a dark spell from her powers, when her Empathy took over and flooded her she had screamed at her mother:

"I do not care where they would go.
They should go and find peace! For all the gods that
may be mighty, mala, I would find rest in the death
of the universe because that it would bring silence
and my head wouldn't feel like stone and mush every
time my guard is down!"

It was then that she had realized how selfish she had been because even now her mother's final words spoken to her sadly, consuming her thoughts with the image of her mother's face wanting her to understand the consequences such a world would create:

"Oh sweet Ana, do you really think you
could handle infinite silence?"

Ana shook her head, shivering from the thought of hearing *nothing* and *knowing* you were alone. That would be the last place she desired to be, in a world of desolation. Her thoughts screamed to a halt when she saw the blackened blood trail that stained the driveway leaving a horrid thought playing over and over in her mind as she slammed back into the present.

Jon directed Mercy to circle around back while he and Ana entered through the front door into a black oiled kitchen to find the empty shell of a TransBot. Ana winced at the smell while assessing the emotional echoes to learn what had happened. Emotions of these magnitudes left signatures and those signatures, to an empathic seer, told a story. To a strong Ahzai born with an empathic sight, the story told could become a vivid replay in their minds. Ana was one of the strongest hidden in the Breach.

"They used her fears of losing us and there was only one who knew of our existence," a small gray ocean began churning in Ana's storm-swept eyes, "Owen knew we have been lifting Sector files from the Department."

"He had to of been betrayed," Jon thought on the concept but couldn't agree with his sister, "He wouldn't gain anything from selling us out. Owen wouldn't risk losing *mala* in the crossfire."

"That may be, but he wasn't there to meet with us either," Mercy crossed her arms in thought, "He drew us out so he could make a strike."

"We gave them what they wanted," Ana whispered trying to find a solution to fix their mistakes, "She has released the goddess."

Mercy tightened her jaw knowing what that meant, "We need to know which gateway Krypt was sent through and which realm Anara could have been taken to. Owen will have no choice but to help, it's the only way to retrieve his Anara."

"He doesn't know about the Vessel," Jon grabbed her arm, "How the hell do you think you'll be able to convince him without compromising her secret? The goddess could wipe this planet clean if *mala* permitted it."

Ana crossed her arms and growled at her brother, "And what do you think she will do if she can't find us?"

"If she is crusading to kill the world, it doesn't matter if he knows because she'll just assassinate him and everything else that gets in her way and it would have nothing to do with Kamenah. She is Ahzai, blood and soul," John crossed his arms and calmly exhaled, "If she hadn't sacrificed what she had, we would have been nothing but dust."

Mercy nodded, "My mother flew to Eere View on an assignment. Zende Dajan was her replacement at the Traverna firm."

Mercy, being the oldest out of the three, was left alone under the supervision of their mother. She spent most of her time with Ana and Jon digging information up on the Projects, specifically the ones involving their fathers. What she hadn't told Ana and Jon was that she reported back to their mother, so Anara wouldn't lose her reasoning like she had in this current event. Meeting with Owen had been a last minute decision on Ana's part—Mercy didn't have the chance to inform Anara of their intentions.

...

Owen Dame is one of the wealthiest snakes in the entirety of the Breach. He was one of the few in the New World who opposed the alliance of the Supremacy, secretly and not for the patriotic purposes he represented. His pride and pursuit for power placed the Supremacy somewhere beneath him, therefore making them inferior to the Breach and keeping him safe from their persecution. They needed him. The Dame Industries produced numerous weapons and inventions to aid the battle to create complete Control over the population. The Breach was a large planet with many to conquer in the most political justifications possible. He saw no equality between other worlds and believed that they must develop stronger defenses and weapons to prevent invasion—even though the enemy was in fact the Superiors and he sat at the top of the supremacy…or soon will.

In the pursuit for Control, he crossed a society known as the Hierarchy. The Darken of the South Run Arkeon, the kingdom which inhabited the Shadoa Moon that never shifts from its spot creating total darkness over a good stretch of the polar South: a land of Black Ice. It was also where he was conceived and also the place where he met Lukan and Damu. It won't be till later that he discovers the truth about the Hierarchy and their devious intentions. Still, his most trusted connection with the society was Anara, and Anara had no intentions of yielding her knowledge willingly.

Ana Halen's connection with Owen was the exchange of information. She would provide a needle in a haystack by sharing the work of her mother and bits of her mother's journals for intelligence and information gathered through Owen's sources after she had gone through and chose significant yet unreliable entries and research. Young and naïve, Ana didn't know that the only purpose Owen built a partnership with her was to keep watch over her mother.

...

Traverna's Dame Towers were built in the center of the city. They rose high and strong with the darkest alloy of the irinoi-core shielding its secrets from the civilization around it. Every floor had a reason and every employee had a purpose of employment and didn't question their objectives. Science—the towers were made for all levels of science and research. Knowledge was power.

The current plan:

Ana and Mercy would go to Traverna and infiltrate the towers using the secretary to gain access to the Hall of Mirrors as their mother had done many times before. Jon would hack into the system and attempt to locate the beacon on their fathers. He would have only fifteen minutes to accomplish his task. They would need a Vacant Transporter to enter the right codes that would take them to the location of Krypt Halen or Kai Thareck: the leaders of the Soldiers sent to find Prophet's Eyes. Ana hadn't yet decided what the exact name of the devices were—as her mother had not yet given any lead to the accursed objects.

It hadn't occurred to them that there were great possibilities in their equation for disaster. The children were in no shape to take on an environment that a Soldier had been taught to tear down. Children knew not the dangers of such threats, especially the ones entrapped on their own planet in the shape of irinoi alloys and steel. The tower stood sharp and straight into the sky, higher than all others casting a shadow that could tell the time of sun-settings throughout the shifting hours of the Breach. It was only one of twelve throughout the entire planet; with prospects of more in the making.

Ana vividly remembered her mother describing Owen as being clever and a greater threat than the entire Supremacy:

> *"Unlike the Superiors who exist and*
> *function entirely on broad generalization, Owen*

prefers working with details and is a master for mass

engineering.   What he sets into motion now will

show its outcome far into the future. I often wonder

if he knows what he truly asks for when he begins a

Project."

Her mother's voice echoed in her mind as they took their first step into the tower.

Normally the first thing they would see was the receptionist that would leak information to their mother on a regular basis. This morning, Starla was not present, the receiving desk and the touch computer was gone with her and the elevator had been barred off with a sign saying "Out of Order" taped to the irinoi-alloy door.

Ana looked at Mercy with her thin rust-red eyebrows raised in questioning concern, "We are not walking all the way up to the damned thirty-sixth floor."

Mercy smirked walking over to the elevator and winked at Ana as she pulled a few tools out of her lavender backpack, "Genius, remember?"

Ana grinned, placing a hand on her hip to stand back and watch her best friend go to work.

She reached under the bar and pried the shield off the controls of the elevator, "I scoped this out when we got hold of the new grids. Starla generally controls the function of elevators and hall doors, but everything has a manual override that is still possible. Difficult to hack when you're being watched, but not impossible when there is no one around," she clamped down on several wires, "you know, there was something else on those old grids that caught my eye. There is a passage that cuts off with no destination. Doesn't show where it is heading too and has an ancient override system built in. I asked mom about it, she said it was built before the score: bolts, triggers and knot-codes."

Mercy and Jon had those things in common; they were incredibly smart where Ana had only her emotional dysfunctional abilities. One of their differences were that Mercy was great at breaking things down and figuring out how it was created and Jon had the ability to *create* something new and undiscovered.

Ana rolled her eyes at the girl who had been the only sister she had ever known even though they were not blood-kin, "Just like your mala."

Mercy wrinkled her brows, "Where did you all come up with the term *mala*?"

Ana laughed shaking her head, "For all the genius, you still have glitches. It's my mother's language."

The elevator door slid open and they both ducked under the bar and slid into it, "Ahzai. I keep forgetting that, she seems so domestic at times."

Domestic was hardly a term you could use to describe anything born of the Ahzai. Yes, she baked and plowed her own gardens, but even the lonely farmer would kill if something or someone threatened their *harvest*. Ana shrugged watching Mercy get to work on the key pad to take them up, "Will Jon be able-"

"Don't worry about Jon. He is better at this than I am. He taught me how to do my first hack you know," Mercy chuckled at Ana who obviously remained in a stone age, "I just wish I could get to my parents and brother and sisters to warn them before things go down. I feel like there's something bad that's going to happen."

Blinking at the new information Mercy muttered while she fiddled with the wires and the elevator began to move, "I didn't know you had a brother or sisters."

Mercy shrugged, finally complete with what she was doing, "Daddy was a busy man. I have three that I know of, there could be plenty more. Oliver is the oldest, he is a cadet on the Naval Star, watches us from above," she smiled to herself, "He is wonderful and probably doesn't know I exist. I am sure he knows that Nathus has many children running around but Momma was sure to keep me secret because of Owen—like Anara does with Jon. Mina is my older sister and Idol my younger. Before Momma was sent away, I got to see Mina once a month and Idol had been sent to the Advance Placement Academy in Keeton. Momma didn't want anyone to know about her either. She said that it was best that Owen *never* found out about her."

Bing. Bing.

Ana froze absorbing the input Mercy was offering, "But that would mean in the time they were on mission, Bioni would have seen either another man or your father."

"One-nighter," Mercy frowned knowing that it wasn't fair that the ball didn't roll in everyone's favor.

There was true-love, blind-love, puppy-love, dumb-love and—mating. Mating was generally the master of one-night-stands. Ana shook her head as if trying to get dirt out of her ears.

"Some have more animal in them than we care to believe," the elevator came to a stop and they stepped out into the hallway filled mirror transports, "Who knows their true origin?"

9

They glanced into the first mirror and hurried to pass it up. The view of smoke and ash was disturbing and neither of them could explain why. What they didn't think to ponder was the possibility that a war had stripped that land moments before and what they saw was Death— except that the scene depicted was on their land and in their world...

There were many other mirrors, each with a different scene reflecting back at them. Some held life in it and others were as still as a painting hung from a museum wall. Ana paused when she came upon a mirror flooded with a land made of only water. She desired to touch it but knew that it would suck her in and drop her into an ocean she had never seen, but the light glistening from the water and the gray storm in its horizon enchanted her with promise of mental serenity. This world called to her and she didn't have time enough to answer it.

The door at the end of the hall creaked open, "-and have the mirrors transported to Eere View to join the collection there."

Owen Dame stepped out carrying a file and suitcase with his pet Soldier, Lyle, not far behind him, "Zende said the archives have been successfully trans-"

Lyle stopped, focusing on the girls who were unable to run or hide for all that surrounded them were other worlds and different realms.

When Owen saw them he smirked and waltzed towards them with his usual arrogance and charm, "What do I owe the honor of this visit?"

Ana studied the man who stood before her, smiling with secrets. His hair had grown out since last she had seen him, what was once a bald head now held a crown of silky golden blond hair. He wore combat boots beneath his expensive hypocrite's suit. She wanted to drive her unscarred fists into his flawless face, Dame was withdrawing from Travena just as her mother

was kidnapped, "When would be the appropriate time to activate Control?"

Mercy gawked at her bluntness, "Ana."

She continued with her hopeless interrogation. Owen may not have been responsible

for her mother going missing but he was responsible for her father's absence and she was pretty

sure that he had a hand in everything else evil in the game of domination and power, "Make us

slaves or prisoners. I mean, really Dame, if you had access to more power than every human on

this planet, wouldn't you seek complete domination?"

Owen let his smile fade and tensed at her implications and use of his last name in place

of his first, "Ana, I would never betray you or your mother."

She tilted her head like a wolf observing a meal, debating how to devour what was

left. Ana withdrew into a subconscious wall to keep his prying eyes from seeing her true feelings,

"Only that the war has begun and you may be the first to fall."

Her childish conclusions and assumptions forced a small, charming chuckle through

his thin lips. He was intrigued by this girl—she was much like her mother, "You are no hero,

Ana. Not even a Soldier. What are you to do with the tools you have been given?"

Ana began stripping his emotional barriers and tasting the feelings he held within his

suit of flesh. His mind was a labyrinth of murky red and faded black with walls of *irinoi* core and

some foreign mineral she had never seen before. She knew her planet's minerals and metals and

the majority of its chemicals and compounds, this wall was made of something frozen and deadly.

She searched for panic, for the feeling of accomplishment…there were none hidden in the depths

of Owen Dame's mind.

Mercy stared confused at Ana as she began walking away, "We need to know

answers."

Ana snapped around grabbing her friend's arm, "We have gotten all the answers he wants to give."

Mercy nodded, understanding that they needed to vacate the presence of this man before he took it upon himself to keep them for whatever reason. There would come a day that he would *be* the Supremacy and the government would bow to him if they still existed at the end of the doom that has come. If there was a time to be far from the Breach, it was now and Mercy wished she could manifest wings and fly away into the stars.

"I can take you to your father, Ana," Owen's lip twitched with his intrigue, "The Mirror Transport we need is not here though. It is at my tower in Eere View."

Ana wheeled around while reminiscing every bedtime story and morning tales of adventure her mother had drilled into her as a child. All civilizations were doomed with a single taint that wanted to control the existence of all that was. There had always been a mortal who would stop at nothing to become a god. They would even entrap the Celestials and Entities that were native to the land, those who were here before the current Majority came, before the human colonies of afar, the Score, and before the Drillers.

The Supremacy of Government, with the aid of Dame Corps, monopolized civilization and continued to explore and search races in need of their influence. They continue to strive for utter Control and now, Ana was positive they sought for more…they sought for an ultimate Hierarchy Control.

Ana stared at him, not really seeing him but seeing through him, dazed from her irritation that she knew what would come. She had even read of it in her mother's letters and journal. What choice did she have but to follow the man her mother spoke of as a half-blood devil who would lay the world to waste while sipping coffee and eating sugar biscuits for his morning refreshments?

She began rubbing the center of her chest fighting back the half-digested breakfast that gurgled up her thin esophagus. A blue abyss of sorrow swirled calmly around the gray of her eyes, agony of ice-gray waves among twinkling icebergs tempting a black hole teetering in the center of a universe of precocious empathy. Her enduring temperament bled through her eyes and was shadowed with her rusty hair. Tears threaten to spill over with pure emotion, she had been trained to control her empathic gifts but all she wanted to do was drown this man in waves of self-doubt to drive the beast mad. Self-doubt was the one emotion Kamenah had taught her that would drive all *men* mad.

"Men are another species regardless to what genus," Kamenah, the cold one, had said in her many lessons. For all the darkness of this Vessel's link, the goddess still wanted what was best for the children of Anara. She taught them to be cold just like her.

The Freeze twinkled in her eyes. Owen watched Ana with passion and obsession over the innocence and the determination the girl possessed. She was her mother's daughter and still persuadable. The best part about keeping the girl around was that she was bait, and she needed to lure Anara to his side—a tool for a weapon.

He knew that Anara would never consent to following him anywhere—he ruined any chances of redemption when he made Krypt disappear. She had already denied him numerous occasions, even when he wanted her to travel to the Tower just to visit with Krypt when it was his turn to be a Runner. She refused and never explained why. She kept too many secrets from him and everyone else. Her entire bloodline reeked of forbidden secrets. Owen had done many tests from the blood samples retained from when she first arrived. He could never understand where Anara was tied into the circle of evolution, the samples from before the birth of Ana was mortal with humanistic character flaws: samples from after they got her into their care were different and corrupt—the samples turned to ash before he was even able to run an origin screen on it.

Shivering from the coolness chafing in the eyes of someone she loved, Mercy reached out gripping firmly on Ana's delicate arms. She shook hard and continuous, "If he speaks true, we must follow. We do not need too, but this lead would be more solid than the *other*."

The *other* being their mother had been abducted and they had no clue as to whom had taken her other than trace emotions left behind by the Transbot which only showed the image of Krypt being shoved into a Mirror Transport.

Ana blinked, her frozen eyes glaring petrified at the reflection nearest to them. Dark clouds plumed over the horizon with a bloody haze outlining the fields of the Wastelands. She realized that Owen had someone spying on the Wastelands but knew that it didn't matter now. She only struggled to keep her jaw shut and her emotions from escaping the control of her mind.

Owen cursed at the picture in the mirror reflecting the Wastelands. The beginnings of a Darken invasion laid waste to the fields of one of his Projects. The center of the territory burned and boiled: the half that belonged in the Traverna territory. It had not yet reached the Gated Forest; he knew this because the sirens had yet to blare through the pale blue sky.

Lukan had severed his alliance with him and now began war with the Superiors of the Supremacy. This was not hard to believe, the Darken had just discovered he had been holding information from him. How was Owen to know the Darken hunted the same game?

"Ana, Mercy, we need to go now!" Jon stepped out of a Mirror yelling, breaking the screaming silence.

They had no choice but to rely on Owen.

"Perhaps he had planned it this way," Mercy whispered to Ana as she narrowed her eyes at the man who looked absolutely irritated.

Ana was the only one he cared enough about to lure into a situation to keep her close to him. He didn't care too much for Jon because he was the son of Krypt and Jon wanted nothing to do with him. It wouldn't surprise Mercy if Jon's finger slipped on a trigger one day and planted a *meinite* bullet between the man's eyes. It was all about Ana, if he couldn't have the mother, Owen would do everything to secure the manipulation of the daughter.

Owen nodded trying to shake off his shock, "I have a-"

"There are Arkeon *hybra* all over the skies. Things, monsters are exploding out of the torsos of people on the street and attacking the humans around it. The Old World is dead—everything is dead," a security guard grunted behind Jon, apparently Jon had been caught hacking and the only thing that saved him was the invasion, "Sir, I believe the Darken have allied with the Supremacy of Governments. The Superiors have hinted that we are not to interfere with the invasion."

He smirked at the wrath Lukan was capable of, the sublime authority and destruction. The Darken were the Supremacies only equal, if not greater on the Breach. They were strategically placed throughout the planet and had been long before the Score. It only just now occurred to him that the King had all intentions of overruling the Supremacy, and overthrowing him.

Owen knew that he didn't need to go through such measures. The *Inoba* virus had to be *Summoned* out of the Nexum and given a host to mature. Owen knew that he, as a mortal, couldn't enter the Nexum and exit it still in his own body. The Nexum was a holding prison for the worst of all that exists, demons waiting to steal your body to escape the hell the Daeviti realm had created. So he sent a Darken, the only species that lives in and out of shadows. The King had returned with what he needed and much more, but he also returned changed.

Lukan had told him it was perfectly safe and easily controlled, what he had failed to mention was that the shells of a corpse that had once been a temple for human souls would become a birth canal for the evolved prisoners of the Nexum. He had gone through a long process of gathering blood samples and distributing 'vaccinations' over the past twenty years seeking an easier method. His closest achievement was left to wither and thrive on the Breach's Prison Islands: Croate, Cenilus and Norvik.

"Lukan now sits as King," Owen mumbled and scoffed at the turn of the table, "his right hand and executioner is Damu, who is his Queen?"

Ana shook her head at the security guard, "We have to go through the city."

Her stern voice and insane suggestion brought him back from his brooding and forcing him to deal with the current situation he had created.

"Face being killed by the monsters exploding out of seventy percent of the population? What does a child know?" Owen snapped sarcastically as he towered over Ana by only a few inches.

Jon grit his teeth struggling not to attack Owen, "We can't go by air because the *hybra* own the skies along with whatever is bursting out of civilian bodies. Where else can we escape to the shores?"

Owen studied the boy before him, a boy he had never seen but knew who had fathered him. He spread his arms out to the hall of mirrors, with a sly suggestive thought, "How afraid are you of your own reflection?"

Lyle narrowed his eyes at the thought that froze his soul, "I hate Mirror transport."

"Let's get on with it," Owen motioned to the office where the Eere View Mirror was kept locked away from all the other mirrors in the hall.

"I've never been transported anywhere," Mercy muttered as she blinked, gazing at a mirror that should have held her reflection.

"There's a first for everything," Owen muttered back with little interest while Lyle took the first step to secure the room. He glared at Jon knowing the last time he had seen his father was when he sent him flying through a mirror transport to greet his doom.

A mirror only sees what's in its reflection, leaving millions of blank spots for enemies to hide in. They stood before the mirror, staring at the room in the other tower, watching as Lyle cleared the room. Thankful there was nothing in it. The desk was void of all the normal things you would find on an office desk telling them that Owen had plans of leaving nothing behind. The walls were the color of *irinoi* core and there were several ancient paintings of their history after the Score. Mercy went next and Jon followed with the security guard leaving Ana and Owen alone in silence.

It would have been if a snake didn't hiss, "You could choose to come with me to the Antilia Tower."

Ana blinked her enchanting storm-swept eyes and reached out to graze the surface of the mirror with her fingertips—and she found herself on the other side, with her brother and cousin.

"Pity," Owen stepped through and immediately was handed a weapon and rifle.

"We can take the third tunnel to the edge of the city," Lyle studied a computer screen and motioned for Owen to look, "It's the same here. We will need to go through the streets. They already relocated the mirror that would take us to Woke Free Base, so it's on foot from here."

They took the elevator lift down through the tower making their way to the underground parking garage for the employees of Dame Corps. Lyle shot the first rounds and cleared the floor as they made their way to the tunnel that would lead them to their next destination. Once they made it to the exit they realized the true damage of the invasion and began running down the street shooting and killing anything that darted their way, including other humans.

Mercy shook her head, "What if they're not one of them?"

Owen knew that the probability of the civilians not having been vaccinated were one out of every twenty. Many of the civilians had refused his vaccination so it left him to poison the city water to spread the disease to the rest of the population. He made sure the children were in school when he had done the deed, the corrections schools didn't tap off the city water, they drank from the Old City mines.

"And so cometh the death of the last Prophet," Jon muttered, remembering a journal entry in his mother's books: knowing that what was-shall be no more. Anara had predicted this moment in their existence that they would face the darkness of mankind. Jon even remembered her telling them that it wasn't the evil of the land but the evils of man that will undo them, *'Control should never be.'*

They ran down empty allies and out into chaotic streets. A woman ran up to them screaming with horror stretched across her face as she ripped her shirt off. A long black glossy line stretched down the center of her torso as blood began drizzling through her skin. The flesh broke and released long claws and black slimy skin riddled with muscle and spikes. A dark roaring hiss of laughter came ripping out as a beast burst into the air sending blood raining down on Owen. It hovered over Ana for a moment making a groaning sound of hunger and began to strike. Lyle opened fire sending the beast to the ground while Ana grabbed the nearest arm for protection: Owen.

10

Gated Forest, the Breach

Markings that were not there before began to appear, and then shimmer away on her glistening body. The fluid motion of her slender figure reminded him of a predator hunting an intruder on its territory. Her hair had darkened and now shined with a glow more exotic than Zende had ever seen in his short existence. Her eyes gazed wide with an amber and copper glow, power flickered uncontrollably with every blink. This was what the Darken wanted him to deliver to them without letting Owen become aware of the meeting. Zende refused to be anything like Lyle, a lap dog that leapt when commanded, no, Zende was one hundred percent mortal, a human.

Anara could feel the frozen fire and rage of her Vessel tearing away at her soul and burning through her veins. The heat of the goddess rose through her cheeks and rippled through her muscles. She knew that the power could now be noticed upon her flesh, she could see her reflection on Zende's eyes. She had already began feeding on his essence.

Anara felt the energy that expelled from the world around her. She could feel the planet's heart and soul pulse upon her cold breath. Her body began to absorb the Breach's energy. The Vessel demanded every drop to be gained. The process would still take time before she could completely control the tides of energy that became a constant caress throughout her mortal body, every limb radiated with unmolested power.

This is what it is like to be a god, Anara thought with sorrow.

She now understood why souls yield to their possessor: the power becomes addicting and a goddess can offer it in infinite provision.

"You seem different, Halen?" Zende mused, with a serious expression consuming his deception.

It took her a minute to translate his question through the constant ringing in her head. She couldn't place that name, 'Halen': she was *Kamenah* now.

Yet there was something that echoed Ahzai in the back of her mind: *focus.*

"I am afraid I have made a *minor* mistake," Anara whispered with an exhaled breath.

Zende's dark eyes narrowed as she smiled insanely, "What do you mean?"

The young woman radiating with divine power demanded worship, *"I was different before I came here, before I gave birth to my daughter."*

He faced her terrified, for she had spoken in another language that he could not interpret, *'Ziat-I tunosai vio, no kai vio he-on doe mui lorala.'*

"I had a habit of bending every rule placed beside my duty," Anara chuckled feeling his fear and something else, doubt? He does not know she could read his emotions—influence his thoughts...

Zende stiffened at her confession, "Anara, are you still with me?"

Anara giggled ravenously at his worry and concern for his own well-being. She was a different person as an Ahzai; cold hearted and calculating, driven by a hunger that none has ever seen the likes of. There was no love in her eyes, only seduction, defiance. She and her goddess were one in the same.

She opened her mouth and spoke in his native language, "Hardly."

They could feel the silence of being watched. She watched Zende snap his head around like a scared animal catching the scent of its predator, *"Mez umai ier-et mez hebrem."*

Anara watched his gaze return to her with a puzzled eyebrow raised, and she answered him, "The wolf leading the lamb,"

The Ahzai could trace the energy-echoes of each Soldier hidden in the field and beyond within the forest. Adding both entities into one divine form created an ultimate weapon. The Vessel could taste the taint of their lust and corruption and their addiction to harm and kill. Not even the traitor at her side knew what they were up against. It was true that the Vessel was still charging up like a black hole ready to consume all within its grasp, and soon she would be strong enough to chill the land into slumber if she so chose, and if Anara consented—which would be determined on whether her children were alive and safe and utterly *unharmed.*

There was nothing subtle about what they were getting ready to do and Anara knew his betrayal matched his master's betrayal—treachery held a scent that would pollute for centuries to come. She knew his treason before they had left her house, even then he smelled of Death.

The moment a traitor is made, Death sets a target on their soul. It won't be before too long that a Reaper will manifest and take the bounty, Anara smirked at the irony of betrayal and that this would be one soul she would have no need to reap because he now had a legion of hunters out to get him.

Kamenah echoed her humor with the Laws of gods, *"If all evil could be dealt with in such ways the responsibilities of a god wouldn't be enacted and I would need not to smite a world of ignorance."*

Anara became aware that the game had taken yet another turn having learned that even gods had rules to play by. She had it in her mind that being intimately linked to a goddess would give her infinite power with no boundaries to confine her vengeance and wrath. No, it would appear that it is Law that the nearest god or goddess, even an entity who held rank and worship would be Summoned to smite or save a world from their ignorance and it is this particular Law that could bring down all the pieces in play for Anara and the goddess. If Kamenah is chosen to correct this world, she would have to stop all that she was doing and obey the Law.

"If you do not, what becomes of you?" Anara voiced the question aloud addressing the Vessel; for a link works both ways, one cannot continue without the other once the link is made.

The goddess sighed, "He *strips me of my right as a goddess.*"

The Ahzai grinded her teeth knowing Zende still studied her as they walked and it only just became apparent that the goddess had whispered her words aloud and Anara wasn't sure which language she had spoke in.

"*Do not worry,*" Kamenah sent a chilling wave of comfort, "*It would not be the* first time I have been given the command to destroy all that exists. We obey, or we fall...*"

"*The cold world,*" was the only thought that rang in Anara's memories as images of a civilization frozen in Death's slumber flashed through her mind.

The sky was speechless and clear, not a cloud staining the perilous periwinkle of the Even-Rise's blue space. The Wastelands generally remained without clouds, and what storms raged through did so quickly leaving devastation and debris for the land to consume. There weren't any hints of the previous storm from the night before: the ground faintly damp and nearly parched as though the earth was dying of thirst. Her residence within the Wastelands was a hungry one.

Anara could feel the immediate suffering in scorching waves of visions and realized that deep down in her own soul she yearned for a dark chill and the slumber Freeze had to offer. As if answering her desires, the Breach echoed with a cool gentle breeze sweeping the dead grass, whispering of an early Winter Wake.

They waited until the foot Soldiers surrounded them in the shadows of a falling sun. Zende gave them a code and waited for them to enter it into a computer the size of their palm with a little pen tapping at a glass screen. He continued to socialize for a half hour waiting for them to receive their orders from their ranking officer until finally they noticed a spark in the girl that shimmered at his side.

Silence tends to scream louder than *Desert Sirens.*

"Is she the woman?" A soldier jabbed a rifle into her back.

Anara exhaled a growl of restraint, Zende frowned at her new persona; "It is what *our* employer wanted."

Another Soldier grinned at her with lust bleeding from his eyes, "What's her worth, her name?"

Zende began to answer when the awakened Vessel glistened with mischief. Anara smiled innocently and offered only riddles like all superior entities offered, "I am the beginning of chill and the end of ice."

They, the lesser, the mortals, had not earned direct explanations. They had not earned the right to question her. In her own world, Kamenah would have slit their throats and used their flesh as grub for the *Umai*, great wolf-like beast with three tails and poisoned bites. In her world, she had her equals in power for they were Immortal. She had a reason to merit such actions among a warrior's race.

We cannot kill them without consequence. With Ana and Jon still not at my side, I will not take such risks, Anara reminded the goddess of what was at stake.

She only received the comforting response Kamenah delivered with insurance; "*I will play by your mortal rules.*"

The goddess paused rethinking her words, "*until they give me reason to* act."

"We shall see who you really are," the Lieutenant chuckled under his breath turning to Zende, "They've been expecting you."

She shrugged at the man noting his address to Zende as they began walking, "It worked for *Him*, had to try it for myself."

They stepped cautiously through the rich evergreen forest that seemed to have breathed its own life. She absorbed the landscape as they walked: her eyes calculating the sky, every branch on each tree, which star shown first face, how the wind escaped the wooded lands. The Vessel needed to do little work because the Ahzai had been trained from birth to adapt and defend: the Ahzai was born and bred for infiltration and delivering Death.

The Lieutenant studied her curiously trying to figure out why, why this girl? He blinked as her eyes caught his with a sly curiosity of her own. Eyes that seemed to glow like the embers of fire around amber stone and within the center was the abysmal blackness that reflected his face as though he were the insect trapped in the glossy amber hardness of eternity and death.

He shook his head struggling to look away and stop thinking with the feeling that she was toying with him. He felt a chill invade his veins, leaving his flesh to feel as if millions of spiders prickled up and down trying to find their way to his bones and devour his soul. He then wondered if he was the only one feeling wounded and molested, as if he had been walking around with no clothes for all to see what he had beneath. Not that any woman would complain, he was a Soldier, he had all the right goods, but it just felt as though something important had been taken away from him or that something held onto him and would not let go until it had taken all it desired to leave only an empty corpse that walked dazed to the world, starved like the dead and with no thought: a zombie to the world that blossomed before him.

The Lieutenant squeezed his eyes shut trying to force out the *emotions and feelings* that consumed him, relying on his training. A Soldier was expected to endure torture and agony like the thoughts that blinded him as they proceeded into their employer's Dome. He fought every urge to run and get as far from this mission as he could possibly manage.

"Zende, why do humans serve so willingly? Is not their souls free?" Her voice seemed to be in harmony with the dry breeze that glided through the forest limbs.

Zende eyed her trying to keep her silent, "Everyone must serve someone. It is the way of life."

"It is the way of slaves. You underestimate the strength of mortality, human souls are strong and yet so weak," she rolled her eyes at his weakness, "To whom do you serve, Zende?"

The Soldiers gasped at the condemnation that seeped from her pink lips. There was a mocking, sinister defiance that hungered in her presence. Before Zende could answer, the Lieutenant saved him with a simple mutter, "That is why humans are obsolete: Naming one god for another, many not even being a god, just power hungry *Immortals*, entities needing fuel for their existence. That is why the Supremacy chose to imprison all the evolved races."

"Thus making the words of humans obsolete and not their souls," she snapped at his remark finding the need to educate them, "Here is a lesson, Lieutenant Brondan Jamicon: *Immortals* were not evolved, they were born that way. They are a race of their own. Half-breed yet still pure blooded and some cannot help but to seek worship as a price for their immortality. It is from willing prayer they receive the food needed to not devour souls or lives. All that exist has a price," her voice fell to a whisper, "They answer to *something* greater as we all do, and by starving them they will evolve or diminish, but either route taken: humans *need* their alliance."

The Lieutenant stared at her disturbed and slightly uncomfortable wondering how she knew his full name because they did not wear their names on badges and addressed each other in code names.

Zende saw the fire in her eyes, twinkling like little stars ready to fall and destroy their world and knew instantly that if she was Ahzai; they had evolved into something greater than anything written in his or anyone's research and Owen would fall dead in his mirrored hall to know that his trusted colleague had betrayed him and given his prize possession to his enemy.

"Don't worry. Traitors have a price on their heads, too," Anara chuckled at the humans remembering a lesson all the Ahzai were taught, "Tell me, slave, if not for an Army, how else would one conquer land and if not for mortality, how else would they take breath? Think upon that before you curse your mortal soul."

Anara neglected to complete the lesson Scarlet had once taught her. It's completed phrasing being: '*If not for an Army, how else would one conquer land and if not for mortality, how else would they take breath—for all that holds control, holds the power to conquer but does not always hold the knowledge to rule.*'

They all stared at her unable to find a protest for fear what the truth would bring, fear of what a lie would lead to.

"Point taken," Anara exhaled following them with amusement, *lambs who serve the wolves and wolves who worship the lions.*

Zende could only walk in silence against her skirmish.

A shadow became apparent not more than fifty-feet in front of them. The wind became still and life was quiet…dead. The soldiers placed a metallic hood over her head before they entered a transport device she was unable to verify. Each technologically advanced civilization had their trademark devices. The Breach functioned primarily on Mirror Transport which would give them long range transportation and Water Holes (Hydro-transportation) which only functions within a single planet or even, depending on the distance of their moons, between their own moons if habitable.

Anara grabbed her chest feeling the shift in Realms opening around her and squeezing her lungs with the pressure: they had walked her through a Mirror Transport. There was something else stirring within her, that she could vaguely depict and yet was familiar all the same, familiar to the Ahzai soul. It had a chill her soul welcomed. She could sense urgency in the air and when she allowed her empathic abilities to reach out, she could sense a raw hunger seeping from the urgency.

A compound built solely for the purpose of science; technology unlike any human creation lined the walls as paintings in a vast museum. She could feel their characteristics with her senses unlike many of the mortals on this land. Then again, she wasn't from this land. The soldiers led them down a hallway and into a cool office. The scent of stale blood stung her nostrils and burned her lungs. It had been ages since last she tasted the rot of death and a long, forgotten part of her yearned for the scent of chaos, almost demanding her to pay tribute to such an offering.

She leapt into the air at the sound of Zende grunting and falling to the floor. Her ears tried to hear the untold secret, struggling to see through the echoes of trace emotions. Humans always left strong, trace emotions just before their passing and Zende's were screaming right now as his soul faded away and became breakfast for Death to devour.

A cool, strong callused hand clasped her face forcing Anara to tense, anticipating a hard blow. The captor removed the hood to see the face beneath, letting an agitated exhale escape his lips as the result of seeing what had been revealed. His eyes twinkled with victory as he glared at her, tracing every line and contour of her face.

"At last, " the words echoed in her mind, prickling her blurry memories with recognition. She could hear the puzzle in his voice and opened her eyes. He wasn't what she was expecting. Here she sought a demon, hideous and demeaning: but this man was handsome, strong and beautiful with the signs of war upon his flesh.

She locked her eyes defiantly on his as those last moments before being shoved into a jettison pod finally returned to her, "Have I been betrayed?"

"Yes," a strong, charming voice pierced her heart, "Anara, you should have known better. Follow your instincts. Zende has worked for us since the beginning of what the Supremacy calls Control. He has misguided you for our cause."

He struggled to keep his mouth shut as he peered into her defiant eyes. She was more than what she had been when he shoved her into the pod and helped her escape her mission. Her orders were clear and they were orders she could not, nor desired to carry out. He would have not allowed her to carry out regardless to whether or not she had loved him. Even now as he gazed into her shifting amber eyes, he could sense that she was *more* than just the Ahzai. She was cooler, as though warmth had faded or had been absorbed elsewhere. Heat still remained, but warmth was no more. The Anara he knew and loved had become cold and calculating.

"Darken," she glanced down at the pool of blood that encompassed her feet, "and this is why you killed him?"

The Darken puzzled over the species that humbled before him, "His contract has been fulfilled. Zende was a traitor, so death is his reward. That is Law of our people, of *your* people. *We* have searched long for you, Ahzai," he knotted his fist within her hair pulling her closer so that their bodies could meet, "Do you not remember your past, *lorala*? Beloved."

The energy of rage would forfeit her control and concentration. Should she become anxious: her heart would race and cause strain to her breathing forcing her to react with chaos as a weapon. She must appear weak to gain the knowledge she needed from him. There was a puzzle to be completed and secrets to be kept.

The Darken began to probe her mind—at least attempted to probe her mind. She chuckled with insanity glistening on the tips of her tears at his vain thirst for knowledge and poor attempt on stripping her memories from her thoughts.

"Dig deeper," she muttered through clenched teeth.

He nodded a mutual agreement seeing that she had become stronger than the defiant child he once knew, "Humans will be our slaves until we find the gates to the heavens beyond. That little transbot that visited you this morning was right: it goes beyond your comprehension," he then spread the fingers of his left hand over her chest, "I was supposed to take you back to *him*, but I must know that you will cooperate with the task we will ask of you."

"Who are you to ask of me," Anara gasped, struggling to fight his invasion and to fight the Queen's desire to take control over her body.

He continued to search in silent concentration feeling a chill unlike any other surround her existence where there once had been a burning oasis that welcomed his touch. Now, there was a colliding storm—that still welcomed his touch.

She pushed away feeling his fingers wrap around her heart searching for her soul, "If I could have gotten rid of it I would have done so long ago."

She gasp letting a tender yelp escaped her lungs in the struggle to eradicate the talons that dug viciously deeper and deeper into her mind searching for something she knew he would never find. Her eyes began to bleed from the energy being shocked through her body and the tension of keeping the goddess silent—and then she collapsed in his arms. The freezing chill of the Vessel began burning around her soul, screaming in fury at his attempts to invade. She knew he would not succeed, would not even comprehend what snuggled within her body offering her infinite energy and ultimate power.

She reached out clasping his cruel face, grinning mockingly with a soft chuckle, *"You shall have great needs to dig much deeper than that, dear* boy."

She couldn't fight back both forces. This Darken was powerful and would have been her equal as an Ahzai. The Vessel's link reached out for the kill, combining his mind with hers. No one really knew the torment within her, the demons inside. The true reason why she fought so hard to hide from the world and avoid the battle she was forced to play in, *everyone had a Role.*

Kamenah soothed her while tormenting him with wave after painful wave of his own techniques, his own assaults return to him tenfold.

He wanted to pull away, but he knew to pull away would make him weaker than the mere mortal he struggled to dissolve. He couldn't risk losing her when so close to what he desired. Anara had always been strong beyond her years and training, she was superior to all of the other Ahzai in her ranks…but this—this was something more. There was a *freeze* where there should have been fire, walls that should have broken in his assault moments ago.

No one had ever survived an invasion of mind such as this; not one of this magnitude. He was one of the most powerful of Darkens. He was the Prince, brother of the Darken King.

He became fascinated as she probed his mind. She began sharing her thoughts and giving dead trails with no ends to follow. His vision was blurred with images that were being created and planted as a defense to block his probing.

"What are you searching for?" He growled huskily while slowly withdrawing to make his second assault, except, he would never make his move.

"*The only thing that matters,*" her voice echoed like a bell ringing in the back of his head.

A voice vibrated through the room, a room she no longer saw, and the battle was over as a sharp, burning stab severed her link. Anara passed out in his arms having found the source of the power, a power that was temporarily stronger than her own. It would seem she wasn't the only Vessel wandering the Breach.

He winced as her visions invaded his sight forcing him to grow drunk from her strength, listening to the voices that screamed in his mind: voices which were not his own. Her soul carried scars unlike any others, foreign and not hers but shared none-the-less. Voices that he now would have to listen to lecture him infinitely or until the event had faded. Oddly, he knew the voice that lectured him...

The man who interfered cleared his throat with humor, "You mind releasing my *lorala*, younger brother?"

He held her close to him feeling her heart beat against his, "I do not think she is *your* beloved anymore, Lukan."

"Ah, but I would still not allow you to possess her," the King chuckled with ever-changing sadistic eyes glistening down at the two entangled, "You, nor any other."

They both glared down at Anara as a soft whisper left her lips while she slumbered, *"Damu bahet Lukan, por mehez anuhl-"*

Lukan smiled down at what he once acknowledged as his beloved and parted his lips with irony stretched across his face and spoke to her, "Now, *lorala*, you cannot have us both."

Damu laughed at his brother lifting her into his arms to carry to another transport, "Can't she?"

Lukan grinned with glistening, reddening eyes, "Indeed, who am I to question a Queen?"

Cenilus Islands

Indistinguishable bone particles littered the underbrush with the familiar smell of decay and rot polluting the air. Broken arrows lay scattered within the trees missing their tips and wings, each blackened with old poisons created by the condemned scientists and criminals who were banished to the Prison Isles. Echoes of hopelessness screamed through a shattered silence, crying for freedom.

"Run! Damn you Nick get your ass up and run!"

A man yelled as something unseen raced through high forest shrubs and brushes. Thorns reached out from every curling branch to claw away at already tattered black uniform. Cenilus was not kind to intruders and it was forever hungry for their blood.

The Soldier, Nick, squalled, catching up to the remaining four, "We need to get to the other group you know: the one with the rest of the ammo!"

An arrow shot out from the shrubs piercing the under arm of Nick, "Denny, Ron, grab him, we're not leaving anyone behind for those things to feast on."

The image of the natives hacking the limbs off of Leigh Cruff stained their minds enough to know not to fall and to not be captured—alive. It didn't take any coaxing to pick up the wounded and haul ass to find safety, if such was offered on the islands of the Prison Isles.

They grabbed his body helping him run, but his body only grew heavier and sauntered to a limp forcing them to literally drag dead weight through the brush. The poison immediately began paralysis throughout his body demanding submission—and it wouldn't be before long that the mutation would set in beginning the next stage of an evolution. Nick could feel his lungs struggle with the weight of bricks on them and his muscles constricted throughout his body.

The small path split into a double fork; the path to their left seemed to lead out into an open hillside and pasture while the other lead to the right and wove deeper into the unforgiving forest. Krypt was pretty sure that it would loop around and they would be shuffling through the same paths they had already taken, offering no escape and cannibalistic death.

"Which one, Austin," Krypt growled, moving over to help Denny drag Nick impolitely through hell.

"This wasn't on the map, Krypt," Austin rubbed dry, bloodied hands over his bald head.

"None of this was on the map! It was supposed to be a damn island no bigger than Safrai Gardens!" Ron yelled, lifting Nick over his broad shoulders.

Austin shrugged, sighing at the strategic possibilities of surviving the night, "We stay in the forest; we may be killed by something we can't see. We go into the field, we may have the chance to fight back and see what's coming for us."

Denny looked at Krypt, "The field."

"Bastard wants us dead, that's the only fucking reason he sent us here," Krypt shouted, red with anger, "There's no fucking Eye here!"

Krypt's only driving force was to make it out and survive this mission so that he could hunt down Owen Dame and kill the man. Krypt reassessed the whole 'dropping them on the banks of the first island that was supposed to be vacant to turn and realize its sister prison islands of Hell weren't in the ocean but attached to the Prison's britches.' Damu had been right each time he warned them that Owen wanted them dead because of what they were capable of. At first they assumed the Darken was trying to persuade them to betray the loyalty and laws of a Soldier, but now—everything that ended with Owen a head length shorter was tempting.

"O'the bastard will pay for this," Krypt garbled, driving his foot into the soil and pushed forward.

They ran through the ending shrubs of the forest and etched deeper into the long grass of the field. They climbed up the first hill turning back to see if they were being followed. If the natives continued in pursuit, they would be forced to commence hand-to-hand combat as they were out of ammo. Short shadowy figures stood at the edge of the forest, their bodies drooling with tribal armor made from crushed human bones to protect them from thorns on the shrubs and bushes. Arrows were sent screaming into the air to test the distances of each soldier. None hit, thus the effort would be more tragic for the island natives to leave the forest. The island seemed to hold more evils and dangers than any piece of land in the world because of what Owen and Owen's father and their fathers before them had turned it into.

"Why won't they come out of the forest?" Ron exhaled falling to his knees with exhaustion and not giving a damn whether something would come up from behind him.

"Probably because there's something more dangerous out here," Austin laughed and mocked at the reality.

"Out of the thorns and cannibals and into the fire of whatever the hell is out here," after the Soldiers groaned in agreement, Krypt laid Nick back and began stripping what was left of his shirt off, "What the hell?"

"It's viral and we don't have the equipment or the drugs we need to slow the progression," Denny assumed and began pulling the arrow out of his arm and patching the wound, "All we can do is keep the wound from bacterial infection."

Ron glared over his shoulder and sneered at the forest, "What about the others? Do we wait and hope they make it out alive?"

Krypt glared off into the tall emerald grass, "No, let's hope they make it back to shore and sail away from these fucking islands. There isn't a Prophet's Eye. This is the second time Dame sent us to greet our death. After this mission, if we survive, we follow Damu's orders," he reached down lifting Nick onto his back, motioning out into the field, "We don't stop moving until we find water."

Nick closed his eyes as his breathing became a panting wheeze. His weight had grown considerable with the stench of death lingering. Once puppy-dog brown eyes—turned to a milky, distant stare. Krypt cursed knowing that he would soon lose *another* friend because of Owen Dame. Why should a Soldier be obligated to a tyrant and anarchist? If they followed the old civilizations and served a king, was it possible for the king to become a traitor to his own people? What was the value of one man's life? But, he wasn't a man, he was a Soldier, and a Soldier was bred for one thing—to *kill* or die fighting.

This wasn't the Northrun and it wasn't the Arkeon, there wasn't a Barrier to offer a moments of sanctuary. It was hot, humid and reeked with decay. Their stench became your stench and those natives were the demon-spawn lurking in broad daylight searching for a meal. There wasn't anywhere to hide and there wasn't a peaceful death after the storm blows through, not like the Freeze. This was hell, unlike the others before, unlike what the Barrier offered, and in the time they spent on missions, Krypt had grown attached to what he thought of as his brothers. They were Soldiers, but they were more, they had become flesh and blood, bonded by all the disasters they had survived together—and they had already lost so many.

"He'll be comatose until it kills him or the infection completes its *mutation*," Denny whispered not knowing why he whispered. Could have been that he saw before him a Soldier greeting Death, or a feeling deep down that demanded silence, demanded alertness and prayer above all, "We need to *kill* him if we can't complete the mission."

...

The decoy Krypt created was working. The island's people temporarily hunted the runners of their squad while the brains of the group fled to the shores. They fought away the constant feeling of being watched from behind the blood thirsty trees and forcing away the thwarted feelings of going in circles. The path seemed to shift every time they turned, always unable to find a clearing. The forest mocked them; it pulsed with a life that only flourished on death.

Kai could feel the land sighing at them because the living still raced in defiance to its hunger. The Soldier's had grown so attached to each other that they had become a different breed of Soldiers. There was a time when it was every-man-for-themselves, but the years worn on their group of Soldiers and they became brothers in arms, they developed a no-man-left-behind concept. Kai and Krypt both agreed it was in their best interest to secure the foundation of their squad if they were going to survive Dame's onslaught. It was clear the hypocrite wanted them dead leaving the Soldiers torn between Duty and Survival.

...and their team chose to become rogue. It wouldn't be the first time they would need to trust in Krypt's keen ability to *survive*. The Soldier had a knack for staying ahead of Death and far from the Cradle.

Kai envisioned Krypt gurgling down a bottle of Black Death Liquor without even a burp of alcohol poisoning. It was almost as though Death didn't want him but suckled on everyone else around him like mother's milk. Kai knew it had nothing to do with the lumps of stones in Krypt's head...Kai found religion over the years, he knew there were things out there that lay claim to the souls of mankind. It is the *link* that keeps Death knocking but locked out.

Kai could remember overhearing Anara hinting to her daughter who was still just a babe cradled in her arms: *"... the land was alive and it would devour everyone who defied it."*

Did that mean that the 'land' was completely different from 'death'? She would tell stories to her daughter about such a place when they begged to go camping in the Deadwoods; bedtime stories that he first thought couldn't be true, but now…

The Arkeon looked peaceful in comparison to Cenilus. He missed the frozen oasis that conjured your worst nightmares every now and then. The irritation and anger from being dragged into the hell they ran through was prolonging him from being eaten. A proper ass-kicking was in line should Kai live to see Krypt's jesting face. He was the one who said, "One more," and Kai was the one who said, "Last one." It wouldn't be the first time that a Soldier had gone rogue; Lance Haeden did just that when his rotation to be Runner had come up.

It was the first time that an entire squad went rogue.

Never in the contract was it written that they would endure a suicide mission such as the one they embarked on. Leigh fell with an arrow through her short little leg and was dragged away by the natives. He could still hear her begging for mercy as they ripped her body into pieces. They had even circled around and went back to save her, but when they arrived, there was nothing left but bones and a foul smelling stew boiling on a blazing fire.

"As if they need heat in this fucking weather, it's hot enough that my brain is starting to feel fried," Kai mumbled running his hand over a bald head.

Kai couldn't explain why he felt some comfort at the loss of Leigh—perhaps it was because she was the reason they were lost to begin with: "Follow the trail," Leigh had chirped while she batted her little blond eyelashes.

She may have had many talents—he heard from the guys—but she did not know a damned bit about navigation, "She was Deck Squad and didn't belong in the field."

Nathus glanced over his shoulder at his voice, "What-was-that?"

Kai realized he had been thinking aloud, "Nothing. Why does it feel like we've been down this same path before?"

"That may be a good thing. We may finally be getting on the right path," Alton grumbled as he nervously looked around for Death to wink her blood-glistening eye his way with spear and arrow fingers ready to rip their flesh away.

A rustling noise from the covered forest sent them into another fast sprint into any direction they could fit. Arrows came raining down onto the pathway forcing them to dive into the shrubs and bushes to avoid becoming victims to the poisoned arrows.

Kai shouted, pushing the group forward, "Move!"

The shores were nowhere in sight, not even the stale scent of the ocean waters gave any sign that they were close. Kai took a short glance over his shoulders just in time to dodge an arrow. He grit his teeth and managed to grin at the irony of their predicament, "I'm gonna rip his head off."

…

Eere View.

Ana followed her surviving group in silence constantly struggling to control her emotion, forcing *fearless* and *caution* to the surface giving the others the essence of *courage* and *stealth*. Memories often surface when the time of desperation is urgent and the desire of a solution is even greater. One of her ingenious strategies to control her feelings was to remember her past.

As children, she and her brother memorized every story their mother had ever told them. It was like following a map that would lead to a rainbow and over that rainbow was not only a pot of gold, but their mother holding a plate of freshly baked cookies. Life was simple for children—in her past: It evolved around coco and sugar sticks.

Ana blinked her eyes letting the memories of her past finally find a silent, safe haven to rest and began to pray that each companion didn't burst into their enemy. They could trust no one in these dark times. A reflection could offer more comfort than the friend that stared back at you in the shadow of war: traitors to thy own self.

"Jon, we should have stayed home," Ana muttered placing her head on her knees to find comfort.

~12~

...release...

Darken Territory, Shadoa Moon.

Exhaustion and annoyance were the only emotions available to her at the moment. She had been invaded and consumed, by not one, but three powerful entities. All that was left was a fire that threatened to devour the universe and the shock of the power her soul harnessed alone—which did not belong to the goddess. Kamenah had chosen her for this reason, the uncontrolled and hidden talents a pure blooded Ahzai possessed.

Anara squirmed at the reality that Damu's and Lukan's assault on her mind and body had rendered her too weak to control the goddess. Her flesh crawled over her bones and muscles, drained and starved for a reboot. She began to awaken with the searing tingle in her fingertips and toes welcoming her back to a corporeal realm. If not for her children needing her, she would have chosen a fleshless existence over her body—a bag of bones.

"I know you're in there, sweet heart," a whisper so soft and powerfully enchanted over her warm, delicate ears, "The darkness is gone now, you are safe and with me."

She blinked her eyes realizing she stared out of a shell and the goddess had control of what lay beneath the Darken. Kamenah rested in the mounds of warm pillows listening to every word the Darken whispered into her ears, unaware of what lay in his bed. It had been long since she last had a mortal role to play, the warmth of toying with this male would fuel her for days to come. She could now feed on his essence, making a link with his life's energy. The goddess would soon begin purging the land of their pestilence now that she had control of the Vessel.

His strong, smooth finger brushed her glistening brown hair behind her ears, "I know you remember who I am. Why am I no longer worthy of your affection?"

"T'is a *dream*," a gentle twitch from tender pink lips parted letting out a silent exhale of frustration, "Worth is measured by reality, since this is a dream, ye has no need of affection."

Kamenah toyed and tampered with every knot this male possessed. He was strong, yet naïve. Was he aware of the evil he had begun linking to? She could taste his taint as she lay beneath him, undetected.

To him, she was still Anara; '*Sleep and be still* sisa. *I will tend to this garden.*'

Anara begged and protested against the goddess but she only failed, feeling weaker than before.

The goddess shushed her and began building a wall around Anara to make it harder for her to surface; '*Sweet lorala sisa, I will see them safe but they have their own role to play.*'

"This is no dream, war I have gladly endured to find you. I have done so with bliss. Our pure blood was forbidden to unite because of what it would create, Breeder, I have searched and I have found you," his voice hesitated wavering in strength, "How fairs our *desi*? Is our child well?"

Kamenah opened her eyes at the inquiry he had just made, the fresh scent of a gentle breeze caressing her face with his breath as she looked up at him cupping his cheek, "Our *desi* is of no concern to you, sir."

The king smiled pressing his lips to hers. He sucked in her breath, tasting her and for the first time, tasting something *more* than Ahzai. The Darken in him wanted to mate and the Unknown in him wanted to consume the energy that perfumed Anara Starfallen's essence. He became mesmerized with the shimmer of energy and power radiating from her eyes. This wasn't the girl he once knew, the innocence had vanished and left only a woman with a mission and the artillery and alliances to carry it out. He knew to tread carefully, but what he didn't know was that it was already too late for him. King Lukan had already fallen through the goddess's frozen trap.

"Will you love me no more?" Lukan chuckled as he exhaled over her flesh, both amused with the predicament she created for him and intrigued with her undying defiance to the role she should have played long ago.

Her amber eyes went cold at the question of love. Did he not remember all that he had done to her in the name of love? She had given him her heart and soul and he stripped it away using his brother as his decoy. This was a man who knew little of how love treats the heart of the loved. That was the Darken way, she knew that before she fell, but his love was unique. She could feel his link to her thicken with the threads of love and addiction. Power attracts power and creates a never-ending addiction for the abuser. She of all people would know its strength. She succumbed to its poison many times...

Anara pushed him away so that she could study his face, "You left me, you abandoned me—you sent me into time and space whilst mine *desi-lorala* slept within my womb! You stripped me of memory and you poisoned me with lies!"

He held her forehead to his letting a tear fall from his twinkling ever-changing eyes and drip down her cheek, "There it is. You hold no love for me."

Kamenah turned her head away, feeling Anara's heart cracking and falling from her soul: he *lied*. A pain which was all too familiar, when coming from the ones you had loved unconditionally, ripped through her chest like splintered ice. The goddess sighed and released Anara for the intimate moment with the Darken and prayed that the Ahzai would dispose of the male like she should.

"Love is infinite," Anara exhaled, staring deep into his eyes, feeling evil shining from behind the watcher, "There only comes a time for resisting. The role of one player has been set and all must play their parts in the game or diminish into the shadows of Death's Cradle."

Her words were final.

"A time of resistance and the act of control," his perfectly handsome face fell sullen with pain, "These were your last words before I helped you escape."

"I *loved* you," Anara whispered, letting her lips brush his dark eyebrows, "I have had not one pleasant dream after the *fall*—visions of what was to come. I *belonged* to you. You were my last mission, and I chose not to deliver you to the Ahzai Council. Numbers and Time are obsolete in life and death, only restraints to simplify the truth for mortal-kind. You let me feel pain, feel death in life and could not once comfort me because you refused to abide by the laws of our people. You abused the system and tampered with the Traveler's Scrolls," she watched him narrow his eyes at her, "Thought I did not know that there was *desolation* and *iniquity* peering through your eyes? I could destroy you, and easily. You knew this then, and now. What do you want of me?"

"You *loved* me—so you do not love me anymore," his eyes filled with a pool of sorrow, "I fear the darkness has the better half of me, my love."

"Half to waste," Anara smirked shaking her head, *"A kingdom can be found behind bindings with an army looking through its gates."*

Words spoken can easily be woven with commands and enchantments. A future embedded and manipulated into a single phrase *Summoning* the servitude of a subject and slave. Anara clenched her jaw together knowing Kamenah had now placed the Darken on the same game board she mastered, moving him unwillingly to serve her purpose. They now had no choice but to eventually build an alliance with one another, she knew all too well what the goddess had planned. A Wiseman once told her to keep her friends close and few, and to keep her enemies closer and on their knees.

He chuckled at the riddle and the power behind each word, "What has my *lorala* become?"

Anara leaned forward pulling his smooth face to hers, kissing his tender lips, realizing that Kamenah kissed him as well. She could feel the interest the goddess possessed as she tasted his soul one lick at a time. The darkness within him was like nothing she had ever encountered; even the goddess was intrigued by the malevolent power churning around the Darken's soul. Anara could sense more than one but was unable to locate how many. Like Kamenah who is a goddess, whatever nested within the King was an Entity, and all Entities cared little for good and evil. Why should they, an Entity lived forever and Time feeds them well.

"I wish you to return me to the Breach so that I may protect those who own a piece of my soul," she pulled away and glared into his eyes which were like pulls of lava, swirling and ready to erupt.

She rose from the mound of pillows that molded the outline of her body, stiffening at his tensed expression. Anara knew that a part of him wanted to force her to stay, but the wiser part, the Darken side, knew it would be feeble to try. Last time he tried to control her she banished him to the Nexum and didn't know she had done it: Anara was only six mortal years when that had happened.

He caressed her face with his fingers, absorbing her touch like an addiction, "They seek the Soldier on the Prison Islands. I still hold love for you. This is why I inform you of our—your offspring's location…they are with the *mahkin*."

Anara's eyes narrowed allowing her cheeks to redden with an all too familiar temper, "You allowed this?"

"I no longer collaborate with the bastard *mahkin*. He lied about *you*," feeling her every discarded emotion, he threw his arms around her with a dramatic frown on his face, "Have faith in the blood that runs in their veins…the marrow that feeds their bones."

His words vibrated like a melody, echoed in a rhythm she had never known. His voice was not his and the hunger that shone through his eyes was that of a galaxy long forgotten. So much had happened in such short time…forever seemed to plague existence throughout the universe…there would be no ending for a long time.

Her hair fell around her shoulders like black blades glistening with blood. She had changed copiously since last she was a mortal. The king was mesmerized as he glared into the fire that calmly swam around her indigo pupil. Her eyes finally gazed up at him with the same love and affection she had in those innocent moments so long ago. He was her soul's lover, regardless to what *He* or the Others demanded of him.

Lukan could feel her heart beat matching his with every touch and every heated breath of air that exhaled. He curled his long fingers around the hair that grew above her cool neck, feeling the pulse of her warm blood—a warmth he could not feel for he was not in command of his own body. The darkness within him wouldn't allow such pleasures to be shared. It starved for the link with the Ahzai held tenderly in his arms.

She laid her head against his chest as she had done so long ago in her happiest dreams of escape, unable to understand why she couldn't push him away. She had hunted him for so long, desperately needing him at her side, needing him to be more than an affair within a dream. Lukan never understood her fascination with him, why she wouldn't let him go…

Damu watched from the great chamber door studying their passion, feeling it vibrate from their bodies and understanding why their love had been forbidden by the Ahzai Council. A human would worship the emotions expelling from them in this very moment. There was so much energy massing in the room, leaving ripples that could have been seen in every color within light and all darkness. A god or goddess could be born with their embrace—and would have been if He had not interfered.

His burgundy eyes narrowed, forcing back a deep emotion he could not afford to show, "Brother, it would be wise to return her to the Breach before her children are completely lost," they stood there adrift in their private world barely hearing the intrusion, "My liege!"

The King looked up at his younger brother, "What is it?"

Damu curved his lip with a sarcastic smirk, "Anara needs to return to the Breach. Her young are to be slaughtered by the Minions. I will assist her in *falling* as you have other business to attend."

Anara glared into his shifting eyes saying nothing—only expelling a deafening emotion. He winced, forcing back pain and the truth, grabbing her arms tightly. Lukan knew what rattled through her brain from the glow in her eyes and for a moment he thought they glistened with divinity—or was it damnation?

He shook his head, pleading, "Do not do this. *Be-an kor johmet.*"

It hadn't occurred to him that the King was capable of succumbing to a woman's manipulation. Damu never imagined the enslavement of his king to an Ahzai. Damu glided to his brother's side, "Brother, kiss her, hold her, and let us part."

"*Lorala, baen-het, lo-sae ahmorai,*" the king did so with despairing reluctance, "Beloved, return, I beg you dearest."

She only smiled at his words and followed Damu out of the chamber without looking back.

"You should have killed me, *lorala,*" the King muttered knowing the position he had just lost and acquired, "*They* are not ready for what is to come."

She walked quietly at Damu's side feeling a slight hint of anger escaping his unchanging façade. Entities were obsessed with powerful life-forms and tend to covet their existence, take favor in their roles and enlisted them in services whether unwillingly or volunteered. He was the one who complicated all things of her past. His jealously was what put her on the Breach and away from his King, even if she had only planned to dismiss him to Death's Cradle. Damu took from her what Lukan should have had.

Damu was as handsome as his brother with sharper and more brutal features. He was born in the form of a Warrior; a being that had no problem with torturing a child of innocence in order to receive the answer he desired. His eyes were contently full of secrets set within an intense, dark burgundy brown dessert abyss and they irritably struggled to analyze the Ahzai that walked at his side—not much had changed since the first time they crossed paths.

Anara paused when they arrived at the end of the aisle that dropped off into a rift of puffy white clouds and plumes of stormy black gloom that held enough water for a hydro-transport. This was the one transportation technique she hated most. If the device failed, she would fall through the clouds and hit whatever hid below the coming storm. If the coordinates were correct, she would step out of a field of mist perfectly unharmed…not to mention that the effects of the hydro-transport on your body were devastating and usually lasted weeks after the dive: and there was no definite way to know if you were sent to the right location because the coordinates needed to be *precise* and can change in a matter of seconds.

This was the Shadoa moon: a moon that never moved from its spot over the Southrun Arkeon and casts an eternal shadow on the Darken Territory allowing the most evil and darkest of predators to exist and prosper.

She glared down at the shifting clouds from the edge of the King's domain, "We all have our place."

Damu stared down with her, reaching his hand out and grabbing her ever so gently. He mused at the electricity they shared when they held each other's hands, and it wasn't just the Water Hole device he placed in her hand.

It was the chill in her touch and the fire that burn in his; there was a time it was the other way around. It was as though, like with Lukan, they would remain infinitely and completely polar opposites. She startled at the tenderness of his hand on her hand as he exhaled a strong sigh of tense frustration.

His eyes reminded her of a dusty, dessert storm churning around a drift of black ice that glistened and hid from the Freeze around it. Anara realized that it was much like her daughters; the storm that rages around the frozen tundra and at times a burning eclipse. Her lips parted at the likeness, she wanted to ask but there was a part of her that did not and could not afford to go *there*: to where truth would complicate the events to come.

"You make my brother weak in this dark game," he lifted her face to his, staring wearily down at her, "I have seen your soul, I know what you hide within and what you intend to do once *you* are set free." With that last silent information he pushed her over the edge of the stone aisle before she could react to his confessions.

He could hear the clever footsteps of his brother stopping at his side. The king frowned at the girl that fell back to the Breach, farther and farther away from him. She glared over her shoulder at the king, whispering a word unknown to them.

"Do you think it is wise to awaken the beasts?" Damu watched as the energy around her formed a shadow of wings that expanded silently around her glyph.

Damu assumed that was either an endearment or a curse escaping her lips—but he was wrong.

The king gasped and gawked in amazement, feeling the words that left her mouth bind his soul to an inferno he had long since forgotten, "What has she done?"

Damu watched his brother's body and soul begin to rip apart and fade away, "She *Sends* him."

He stepped away from his brother, "Lukan?"

The King was gone.

~13~

... thin line ...

Eere View: Dame Towers

"For the last time, we need to get out of population!" Ana and Owen growled at Lyle who continued to be stubbornly adamant about remaining locked away in the towers.

Dame's plans to complete the first stages of Control over the Eere View had gone terribly wrong. Lukan had began an invasion and Control over the Sector would have to remain, yet again, unfinished—until due time. Owen now needed to reach water before the Darken lifted their old shields preventing all within its range from escaping. He had no clue of the exact amount of power the Darken had or the intelligence they had collected.

Owen winced realizing the short time that remained for him to escape, safe and sound on his way to Croate Island for his departure to the Naval Star before Protocol landed and cleansed this territory. Owen had an idea of the range the shield could reach. After all, it was the Old World's fallen shields, another creation of his family's advanced technological developments. It would leave Antila free of Traverna and Eere View's burdens.

Antila was one government like all others but with a separate rule. They had succeeded Control without the biological assistance of Eere View's current situation and were now in the advanced stages of Control. The shield would rise and Antila's defenses would force it to simply *bubble* around her creating a partial dome, leaving gaps for escape and reentry. They need only be thankful that it isn't the Ahzai that were invading. The Ahzai were capable of placing a shield around an entire planet and had operatives capable of hacking through any technological defenses with evolved and divined interferences. It was already far too late for Dame's territory to be properly defended from any foreign tyranny.

"We can use a Mirror-transport to Woke Free Base, from there a hydro-transport that should take us to my yacht on Broken Bay. It's slightly backtracking off the Eere View coast but it will get us out of the city and onto water," Owen set his face grimly, knowing there would be several difficulties he could have getting to Croate Island.

He needed the exact coordinates for the instaports to get to the *Naval Star*, and not be lost in mid-transport. Instaports were never reliable. They were only convenient for escape and a mortal body can withstand only a minimum amount of molecule disruption from such means of transportation. Owen wasn't sure if the children would survive the Mirror transport so soon after their previous to make it through the Water Hole, and it would be a matter of hours before a full recovery: not nearly enough time to attempt travel through an Instaport. Owen knew that if anything happened to the children of Anara that she would hunt him down and Send him to Death's Cradle...or worse, the Nexum prison.

"We will need to travel by foot after we get to Woke Free," Owen began entering the coordinates for the instaport to have it ready. There was little choice in routes he could take to get to his destination and escape the Protocol, to escape the shield. Two of the three were children of an Ahzai, the third, Mercy, would only be collateral damage.

Ana read every ounce of guilt and remorse Lyle held hidden and buried behind his Soldier's demeanor. She could also sense that Owen would leave them with a ticket to Death's Cradle if it meant saving his own life. It didn't matter who their mother was at this point, Owen had an agenda and they only created obstacles. As they followed him to the Mirror they would use to get to Woke Free Base, Ana studied Mercy and frowned. Mercy hadn't fully recovered from the motion sickness that came with the last Mirror transport. Her curly dark hair branched out like a storm battered vine tree and she had bluish bags under her eyes. When she turned her attention to Jon, who glared murderously at Owen, he knew Mercy was hurting from the last transport.

She wanted to push for the option to travel through the city, but that would be condemning them all to death. Ana knew that Owen reviewed the option as such, and she knew that to him, Mercy was expendable. She reached out and grabbed Mercy's hand and refused to let go. Her mother once told her that Mirror transports could rip you into another dimension if you weren't strong enough to focus on the reflection before you. Right now, she glared with determination at an empty bunker with nothing but shadows to occupy its corners. Ana could only hope Mercy would do the same, either way, she wasn't letting go of her hand. So if Mercy fell off track, Ana would fall too.

Jon watched as Lyle took the first step into the Mirror and waited until the Soldier's reflection in the mirror gave an 'all clear.' Owen didn't bother waiting, nor did the guard. Ana motioned for Jon to proceed, he shook his head and held his arm out for them to lead the way. If they didn't wink back at him in the mirror, he wasn't going to be stuck with a Dame and a lap dog.

They entered and slouched on each other waiting for Jon. Mercy was showing much more fatigue than everyone else in the room. He stepped through and stumbled into the guard's arms, grinding his teeth as he shuttered from the transfer. His stomach curled up wanting him to cough up his guts but he wouldn't allow it, and to think, they still had more traveling to do. The worst had yet to come: it was the Instaport that could be their last tribunal.

...

Anara hit the ground hard with a splash—and irritated that she was being thrust back into the games of who-is-in-power-now. She lifted her head into the air wiping blood from her forehead, cursing at Damu for throwing her off the edge of a kingdom thought to be a Hell but was, in comparison to the current condition of the Breach, a step closer to the Heavens. She was back in hell all over again. She began brushing dirt from her dress—dress?

They didn't even give her modern human clothes when they pushed her back down into the Breach. She couldn't recollect them having had changed her clothes to begin with. Why worry about the traitor's blood that had been splattered all over her? She was just going to add more of life's-fluid to it.

"Sheer, of course, what else would a man clothe a woman in—other than flesh," her gaze focused in on the distant field with figures running her way, "Nor did they supply me with a proper mortal weapon."

A soul is the greatest weapon to have, Anara, the goddess echoed in the back of her head like a soothing—migraine.

The small group came to a stop, obviously shocked and weighing the chances that she might be a foe or…a foe.

"Bet they have big irinoi hallowed weapons," she growled staring up into the sky while standing alone in the middle of a war, "Another *folly* for the game, *sisa*?"

A loud sound echoed in her ears, a shot fired her way. She didn't flinch, knowing it wouldn't hit from that distance—even if she were capable of dying: *together forever.* Anara only glared at what pranced in her direction and irritated that of all the places they could have dropped her: they placed her alone in a field with trigger-happy-children running straight for her with their guns waving carelessly in the air as if trying to pop balloons. Wasting precious ammunition—children…

Anara took a step as they became closer and more apparent. Her heart shuddered at the faces that stared back at her, "Ana?"

They stood there confused and leery, not wanting to believe that what they saw truly stood there, calling for them. Owen took the initiative and lowered his weapons. Not that it made much a difference with his lap dog at his side ready for battle, ready to take a lightning bolt in the chest if he needed to.

"Anara," it was Owen Dame who raised a thin eyebrow of satisfaction, "What happened to you?"

"Ana, Jon? You look distraught," Anara smiled at the awe in his voice but chose to ignore the power hungry half-breed with the tainted energy of Darken seeping recklessly off his aura.

"*Mala*, where are your clothes?" Jon snapped, half angered but fully relieved that she was alive.

"Don't have time," Ana shook her head as she threw her long arms around her mother, "but, really, mother—why are you wearing a transparent, indigo gown."

Anara chuckled gently staring up at her daughter and kissing both of them on their foreheads. Had her daughter grown over the short time she had been away? Not even a full day had past, "I don't have good news and we don't have time to share. Mr. Dame, do you still have your little boat in Broken Bay?"

"Little," Owen scoffed at her sarcasm, "*The Irinoi Queen* is our destination."

Anara exhaled knowing what ran through his mind. She could read his 'feelings' as they seeped out from his body like a plague, "Why are you running on foot?"

He rolled his eyes knowing that if she had been on this planet within the last hours she wouldn't have been so clueless, "If you haven't noticed, we have been invaded and transportation on any highway is just short of suicide."

Play the idiot and they will not follow, Anara wrinkled her eyebrows, hiding her annoyance behind sarcastic expressions, "Any other means of transportation?"

Owen stared ignorantly along with everyone standing there, "Where have you been?"

Ana narrowed her eyes shaking her head, "*Mala*, people are randomly bursting into biological some-things."

Anara nodded as she glared amused at Owen who pursed his lips, "If we don't get waterlogged we will be dead when the shield rises. The longer we are on land, the closer to death we become. It won't be before long that the *hybra* start jumping up out of the ground wherever they smell meat."

Owen gritted his teeth, struggling not to grab her by her arms and shake her until she told him where she had been like a jealous, paranoid husband that he clearly was not, "We head for the shores of Broken Bay right now, and for your information, we just left Woke Free Base. I have the Hydro-transport in the hull of the *Irinoi Queen*."

Anara curved her lips into a smile still debating whether Owen had anything to do with what was happening right now, "Well, that is clever, but there is one last stop before you escape—evacuate to the *Naval Star*. We need to rescue Krypt and all surviving Soldiers you assigned to Cenilus."

Owen bowed his head knowing he had been caught, "That is hardly necessary. They were provided with the proper equipment to evacuate when their mission was complete."

Anara glided forward to get close enough that only he could hear her words as she hissed into his ear, breathing cool air onto his flesh, "That's not what Lance said."

...

Broken Bay was just another research compound owned by Dame Industries and specialized in collaboration with aeronautics flight research and missiles. More missile than air-transport…the key to making Owen Dame the most powerful man living was his ability to monopolize on the world's weapons and defense departments, abruptly turning all continents against their realm and making them paranoid of invasions from other sharks in their own sea.

It was thankfully void of all predators with the exception of the one walking at Anara's side. She made a point to keep him far from the children. Owen had a knack for getting innocent people killed and Anara had no intentions on him befalling Ana, Jon or Mercy.

The land mourned as the mutated dead mortals rested until the next wave of invasion would commence, a wave that was only a great shield that would imprison all that was within its range. Anara had yet to decide how to label what became of the civilians that exploded into creatures who hungered for blood. They obviously thought like animals and flocked like beast, the human soul had passed on leaving a mutated shell open for what occupied the flesh now. The way the children explained what had happened as they traveled, it was a rapid combustion which meant that there was a reactant used to complete the metamorphosis. They had either consumed a forbidden chemical or mineral by air, mouth or injection; by the random infection, she knew it was by injection.

Anara knew better than to rejoice as she watched the worries fade from the children's faces. In the eyes of a mother, they will always be just infants cradled against her heart. She studied each child as though picking their names from a roll-call list: making sure that their names weren't going to pop up on a Reaper's scroll, and if one should, she had every intention on destroying any Reaper that came to collect. Sight was never welcomed when you would see that Death would rape a child of its last breath. She hated the combined energies of the Ahzai and of the goddess. The powerful blood in her children's veins would always attract the deadliest of entities.

Owen knew what his joint technology had let enter their world, assuming he had control over higher beings when he had yet to ascend. He was only *half* of what they are, deeming him weaker. You can't ascend without Death, and you can't control without evolution. The law of foreign science he should have known. After all, he was playing the same game. Owen Dame should have known that he wasn't at the top of the food chain, yet. He should have known he could and would never be able to control the Ahzai without manipulating the possessions that are dearest to her.

Anara's only curiosity was: who was pulling his strings? Mortals change sides so carelessly that it was impossible to understand the reasoning for slaughter and chaos, betrayal, treason. Who did the Dame answer to? She knew his ties with the Darken had been clipped and knew that he still sought the collective of Prophet's Eyes that were still on this planet, but did he know about the ones that had been scattered during the Score or the price that followed the use of one of them? They were dangerous in the hands of mortal men, almost enough of a threat to *summon Divine Intervention.*

The bright shoreline became visible on the near horizon. The scent of the ocean rose into their nostrils and they could already feel the sand mixed with soil beneath their feel. Anara curled her toes in the warm sand not caring for the minimum of clothing they had left her with, the *bare necessities.* With an active war raging around her, she would have to find boots to get her through the obstacles ahead. She might have become divine in the past seventeen years, but she still occupied a mortal body while she existed in a corporeal realm. No magic on this planet manifested clothing; hell beasts and plagues, but not clothes.

"*Planters,*" Anara watched tiny specks race in and out of shadows, waiting for a host to occupy.

It would seem that all the dark things in this universe had come out to play on the Breach. She glared at Owen with a subtle, I-know-what-you-did-but-not-who-you-did-it-with, expression directed at him for him to see. Now that the Solar Gates are opened, all gates are accessible with the proper invocation and coordinates. How he achieved opening those gates without assistance she had yet to discover, nor had the time to dig.

The *Irinoi Queen* glistened at the docks with silent envy. The white paint shined and twinkled like mirrored glass with the reflection of the still bay waters shimmering across the irinoi that intricately encircled the yacht. Each movement they made disturbed the waters and sent a ripple through its flawless glossy contour.

"We need fuel," Owen muttered to his bodyguard.

Lyle chuckled with his arms crossed as he glared at his employer, "I thought the damned employees you had were taking care of your little sail-boat?"

Owen shrugged at the mute sarcasm, "What the boss doesn't know can't hurt them. You of all people should know that."

Lyle grunted with a beefy shrug as Anara entered the captain's room with her arms crossed. She had been listening from behind the wall. You could only resist time for so long before it turns and gives you a slap in the face. She only stared at them debating whether to burn them on the ship while the others still waited on the docks, or to save them for something more tormenting: patience always prevails.

"We can get the fuel from the other boats," she turned exiting onto the deck, leaving them to grind their teeth, "You guys stay here with Owen, Lyle and I need to get fuel and water."

Jon shook his head refusing to lose his mother, "I can do it and you stay here."

Anara smiled, pointing her finger to the small door leading to the deck and sighed. Jon needed to grow up and she had sheltered her son for far too long. She knew it would take longer for just two to do all the work and it would be safer for them to be near the docks in case the Shields rose.

"You go with Lyle to get fuel," she tilted her head studying him with sad amusement. Even now he was defiant whether his life was in her hands or not, "I will go get water."

Ana watched them leave the *Irinoi Queen*, shaking her head, she proceeded down to the captain's chambers where Owen was setting out weapons he had stashed in the cabinets. His shaved head perspired as he knelt into the cabinet shuffling with the ammunition that he had stored inside. She traced his shoulders and sized him up while reading his emotions and desires. There was a definite infatuation and a deep desire he forcibly ignored and subconsciously built a thin wall around: frustration being the mortar for each layer.

Ana took in a deep breath and began manipulating the energy in the air causing all of his feelings to heighten and sting, "What kind of relationship do you have with my mother?"

Owen raised his head up, hitting it on the counter-top, "Business, that is all she would ever allow."

Ana narrowed her eyes at his directness sensing restraint in his demeanor, "Do you love her?"

"As a giddy child does a possession," Owen smirked, amused at the young girl who questioned his heart as if he had one functioning in his chest, "Love is a sin neither your mother nor I are capable of."

Ana knew that it was partially true. She and Jon were the only things in existence that Anara Kamen has ever loved unconditionally. It was their fault that their mother had been abducted. If they had been where they were supposed to be, Anara wouldn't have been lured into the trap. An Ahzai was powerful, but not the strongest species in the universe, definitely not in the Daeviti realm.

Mercy eyeballed Ana fearing an argument approaching. She could tell by the storm brewing in her eyes that Ana's temper was due to shatter within moments. Ana had always struggled with controlling her emotions and one could not blame her because she focused every ounce of control in not feeling everyone else's emotions, "Mr. Dame, I need help with the buoys. Anara wanted them up and ready to get out of here before the shields rose."

Owen cursed under his breath and followed Mercy out of the den, "Ana, finish loading the rifles and setting out the moranite shells."

Mercy pulled a buoy in, avoiding Owen's glare. She was content with silence, not speaking to him or answering his questions. Her mother taught her long ago that the less spoken is less given. Mercy didn't intend on giving Owen anything more than what he disserved.

"Ana could have helped you do this," Owen flexed his arm as he reeled in another buoy.

Mercy shrugged keeping her face void of expression, "Could have."

Owen grinned, sitting back to look over the docks, "She has a crush on me, doesn't she?"

Mercy forced back a gag and chuckled, "Don't flatter yourself, she misses her father. In her eyes, you are to blame for him leaving. After all, you were the one who sent our fathers off."

Heavy footsteps shook the docks, disturbing the water and silencing the air around them. If there were birds still around, they would have fled as well. Lyle and Jon flew—ran yelling for Owen to raise the anchor. They watched as the water beat against the boat with more force than before. The silence soon fading answering to the new sound of shattering planks as the 'Darken' shield began to rise.

...

Anara kicked the Food Mart's door open grabbing four, two-gallon jugs, two in each hand and hugging onto the other two. The silence of the store ended with the sound of yelling echoing inside. She ran out the door to see who was yelling and what for. Her jaw dropped as a dark shadow devoured the docks, the shield had been activated and the perimeter was being made.

From behind her she could hear a shuffle, forcing her to turn her gaze from the docks. A man grabbed the two jugs from her and added another under his arm and they began running down to the *Irinoi Queen*. Anara couldn't count how many mobile transportation devices Owen had named "*Irinoi Queen*" and knew that he would name the world 'Irinoi' if he could muster enough power to do so.

The wood from the docks splintered into the air sending shards of debris in their direction. They threw the jugs onto the yacht jumping in as the dark shadow nearly engulfed them. Anara could feel the splinters prick and scratch at her back as she tumbled over the gallons of water, rolling like a feline ready for another attack.

"What the hell is that?" Owen shouted as he glared up the wall of darkness. The last he remembered, a shield was translucent and not murky with shadow. The Darken modified the shield making it temporarily stronger to serve their purpose.

"As if you don't know," Anara hissed, throwing her hand up to present the barrier that sought to entrap them, "A perimeter."

The man from the mart looked at her, "Why now? Why didn't they do it during the invasion to keep everyone in?"

Owen glared at the wall deciding to bring Anara's position to light, if he could, "They know what you're up to, Kamen?"

"That's right, blame me," Anara laughed at his accusation fully aware it was she they feared, that it was Owen Dame that held their only threat. She looked at the others to answer their doubts, "Takes a minute to get their towers up, to modify our beacons," Anara was passably disturbed as they set sail to the Prison Islands, "You know what Protocol is, Owen. You helped Eureof pave its foundation into this Daeviti galaxy. We need to get off this planet before they send the Sleep and Eliminators and then drop the *bomb*."

Owen smirked at the image of the entire Breach being compromised and becoming a spot of dust in the vastness of a Daeviti universe—if only it were so easily disposed of. Until that day had arrived, he would have to settle with worldwide Control. The first step to Protocol was the Sleep, they would detonate a neuro-gas that would make the mortals fall asleep. Some would die in that sleep, others would wake to complete silence—the affects differed due to the variety of genetics and species on the Breach.

The Eliminators would descend and kill all threats that survived the Sleep. It didn't matter whether the threat was truly a threat, all within Quarantine were considered contaminated and compromised. The Eliminators were genetic machines created to have no feelings, they could not observe compassion or pity…they had no desire to preserve life.

The 'bomb' in query would target only the invaded territories whether it had been evacuated of all citizens. Not much of a loss considering that the majority of their population had been reduced significantly with the virus he and Lukan had created when they were allies. The territory would be used as a reason to enact Control throughout all of the Breach.

Dumbfounded and petrified, Owen clenched his jaw at the thought of yielding his place in the Supremacy—forcing him to take a defensive position only to realize that his position lay now at the heels of the woman glaring hungrily at him. He narrowed his eyes as he examined her eyes, which were literally a bowl of twinkling stars glittering in and out of existence as they orbited the black hole in the center waiting for a reason to devour all that reflected on its glossy infernal surface.

Owen released a dark chuckle, his eyes glistening at Anara as he summed up his new threat, "That would make me your prisoner, wouldn't it?"

"The tables have turned, Owen," she hung her head mockingly at his remark, "It took you this long to realize who controlled your place in this game?"

Owen Dame puzzled at the dark fact that someone held a part of his position in a game he had been manipulating for over a century, and definitely long before Anara Kamen had even fallen into the Northrun Arkeon. There wasn't any need for words or rhetorical responses, his demeanor showed his unequivocal sentiment. One of the wealthiest and most powerful players on the Breach had been played—and was now conquered with but a single stroke of the hammer.

"You never crashed here, you were placed," he growled out the words as though they were his last.

Ana glanced at her mother and realized she no longer wore the black necklace or the cuff-bracelets. She narrowed her eyes at her mother wondering if the woman standing on deck with them was even her mother. Something churned in her mind while she watched the glistening aura that her mother leaked through ever-changing eyes of burning amber and blood-stained blackness.

The former Ahzai, Anara Kamen was no longer in presence. A Vessel stared through her eyes in a constant battle of strategy, power and possession. Oddly enough, she knew that her father would be saved, and Owen was no longer their immediate threat.

The Prison Islands

The Supremacy of Governments assigned these islands, not caring what natives lived among the land or the history it had. It had become the Prison Islands for all those who broke the law and were stupid enough to get caught. This was the Breach's own mortal Nexum, only the most deadly were sent to these islands.

The Norvik Islands and Croate Islands became a focal point for science and experimentation, north and south. Owen made sure that what was being experimented, were never known. The civilian public only knew that it was dangerous territory and to steer clear of their waters.

The southern islands were the Croate Islands, four small islands made of several small volcanoes which were part of the reason for the energy spikes in the Northrun Barrier. It also provided enough energy they easily converted into a variety of transportation uses involving Hydro-transports, instaports and even Solarun Warps which were used on their more advanced spacecrafts.

Directly in the center of the island chains were three larger islands, Cenilus. Those who sought to explore these islands have yet to return…alive. This was the one they usually banished their convicts to and it was also the islands that were mostly populated by natives— cannibals.

Never once had it been written that there might have been a hint that the islands would ever unite and form a single landmass that would terrorize intruders. The prisoners of the island would now have access to the laboratories stationed on Croate and Norvik if they could overtake the security. With an island filled with mad scientist and trained assassins, it was a task that was not impossible.

Transparent diamond and sapphire waves glided gently across a silent and desolate ocean. No hint of life or supernatural activities grazed the minds of those searching for the ominous Prison Islands. Their destination had been the Croate Island, but to their shock, they had been taken elsewhere. There before them rested a single island mocking and taunting their arrival with gentle yet deadly waves set against the boat. This mass island defied normal geology.

Weary from sea-sickness, the young crew of the *Irinoi Queen* lounged impatiently under a heated sun. White rays reflected generously up from the white and irinoi-chrome outline of the yacht sending a beacon of forewarning to any predators out there. Clear as the sky might have been, a haze crept across the ocean surface. Shallow waters triggered the sonar, waking the crew.

Owen sent the anchor diving into the rapid waves to keep the currents from sending the *Queen* back out into the silent ocean of the North Channel. He was no longer wearing a shirt and his expensive pants were rolled up to his knees, doubtlessly creating the dreaded wrinkle that no rich man cared for in a well tailored pair of slacks—a slight price to pay when weighed next to his life.

Anara could see the distant flags of the Prison Islands like a beacon warning off all those who sailed by. The beach was stilled with a void that screamed 'trap' and 'death'. She could see a scatter of ancient bones littering the forest-line with forewarning.

"The islands shifted to welcome a deadlier world," she muttered at the irony that the Prison Islands were in truth, categorized as a Traveler's Island.

She frowned at the movement knowing it was a result of the Breach interfering with her plans. Now that they were joined, there was no telling what kind of hell they dove into and she didn't know how long they had been joined. If the planet wanted a reaping of souls, it could only mean that there was a shift in balance somewhere and a leak in the Cradle. No, it wasn't a Traveler's Island, it was a Breach Island—a giant fly trap. The difference between a Traveler's island and a Breach island was that one avoids suffering while the other welcomes the blood, yearns and starves for a squirmy meal.

"Finally, land," Mercy groaned with desperation. She hadn't fully recovered from the last transport they had taken. Her tanned skin had even paled beneath all the sun. Mercy spent the duration of her trip constantly visiting the edge of the yacht to spew out every meal and liquid she had consumed due to sea-sickness. She had now decided that she would gladly jump into the nearest hyper-transport if it meant saving her from the salt water that surrounded her now.

Anara laughed staring at her with a concerned seriousness that silenced all the children, "No, you will stay on the yacht with Owen. Lyle, Mr. James and I will be going on land."

Jon stared at his mother annoyed, "Why can't we go?"

She closed her eyes deciding that truth would be the greatest respect to offer her children under the instance of a fare-well tiding, "Because, there is a chance we may not return. Owen, you know what you must do. This is obviously not Croate. By the look of the thorns and bones plaguing the shoreline, I would assume that this is half of Cenilus and half of Norvik, which means just beyond the forest-line would lead into grassy fields and the entrance of Croate."

Owen glared at her annoyed and about to object. He needed to get the coordinates from Croate and had every intention on getting them, with or without Anara present, "You can meet us on the other side of the island if you survive. Their only chance at survival is if I get the coordinates from Croate."

Anara held her hand in the air knowing that whatever objection he had to offer would be much like an empty promise, "We can get the coordinates from the Soldiers you had deployed here. Owen, you are too important to be lost to this island," the word 'important' tasted like vomit in her mouth when used in reference to Owen, "You *do* plan on taking as many innocents with you as possible, yes? You did give the men the right coordinates?"

Owen smirked and bowed his head smugly. He did give the Soldiers the right coordinates but chances of them still breathing and not licking the lips of Death right now were slim. So a rescue mission in hopes of getting the digits from dead men was pointless.

It didn't matter what he said because the odds were that the three setting out were never going to return, "I have enough Instaports for those of us remaining on the *Irinoi Queen*, and much to spare for *when* you return."

She nibbled on her lips and narrowed her eyes at his subtle sarcasm. Owen had every intentions on leaving them once they faded into the Veleriruin shrubs and Cradle Trees.

Clever half-breed, Kamenah thought to her host, *whether you allow it or not, Anara, I will see his head roll before this is all done and over.*

Anara chuckled aloud and turned to her children bowing her head, "Never stop," she leaned in and pulled Ana and Jon closer and whispered, "You have the blood of gods in your veins."

They slung irinoi rifles over their shoulders and grabbed what weapons they could find on the *Irinoi Queen* before leaping off into the warm waters of the Prison Islands. Ana could feel the absolute power that seeped contagiously off Anara as she watched the Vessel wade through the waters of what seemed to be a dream whispering memories of her past. She could feel the change in the air, a potent taint she couldn't destroy. The Breach was coming alive and it would alter the existence of all mortals within the Daeviti Realm.

"What can the Pawn do?" Ana whispered to her brother, "When the Queen is playing all the moves."

...

At first the glistening lights before them seemed nothing more than illusions toying with their desires. Kai groaned at the white shores lined with black debris expecting the next pin-up model to emerge from the shallow waters holding a cold bottle of Starlyte foaming down her hand. Every man's dream began with something shiny and ended with bare flesh. He couldn't ask for more if these were the last steps he was ever going to take again.

"I see a beach!" Nathus yelled, his voice reviving their hopes and sending them into a sprint towards the sweet smell of shimmering ocean water.

Their eyes narrowed as three bodies began rising out of the water. The first thought that plagued their minds was that the damned cannibals had learned to swim and were waiting for them to trip into an unseen fishing net of poisoned wire. Their first emotion was the odd sensation of gratitude and none of them could place the reason for it. A Soldier showed little gratitude when facing Death; they were fighters and with no ammo to light their way into the Cradle. If it was the natives: they were on their way to greet Death with not an ounce of energy to see them on into a Soldier's heaven.

Relief washed over their faces as the pin-up woman got closer and shadows became detailed images of a past memory. The illusion grew more real and substantial with every step. The familiar sway of the woman's hips and the sure, agile legs slicing through the waves like the presence of a goddess had began to approach them. The bottle she held became a seven-inch long range hand gun and the bikini they imagined morphed into a belt lined with moranite shells: precious ammunition.

They had to be dead and that was the Reaper retrieving Death's lunch for the day. They had, after all, been evading her kiss from the moment they were stationed under the care of Owen Dame. *She* had finally caught up.

Kai bolted at her with his arms spread out like a bird ready to take flight, "Anara."

She closed her eyes hugging Kai, amused at his emotional state while pushing him away searching for Krypt, he alone had coordinates they needed, "Where is he?"

Kai knew who she was searching for, she hadn't seen him but once in the last—he had forgotten how long it had been since they began retrieving the Prophet Eyes, "They went deeper into the island as a diversion so the rest of us could escape or at least get a head start to shore. We landed on the other side. The mission remains incomplete."

They looked at her and back at the forest and growled, "There was never an Eye on these islands."

Anara forced a smirk to scar her face, rolling her eyes and staring up into the clear sky sighing at the *folly* she was contending with. Before she could speak Nathus leapt forward and took a heavy, calculated swing at Lyle. It landed just before Alton wrapped long, weary arms around him, struggling to restrain him. Nathus shook him off and brushed his chest to recollect his nerves. A Nathus punch would normally knock a man out. Anara had witnessed this, what few times he had allowed his anger to boil.

This time, Lyle only grinned and rubbed his jaw, which had already begun bruising. Anara knew they were drained and weakened from their journeys, she could feel their emotions and nerve rip away even as they stood before her as Soldiers. She was concerned that they wouldn't have enough energy to enter a transport of any magnitude. At their current state, a simple Instaport could shred them.

"The tide is taking everything out, stay surfaced. Go with the flow and you'll reach the *Irinoi Queen*. Get some rest and sustenance on the yacht. We'll go in and save what's left of the Soldiers," Anara gestured to the rich liner that bobbed in the blissful waters.

"I'm going with you," Kai volunteered, tired and dripping with blood, "We need more ammo."

James shook his head knowing that any of the men that were heaving from exhaustion before them would only slow them down.

Anara sighed at the man she had come to know as a brother, "We didn't bring an arsenal. You're dripping with your own blood. Get on the *boat* and get patched up," Anara tilted her head with wide pitiful eyes, "I need you to protect the children. The Darken has set a perimeter up and the shield will doubtless be complete by nightfall."

She motioned for Lyle and James to continue into the forest and grinned, "Owen is on the yacht, I'm sure you have some catching up to do."

Alton stopped them with a warning in his big, chocolate-brown eyes, "The natives are cannibals and they are waiting for you in there. Their weapons are dipped in poison, be careful."

"The arrows will change you, do not touch them at all-" Kai finished their warnings knowing time was of the essence, "It's nothing but thorns and vines from here on out."

Anara held her hand out, with a sly grin on her face, and pointed up to the treetops, "You neglected to look up."

Kai narrowed his eyes at the woman that stood before them, noticing she had changed since last he had seen her. He was never told the secret about her true origin: that she was Ahzai and wouldn't hesitate to be his best bud one moment and slit his throat the next, "When did you become a monkey?"

Lyle smirked, staring at her with the bit of information Kai just gave them, "I would assume when she was abducted."

"Whoever said I was abducted?" Anara challenged the men who tuned into her history of the past hours, the Ursan sun barely in her zenith. She smiled smugly towards her companion, "Hurry onto the yacht before you bleed to death. Ana will bandage you up. Owen will go to Croate to get coordinates for a hydro-transport, make sure you're there and you get them, too.

Make sure they are the same as the ones he gave you for your Instaports," she paused again, "try hard not to get eaten by sharks or *baefish.*"

Baefish were giant silver leeches the length of a human arm and were native to the Prison Islands. Kai shook his head knowing this conversation had reached its end like all debates with Anara became, "Be careful."

She rolled her eyes lifting her rifle up and aiming at them, "Come in after us and I'll shoot you myself."

"Now that I can believe," Nathus turned and left them to trek through the palm trees and fruitless tropical brush.

...

Lyle watched Anara analyze the land around her as though becoming a part of the earth. Her body even began adapting to the rigid habitat, strengthening into a predator. Her hair lay flat to her body as though it were a living extremity of its own with a conscience. He forced himself not to goggle at the Ahzai that manifested before him without a second thought of why or what she really was or what she was doing. She just became. This was the weapon men could and would willingly fight and die just for the right to breed her.

Anara lowered her voice and let it sail on the wind in such a way that they could only hear the vibrations of every word, "They're close enough for us to jump from tree to tree. It won't take long to get to the fields while we're above the maze. We must get through quickly because it won't take them long to figure out where we are at. No matter how high up we are: *they* have the upper ground. We must understand that."

James stared dumbfounded at the woman who glared through the face of a fragile young woman, "You want us to engage combat in a tree?"

147

She nodded sincerely and almost insanely, "Yes Mr. James, first come first serve," she swung her rifle over her shoulder and began climbing the tree trying to avoid the thorny shrubs, "They trekked through a shrub called *Veleriruin*. The reason why they felt so lost inside the shrubs is because the thorns emit a toxin that causes delirium. I'm surprised they made it out at all. Silence from here on. If we get separated, use your compass and find your way. Don't come back for me. I won't come back for you."

Lyle stared at her as she took off leaping from one tree to the next like a frog or gliding squirrel. Her nimble legs stretched across thicker branches as her feet pivoted precisely to each step. They looked down to see moving shadows that hid under little huts built within fatter trees and beneath larger bushes, perhaps the natives even burrowed into the ground for shelter against the life-sucking nature around them. The habitat offered the perfect protection from intruders and for prey.

Lyle prayed that they moved unnoticed, because to engage in combat from the treetops would be insane. Sweat dripped down their faces as they pressed forward cursing under their breath at the heat and constant struggle not to fall. They had made it half way through when Anara paused, calling them to a halt.

They had been spotted and an arrow screamed through the air hitting the tree Anara clung to. Lyle had already sighted the thing that pursued them and took the first shot and continued on jumping from tree to tree. They took to walking on tree limbs that stretched out long and strong, giving them a break from the impact of jumping.

James and Anara walked on the same limb just as she began to make another jump, Lyle leapt from the tree behind them onto the same branch. Lyle's weight proving to be too much when he hit: their branch snapped beneath them.

Anara hissed and they leapt to the nearest tree as a dart shot out and pierced the bark right above James' hand. The natives were getting too close. North of them, about twelve jumps away was the clearing to the pasture and hills. Just beyond those pastures were stakes ascending to the sky with enormous beasts impaled on each as a native warning. The dead grass blew in the wind with a dull luminance making their destination all the more undesirable.

Anara frowned and pointed to the clearing, "Descend, now!"

"Run through the brush?" James yelled frantically close behind her, "With the toxic thorns?"

She nodded stepping onto a weak branch almost losing her balance. She wasn't on it long enough for it to break. The forest was easier to navigate when leaping through the treetops. Through the thorny shrubs that threatened navigational delirium, it would have been easy to get lost and spend weeks trying to break free like the Soldiers before them had suffered.

James was the first to hit land and began firing at the natives to give them cover. Lyle landed next catching Anara as she leapt to avoid the poisoned thorns. As he caught her his arm scraped up against the thorns and he immediately began to doubt their position. Lyle fought the urge to go forward, into the forest, and back to the beach. Anara grabbed his wrist and shoved James in the direction of the fields while dragging Lyle at her side. If all else fails, the big Soldier would make for an excellent shield...

The dry perfume of the grass welcomed them as they found the end of the trees and shrubs. They frequently glanced over their shoulders to see if the cannibal natives still followed, and they were. Arrows still soared through the air and the sound of twigs—or was that bone—snapping as their padded feet moved in on their prey. They hunted with determined vigor: they had already lost one meal for the day.

"They stopped following!" James shouted as they grew farther and farther out of firing range.

Lyle and James heaved their rifles up and aimed at whatever stood before them. The look in their eyes and emotions that bled out of them sent Anara on alert as she snapped her head forward in mid-step just in time to fall backward and onto her rump, cursing at the wall she had ran into. The man standing above her was thinner than the last time she had seen him, and exhausted beyond belief.

She exhaled on a choked voice seeing who had floored her, "Krypt?"

Anara puzzled at the man who had the misfortune of finding her in the Northrun Arkeon, *he doesn't recognize me.*

A tooth had been missing from his mouth along with a huge pulsating bruise encircling his shoulder. His face was rugged and worn from exhaustion and finally showed age with the shadow of Death kissing his eyelids leaving little, yet noticeable red spider vines. She wanted to look away but knew it was pointless. This was the evolution of a mortal, the *natural* evolution. Krypt was no different from the other mortal men, whether he was a soldier or an evolved race, he was still mortal.

Even if she could offer him youth in his existence, he would still fade like the other Soldiers. Death would soon taste everyone's flesh with her black beak and feathers. It was only a question of whether you lay down and died to be dined on, or if you fought her seduction to plunder for another day.

"Carrion, all the mortals lay waste to carrion," Kamenah exhaled in a raspy whisper, and Anara clenched her teeth realizing she had spoken aloud.

The man glared at her, slowly recognizing the glow of the Vessel, "No-" a familiar growl vibrated through his throat, "I told you to stay home!" Krypt lectured turning away to push forward through the grass, "You can never listen can you?"

"Guess I learned a thing or two from you after all," Anara rolled her eyes; "What did the Darken tell you? And by-the-way, I'm here because you have made a complete mess of things."

Krypt narrowed his eyes to her shrugging, "There were no fucking Eyes here to be had! Owen set us up."

"Krypt, listen carefully. Owen is without a doubt, heading in the direction of Croate. He is retrieving the coordinates for a Waterhole," Anara looked at Lyle to see his reaction, to see whether he knew what it was. His guilt flooded like the Niasar River every moon-tide.

"Shouldn't they be the same as the ones we have for the Instaports?" Krypt glared at her with sharp narrowed eyes, "I'm going to kill him."

Ah, Krypt. Instinct to survive but none to escape, Anara looked up into the sky, "Not yet you're not. He needs to delay Protocol. Only a specific human gene can go through this Waterhole. It's just like the Instaport except where that takes one passenger, the Waterhole can transport millions—it only holds for a short time period though. We need only to turn it on with nanytes that will locate and signal other beacons that have been set wherever Owen decided to set them for his own use and it will automatically triangulate. All that is water becomes a transporter for the remaining human survivors to escape to whatever destination Owen has set the master-beacon at."

"That's not encouraging," Austin placed a fist on his hip grunting from a sudden stab of pain in his leg.

Krypt narrowed his eyes at her noticing the look of shock on Lyle's face, "He doesn't know about that, does he?"

Anara glared at Lyle and tilted her head, "No, not completely."

"The Towers," Denny stopped and glared at Anara knowing how such devices had been placed without a word of knowledge leaking into the press, "This is one of *your* Projects."

"As to your first assumption, no, it's Hydroport, they need water and therefore, a beacon within the water," Anara couldn't stop her hand as she forced her finger into one of

Denny's wounds. Last time she had seen him, he was a transbot bleeding black oil. He jumped ready to strike, "Sorry, just making sure you bleed red."

"Anara," Lyle wanted to know exactly what she had done to his master's projects, "Proto-."

"Wrong," stopping his very thoughts, she shook her head at his naivety, "No, Owen keeps his confidants in the loop. Protocol will be launched. Yes I know he found a few of the beacons…and I am sure he tampered with those few."

Krypt's eyes reddened with annoyance as he had done so many times, years ago, "No! You tell us what the hell is going on. You always do this encryption bullshit. Explain yourself."

She glared at the ground knowing that he would have to know a little of why her partnership with Owen Dame existed. He refused to move and crossed his arms over his chest, like he had done so many times before when questioning her about her deeds with Dame. She didn't have to tell him anything, it made no difference because she knew this would be the last time he would ever see her in the flesh.

"Wasteland territory is to be made example of to secure Control in the entirety of the Breach realm," Anara shrugged and glanced over at Lyle who knew what she would tell them, "Every machine has a sign. Those signs are destinations, one linking to the other. I can't go into details because we have little time before they execute Protocol—Owen is in a rush and will leave us."

"Blah, blah, blah," Krypt muttered turning away from her.

Lyle chuckled under his breath now understanding his boss' interest in Anara Kamen, "Always planning ahead, you knew what would happen."

"I can't save a planet that doesn't want to be saved but I can save my children and open doors for those who are of interest to me. Owen had every intention on treason," her eyes snapped at him with the evil glance from her husband, "It was business, Krypt. Even *I* have orders."

Krypt shook his head at her knowing every lie she had ever whispered to cover her research, "You always said that a Daeviti world must not be compromised."

"So long as one Carrier remained innocent, the rest of the world is not needed," she shrugged with a smirk hidden beneath her tightened lips.

Anara blinked as the grass whistled at their waist with the sweet scent of the tangible rich soil beneath their feet. Occasionally the stench from the rotting flesh of Nick Ansel would catch the tender breeze wrinkling the noses of the Soldiers. Another whistle glided through the air, foreign to nature yet as delicate and well hidden to man. Anara stopped to glare over the grassy land, shaking her head at the false sound.

She turned and caught up with Krypt struggling to frame comprehensible words to speak a warning. For a moment, it would have seemed they were taking a peaceful walk through a field of dreams: If not for the whistle that sang only in her ears, bringing her and Krypt to a complete halt. She motioned for him to listen.

He shrugged at her request as another whistle glided to her ears on the gentle wind, "You don't hear it?"

"Hear what?" Krypt shook his head looking over the tall grass, "All I see is grass."

Denny set Nick down watching her close her eyes and smile at the sound like a junky with an addiction. Her face beheld such serene pleasure that it stole the breath from her lips as she seemed desperate to taste the melody only she could hear. They had never seen her so immersed in what was, to them, a delusion of the weak. It then occurred to him that even Nick began wheezing to an unknown rhythm.

"It sings to us," the sound became hypnotic to her ears as she exhaled with such immense pleasure that her cheeks began to reddened, "Sugar on the tips of a flutist's delicate fingers, gliding over such virgin wood."

"Darling, focus, what are you talking about?" Krypt spoke with a subtle sarcasm with slight concern. He had never known Anara to allow herself to become so distracted. He looked to his Soldiers with questioning, and all shook their exhausted battle-torn heads, 'no.'

Austin looked at his brother muttering, "What the hell did she say?"

Krypt rolled his eyes as her arm slipped away from his grasp.

She pulled her hair down to let it catch the wind as she grabbed her neck just to feel flesh against flesh, "It calls to me—" Anara grit her teeth with annoyance, "If it knows my name, I have been marked—I am being Summoned by a *Maestro*, but whom would have such power here on the Breach…"

Krypt stared endlessly confused at his lost lover as she pulled her hair back into a bun and returned to her 'kill-mode'. A personality he knew all too well, and respected because it revealed the little piece of humanity he would ever see in her. That moment she pulls her hair back like a man would roll their sleeves up prepping for a fight, she became mortal. Their false-marriage had been one hell of a war that he gladly retreated from—the woman was always right. He decided that when all was over, he would never marry again. Being a whore was less complicated and you didn't care about the females you bent over.

"Stand alert," Krypt ordered the men.

Anara focused her eyes, shaking cold and feverish from the assault being made on her, "I'm being hunted. We need to get out of this field—now."

Krypt puzzled at the woman he thought he knew. He had never seen her being assaulted by something unseen. He puzzled even more, wondering what a maestro was. Ron stood behind her with his rifle aimlessly pointed over the tall grass, much like the way he thinks. He spoke with a lowered voice, "Why you?"

"Why anything, Ron: we're on an island that shouldn't exist, why does anything ever happen?" Anara snapped at his ignorant questions.

If she said she was being hunted, than damn it, she was being hunted. She was barely able to walk straight and could feel a blistering tingle run down her back like hellfire with the urgency to obey the call of the melody Summoning the Ahzai in her to answer. If not for the goddess she hosted, the maestro would have succeeded in entrapping her. Anara knew that only a powerful maestro was capable of Summoning servants to do its bidding. She awaited the physical attack as she battled the mental battering.

A swift movement dashed passed Ron's leg, sending him falling onto his back and setting his leg on fire. While Austin hustled to put the flames out before the entire field caught and went up in an infernal blaze. Another attack sent Krypt flailing down face first. The shades of the creatures could only stand sunlight for brief moments and the tall grass provided them with enough shelter to snatch a meal and drag it back into the forest to feast with the native cannibals.

"Run-" she yelled as a shadow reached out dragging her into the tall grass. She shrieked once she saw what held onto her ankle and whispered to it, *"hello, Drifter."*

The Drifter had manacles with a mouth full of sharp black, slimy teeth. Its eyes glittered pale blue as the ice would glow on the Arkeon when light touched its black ice. Attached to its large hands was moranite powder, a substance that burns once it comes in contact with flesh. What the Soldiers used in ammunition shells. The Drifters used armored gloves dipped in the powder to stun their prey, what were they doing on the Prison Islands, so far away from their home?

Krypt dove in Anara's direction and latched onto her wrist keeping her in eyesight. The shadow hissed and shrieked as the sunlight solidified its flesh, expelling a putrefied smell as it singed beneath the Ursan sun. A Drifter never sees the rays of a star and avoids light as much as possible, Krypt now understood why. Even if he had never seen a Drifter up close, he cringed being so close to one.

"A Drifter," Denny gawked as they took off running to a clearing where a fire had seared the grass.

Anara chuckled with irritation. They knew so little of what dwelled on their planet that it was amusing to her that they would succumb to what lay beneath, entrapped in the planet's core. All planets function as both prison and shelter, if the human mortals knew the truth of what the Breach contained, they may choose the Nexum or Death's Cradle over this land known as the Breach.

Kamenah chuckled with her, exhaling the reality of their universe, "*The Daeviti was created for one purpose: Control, a giant trap for all that is good and evil.*"

Austin laughed sarcastically at Anara mocking her, "Don't sound so flutist anymore does it?"

The Soldiers didn't understand what danger they were in, what danger she was in for that matter. Anara was being hunted and didn't know who sent the hounds in for her. She had an enemy and didn't know who—*not that it matters who, the Ahzai has many enemies and no friends.*

They made it to a dead path as the sun slowly passed its zenith and would soon hide behind the tall Cradle Trees. The scent of something rotting and decayed filled the air with the aroma of death. The path led to a long line of impaled male hybra that towered over their heads with their guts falling out; dried from the day's sun. Male hybra have no wings and they were the size of an ox or buffalo with four black horns protruding their heads, and their flesh was the shade and texture of black leather ripped with muscles. This could have been a warning for trespassers to stay away or a gory expression of power. A single hybra was an ominous threat, to have a row of recently impaled male hybra spoke deadly words.

They pushed on following a map that had been drawn before the Prison Islands joined together. The path they followed was not found on the map. Anara finally grabbed the map from Austin who began cursing at her.

"This is wrong," she pointed out, "The islands have combined. This was the shore you were suppose to land on, the dead hybra lined Cenilus' borders so that is Norvik and beneath should be enough water to create a Waterhole linked into Owen's coordinates."

"Are we there yet?" Denny laid the body back to the ground.

Anara came to a stop staring down at the ground they stood on and began toeing the sand and watched as it moistened, *that will do.* She held out her hand expecting them to give her the nanytes they should have had.

"How do you know it's enough water?" Krypt stared at her slightly annoyed, "Is that something you and Dame did behind closed doors, too?"

She grinned while handing him the map, "Did Damu give you a jar of what looked like water but is really nanytes? Or did you already drink it? I know how you like to get to the bottom of the bottle as quick as possible."

He pulled a small vile out of his waist bag and handed it to her with murder in his eyes. She pulled a device out of her ammunitions belt and jabbed it into the ground. The Soldiers watched her as she meticulously set the device to link with the others she had set throughout the perimeter.

"If you're not human, step off the sand please," Anara frowned at Nick, not sure if he had mutated so much that his genetics had shifted with the poison.

She opened the vile letting a drop fall slowly to the ground not wanting to use too much in case it really wasn't enough water. Light shot high up into the sky as the dirt became water and the Soldiers began to sink into the ripple. Success cried from their lungs as they began their drowning escape while Anara was sent flying back into the grass with wide eyes of horror.

Krypt glared with confusion swirling in disturbed blue-gray eyes. This was clearly not a part of her plan. He could always tell when she had been stumped.

"C'mon girl, jump in. The water's fine!" Austin yelled out at her as he faded completely into the Waterhole.

Anara shook her head. Fiery eyes never leaving Krypt's confusion, her lips unable to voice the words frozen in her mind, "Dame."

He nodded feeling the anger pull him under, drowning in the creation of his adversary. He may not have loved Anara as a husband would a wife but he respected her enough to want vengeance in her name. Krypt felt the portal rip his flesh and contort his essence as he was sucked through a compressing amount of energy. He raked his hands over his head and screamed from the ringing in his ears as a woman's voice echoed in his conscience, repeating over and over the same words as though writing his mission upon a forbidden scroll in a forbidden dialect he shouldn't have understood.

"A warrior for his goddess," her command Summoned from him, *"A warrior for his goddess."*

~15~

Shock is often cured through memories: A happy thought or a past story told to someone to cure their shock. Anara focused on the past trying to find where she may have made a wrong move, or if there was a cheater staring over her hand. A story of *home* came to mind, one she told many times to Ana when her daughter was overcome with visions of a future that would never be promising.

Anara blinked her eyes bringing the memory into thought, manifesting every detail of that night in her daughter's room with Jon sleeping on her lap. Ana lay curled up in her arms with a storm beating against the walls of their lost home. They had hoped for good news from Owen and all they got were tree snapping gusts of wind and rain drops that stung upon impact. She could remember wiping warm tears from Ana's high cheek bones and promising that the storm would end when the land had drunk its fill—which had been twelve hours later.

She could remember her daughter's sigh and smiled,

"It gorged itself, mala."

"Tell me Chapter One," those nights always began with Ana begging for a fairy-tale to cure terror and fear.

"I will tell you of a land that raged worse than this night we slumber under. It sheltered few and saved none. There was a girl and her family was of great power in that land. A family with no name: immortals of unknown origin. They first arrived to that planet and grew a garden for their first daughter, the Gift. This garden was of such ripeness that the flavor of the fruit could last days before washed away with the wines of the harvest. There was nectar worthy of divine banquets and eternal contentment.

"There came a night when their moon rose high with the shadow of their sun twinkling in and out of

perfection, and the girl stared up at the sky, captivated by the shadow and the light as they danced in and out of the other. She made her way up the hill to get a closer look, and found, up on that hill a man of great beauty, fearless and with determination radiating from his aura. This girl knew that she was forbidden this man and she knew that she would forfeit eternity if she embraced his existence. So she looked back to the sky and smiled mischievously.

"She said to him and to the shadow within the light: 'Find me again and I promise a name.'

"The man smiled gently back at her peering through the most pleasing eyes of darkness she had ever witnessed: 'I need not search for that which completes me.'

"The girl giggled stepping away: 'Then I shall seek you ahead of the shadow for the light shines through me.'

"The man chuckled at the girl as she turned away from him to glare over her shoulder: 'If all light shone as dark as yours, I would live forever in the shadows awaiting your grace.'

"The girl felt his presence fade and returned to the festivities of the night, but when she looked on to her world she only saw darkness. A cold abyss ascended

*upon her land with a chill that bit so hard that the
flesh of her garden split open and shattered like
glass. The people of this land retreated into the
ground to suckle the warmth of the core, or perhaps
they traveled?*

*"She had disobeyed the Law placed upon her. The
girl wept at the night as she knew daylight would
never return until her mission had been completed.
When her training was complete and her mission set,
she became the Ahzai she was bred to be. Fairytales
were over and deliverance had begun."*

By the end of her story the storm had ceased and her daughter had fallen asleep in her arms with her son snoring gently at her side.

Anara closed her eyes allowing a single tear escape down her cheek. The air was cold on such lonely shoulders bare from thought and care. The succulent taste of freedom now nauseated the roof of a dry, weak mouth. Language became foreign to a mortal mind that drew blank from reality and awareness. Only the events of the past two days plagued the dumbfounded mind of a great dreamer.

The Vessel was only a fraction of her DNA that clarified her evolution, a calculation that Owen should not have summed. There was something missing to the equation that gnawed at her mind like a tumor to a migraine. It was the ten percent of what made a human taint, at least that's what Owen believed. It was a void that should have been unseen to the mortal eyes.

Surely the scientist would have made the accurate calculations to allow such exceptions—but then again, Dame Corps were swamped with traitors. Owen Dame would have substantiated the Vessel line that flowed through such thin veins without knowing the Vessel

161

existed within her, so long as he followed her instructions. No, Owen would only think to secure his place amongst the heavens and doom her to this Hell.

"There is a reason for all results," Anara hissed while calculating all events and what would happen now. The product outcome had reset and left her to begin the process of elimination when the answer swam within her, the goddess.

She touched tender, shaking fingers to the water that flowed before her. Only to pull back at the sizzling noise that accompanied a burning sensation that traveled up her hand. The heat so scorching that the tips of her fingernails were seared black, leaving molted stubs to point out her imperfections. So long as her children had escaped, it was a sacrifice she would make; and if they had not, she remained at their side to protect them. It would be easier to find them when she shared the same land and the link they had was thicker for that reason.

The Waterhole faded and the thin stream returned to moist soil that would soon become a dried and cracked riverbed. Her light footsteps trekked sorrowful and confused through the tall grass leaving no true emotion for the shadows to feed on. She was a shadow in her mind allowing Kamenah to surface in her isolation. Existence had faded away leaving only the reality of a curse she had brought on herself to laugh at her and mourn with her as she walked as a Vessel bleeding with raw fury. Anara had no control once she chose to set herself in seclusion. She gave in to the goddess who used her dark feelings as a weapon against the hunters who furiously circled her at a distance, unable to come near for fear of the goddess devouring their essence.

With the goddess in control, energy entered her body abundantly and the goddess dined maliciously upon all that fell too near to her frequency. Anara gave no boundaries while she contemplated the next plays she must make and how to position her pieces. At the rate the goddess attached herself to the Breach; she would devour all that dared if her Vessel did not stop her.

She would throw a tantrum, but it would serve as a homing beacon for the Darken to find her. For some reason she found herself shifting in and out of control. One second she wanted to fade away allowing Kamenah to take over and the next she refused. The Ahzai within was strong, if not stronger, but it was her desperation of needing to be free of her duty that betrayed her so deftly. No matter how far she ran, it would always catch up to her.

"If the entire planet chooses a Controlled Existence," Anara exhaled with exhaustion, "who are you to interfere?"

"No single mortal has the honor to uphold the Law of Existence," Kamenah chanted through Anara's lips, *"The nearest Entity will be given the duty of smiting this world."*

"That is why I am forbidden to leave this land," Anara growled, upset for not seeing this obstacle before she played her previous moves, "This is the outcome of not killing the King. You were sent to me for this moment."

The goddess retreated into the walls of Anara's mind. The truth had been revealed, the Ahzai was here for a reason. Not simply because she fell from the stars in mid-labor, but because a higher being had *summoned* her.

...

The night turned agonizingly into a dim morning as she ran through the thorn forest not caring if she were to fall and feed the cannibals or live to suffer another day until the end was near. Even the natives could sense the change in her, the danger that warned them to stay away. The only comfort that stirred hope in her mind was that her children were safe above her looking down on her as she dragged her feet through the burning sands of Hell's Breach. She then realized that it hadn't been mere hours that had passed as she meditated before the fading Waterhole, but several morning rises and even falls.

Her eyes glared fondly at the yacht that waited quietly for her, empty and void of company. She would sit and wait for the last shimmer of the Hydro-port to fade before she would tread into the ocean waters of the North Channel. With an instant void that expanded over the water, the transport had ceased with a final pulse. The water rippled to a calm expanse and glittered with only the rays of the Ursan sun. She set sail expecting Protocol to incinerate all that was within the Darken shield and realized that those within its perimeter wouldn't have had the opportunity to escape.

"The shield," Anara exhaled, setting the coordinates for Broken Bay.

She closed her eyes and let Kamenah taste the links they had made; locating those Anara had had a physical contact with at some point in time. She could feel Bioni and Cara both still lived; one with strong and furious vitals and the other seemed to be on the run from something she couldn't place, because Cara didn't know what it was. Her heart sank deeper and deeper as the guilt grew heavier and tighter around her soul—what was left of her soul.

History seemed to be repeating itself no matter what she sacrificed or what had sacrificed her. Is that what lurked beyond the shadow; a reflecting light that was just an echo of the sacrifice? There were reasons the Oracles place a mark on the heads of a target or entire species, it was this moment that formulated that reason. Lukan had brought this to the Breach. He had brought the acceleration of Control to this sector of the Daeviti. Anara knew there was only one to blame for the disaster triggering a deadlier evolution for the Breach.

The ocean remained calm and lucent with the occasional bubble breaking the surface of the water to greet Anara on her journey. The geography had changed much since the first day of this assignment; with the curse of science always there to urge nature on unnaturally. The shores of Broken Bay were shadowed with blood stained water. Bodies lined the dying beach leaving it contorted with grim beauty. A small hint of life rose in several corpses, yet there was no *hope*. It was hope that they would need most of all.

"A sin that may have faded away in all their torture allowing the demons their infinite portal into this faltering world," Anara cursed as she entered the mark of a new era for the people of the Breach.

Did the Darken know what they tampered with? Evil works through the eyes of the good, convinces the innocent of heart that it is the right decision to sacrifice their free will and give Control to those who are stronger and intelligent enough to create a 'perfect' existence. They will build a paradise in the name of Evolution with Control as the foundation and security in which this perfect world is created. When in truth it is only a way to peacefully segregate and enslave those who do not fit into the irinoi shell of perception: the strong, the powerful and the indestructible.

The Breach, unlike many other Daeviti worlds, discovered a way to entrap powerful entities and Celestials. Therefore, the Supremacy of Governments deemed themselves Superior to all others. Now, they wanted to Control everything beneath them and claim the names of 'gods'. The Wastelands were in the first stages before the Darken invasion. It is the invasion that will set forth Control throughout the planet...

Anara sighed as she took her first step onto the moist, burgundy sand, "I should have killed him—at least imprisoned him. He may be contained for the moment, but the event that I should have prevented with his death has sent this planet into a phase of evolution and closer to intervention."

The thought of condemning an entire planet to death with her simple act of not acting itched at her conscience. The second thought that infected her nerves was that she would be the one responsible for smiting the planet because she alone possessed a goddess—not just an Entity or Celestial, they had already been captured...but a goddess, and no earthly mortal was capable of entrapping a goddess. Kamenah was a goddess who possessed divine rights and had already smited worlds before this one.

Anara froze and fell to her knees, "You."

Kamenah remained silent.

Anara ripped her fingers through her hair hoping the goddess would feel the pain as she did, "You were the one that forced our people to go below or beyond!"

Kamenah inhaled without falter, *"Yes, and you were the one who disobeyed the Law."*

Anara's heart shattered as she slammed her fist into the sand around her, feeling sharp debris puncture her left fist, "I was a girl!"

"You are Ahzai! As is your daughter, there is no such existence as desi, child amongst the Ahzai," Kamenah countered, *"I have seen to her safety where He did not want me to. Ana was to be your punishment for disobeying the Law. It was her soul I was sent to collect for the price of sparing Lukan, Master of that which He condemned and evil of unknown."*

"And it is my fault that this world suffers," Anara flexed her fingers through the course sand. Her heart pounding against her chest threatening to break through her ribs and burst in panic: Ana was the price of her folly. The One God Kamenah bows to, wanted the life of her first born child as payment for the events that have come to pass.

"It is not your fault that they suffer. The Oracles demanded Lukan's head knowing your love for him. It was too much to ask of a girl. It is the Oracles fault for not choosing another for the task," Kamenah corrected her Vessel forcing Anara to rise from her knees, *"You can still change the Ripple in Time… you alone can force Time to resist."*

The Ahzai stood, glaring at the shield, searching for a weak point, "Why did you choose me as a Vessel? Was it His will?"

"I chose you because you are free," Kamenah withdrew into Anara's conscience, refusing to answer any more questions.

Anara's eye began twitching with irritation. She was a pawn for the goddess and she had just been played. Her hands shook as she forced her feet to move and take heavy steps toward the shield. The sound of a gasp took her attention away from her destination and she found herself kneeling at the side of a woman wearing a sundress that was stained with dried blood.

"Water," her flesh was pale and her eyes fluttered up at Anara as she parted her dried, cracked lips, "I thought you would pass me by," she gasped, "Who were you talking to?"

Anara clenched her teeth wondering why she couldn't keep Kamenah inside her head anymore, "Only to myself."

The woman closed her eyes still wheezing. She had to have laid there for days, "They took my baby."

Anara wanted to look away, she wanted to shut the woman's pain out and not feel her agony, "They have taken so much more than that," the Ahzai in her was trained to not sympathize but the mother in her felt every wound opened, "Be still, *Sisa Mordai dom or-vae.*"

She unlatched the irinoi blade from her shin, "Be still, Sister Death has come to claim you," Anara repeated as she struck the woman in her chest, driving the blade through her heart, "The Cradle calls."

A tingle began in her fingers forcing her to drop the weapon. She watched the knife fall slowly to the sand and looked up. Anara pressed her lips together seeing what stood before her, glaring down at the corpse of the woman that lay still upon the beach. It knelt and laid a slender hand on the woman's chest, absorbing the soul's essence, devouring the spirit as it had been commanded to do.

"The List has been written long before you decided to disobey Him," the Reaper spoke as soft as a gentle wind sweeping through. Her thin, black robe cascaded around her slender body as she squatted to look Anara in her face, "You are on my List as well, Anara—Kamen."

Anara immediately looked around her for predators that wished to end her life. She stopped when the Reaper began to chuckle, still staring at the Ahzai, "Soon. I will return to collect your soul—only to find it missing."

Anara narrowed her eyes and tilted her head, reaching for the irinoi knife, still saying nothing to the Reaper.

"Yes, you continue to evade the List. On that wretched planet of yours, in that evacuation pod, in the Arkeon, in the arms of Damu, and then in the arms of Lukan, and now, as you stand before me, I cannot reap you," she pulled her veil back to show her face, serene and hungry eyes peered at Anara, "why is that I cannot collect *you*?"

Anara found her lips curving into a smile as she stared at the Reaper starving before her. She then began to laugh hysterically, her chest heaving up and down as she took in the oxygen that was vital for a mortal body to function. When she stood and glared down at the Reaper, the Reaper suddenly appeared a few yards away from Anara.

The Ahzai moistened her lips with stars twinkling in her eyes. The Reaper watched as the power shifted around the mortal's body, enveloping her like a nebula with the colors of indigo, winter ice and ember sparks lacing throughout the center. It realized that she was not the only thing that hungered and knew that if she was not careful, she would be devoured just like she had devoured the soul of the deceased woman.

"A Reaper does not kill a Reaper," Anara took a step towards the shield, no longer worried about the Reaper who held her name on a List for Collections.

"There's an opening outside Traverna," the Reaper took a solid step back, "but your place is in the Wastelands."

Anara felt no need to question or speak further to the Reaper.

"I am Sasha," the Reaper smiled innocently, pausing as she began to fade, "Yes, tell Cara she is Summoned and give Bioni a pat on her back."

This got her attention, "Cara?"

"Is not on *my* List," Sasha purred, glaring through quicksilver eyes that swirled around a diamond center.

"I will tell her Reaper to wait so that you may see her into Death's Cradle," the Reaper frowned knowing Anara's thoughts, "You cannot save them all—not this one. She has purpose, her soul must Travel for you to succeed the next vital move."

Anara knew this was true. She could feel the weakness of Cara's link before she left the Prison Islands and it was weaker even now, when she was so close. Sasha stood above another twitching body, giggling as she reached down to reap his soul before she faded from Anara's sight.

She glared up and projected a thought to the Ahzai, *"We are not all your enemy."*

"Nor are you my friend," Anara muttered feeling a surge of energy stir within her.

The goddess warned her Vessel, *"Do not underestimate Death. She always receives the names on her List. She will Collect in one way or another."*

"Not that you would let her have my soul," Anara snapped knowing the goddess had kept her alive in more than one event.

Kamenah would never let go of her *soul*. The goddess had no intentions on sharing what she had claimed. The matter of the Vessels body was a different subject. Death will take whatever she could get her hands on, and will send the most powerful of Reapers, if need be, she could summon a god or goddess to Collect what is hers. Anara understood the allure of the Cradle, and knew that she could only resist her last breath for so long before she gave in and desired to free the soul body and flesh. The need for such freedom would drive her insane in the days to come now that she knew she had been marked by her end. An Ahzai of her rank could easily borrow time and evade *her* succulent kiss.

Anara shook her head and only looked forward to what she now faced. Seeking what was beneath the shield and offering a way out for those entrapped. If she wasn't too late, she could possibly prevent the world from being destroyed.

Whether it was her destiny or not, she would not allow the responsibility of the Breach and all of Daeviti fall to Ana and Jon. Anara sighed at every memory that flooded her mind: Ana's nightmares and visions as a child, Jon creating *things* out of simple thought—thoughts which became solid and real. Unlike her own parents, she would not force them to do anything they chose not to, and definitely had every intention on keeping them far from the battle. Though, it was not her choice to make.

Part III

... insanity's hands...

Wastlands, Breach

Slaves.

The stench of death and the searing ache of defeat, life was no longer a privilege for mortal humans. The Darken made quick work of conquering the territory, yet she was still unsure for what purpose and what they truly searched for. Anara had another problem she battled, Death's mark. After her brush with the Reaper Sasha, which was not more than a few morning-rises past, she had began talking to herself, to the goddess, and to her past self.

"The face of a girl with rusty-red hair and storm-swept eyes smiling to another face continues to bring me back to reality. Shoveling graves and blessing corpses with a proper ditch—burial. There is also the vision of a young man with honey for hair and hawk eyes that keeps me from losing all hope."

Anara drove the wooden shovel into the soil that had many ages ago been poisoned by previous wars, "I will not flee, yet, there is much I must do first. "

Anything that would be a threat to the Darken was exterminated like roaches and ants. They had been absolute in their invasion. They controlled not one, but all three towers in this sector. Anara's entry into the dome was simple, her journey to the Wastelands, more simple…her ability to fit into the demoralized mortal crowd, impeccable. She found Cara, and gave her the last breath, then took her place among the slaves that scurried the, what they now called, Blood Fields—Bioni was not far away from Cara.

"How did Lukan allow this atrocity? What was there to gain in destroying a civilization?"

Anara continued contemplating aloud, "They buried all religious figures such as statues and even the ordained, alive and kicking."

"That might have been a blessing," Kamenah became amused with Anara's state of mind, she had become completely unpredictable.

"The unworthy had always begged a God or all the gods to save them. Now they all will rest beneath the soles of the survivors, the *witnesses,* all together," she muttered as she dragged a half of a corpse to a wooden skid they would drag to a less filled ditch.

"I can recall a Red Priest who had been discovered hiding behind the façade of a slave man screaming: 'Our sins have drowned us all! Repent that our Lord will save all our souls!' I doubt God can see through the bloody haze of war and black pools of rot."

"The humans had failed to understand that an Entity and Deity gain their power only from the worship of mortal souls: The purest form of energy that provides the eternal life and death of the idol in worship. That is why They requested and ordered that there be no icons and idols. *He* cannot protect his children if they are worshipping another Entity or Deity that has no love for them. Not the love that He has for us—you, it isn't shared, I assure you."

The Darken opened the doors for Pro-Control when they began the invasion. That isn't even the worse of it, with the decision to enact Control planet-wide, the evil creatures entrapped in the planet had been given a bridge to cross into the weak of soul and in time, they will surface within their own flesh. If they cannot turn the Ripple in the Time, the goddess would be Summoned to defend or to destroy. The prisoners and exiles of the Nexum had bodies, but their time spent in the other realm had made it unstable in the corporeal realm, therefore they absorb through the forms of the weakest of human souls; possessing them until they devour the soul or offer it up to Death's Cradle.

"They devour the soul of the living and enter through the realm of the dead. Poetic, don't you think? That it is the humans who must provide the vessel in which a leech can cross. Where has the Gate Keeper gone?"

"The Darken work as servants and spies for a Hierarchy, a breed of demon from another world," Kamenah hissed while dusting her hands off to remove the crusted blood of the decaying body they just threw onto the skid.

"Such alliances are made to destroy the land of man. Why can they not see it for what it is?"

Anara looked up at the sky frowning. Whenever she thinks of Lukan; her head immediate falls back and seeks the storm clouds of Shadoa. It was childish of her, knowing that she had sent him to occupy Akisma in the game of Celeston.

"You can't just ward them off and curse them away. Rocks and stones won't break their bones."

The woman who stared back at her with irritation fought hard not to interrupt Anara's insane narrative.

"Days are red and scorching. The night yields to darkness and summons a blessing coolness that ends with a clammy sweat in your palms and on every breath," Anara drew a deep breath in, savoring the stench of death, "This wasn't expected. The Breach should have been dust by now. What reason has the Alliance kept this piece of land intact?"

After weeks of picking up dead bodies and scraping the contorted limbs and bones of their neighbors from bloody mud, sweetness was a myth in their eyes. The goddess had retreated in the humor of Anara's insanity, a defect caused by the knowledge that Death hunted her. A mortal flaw she should not have to suffer, Kamenah would not let the hungry sister devour her Vessel's soul. Yet, Anara muttered and mumbled on as she cleansed the land of corporeal debris.

"I know all of you have more than once fantasized about wrapping your hands around the necks of those trespassers and slowly drain the life from their blackened eyes for they betrayed us to the Nexum and Death herself. I know I have. I won't lie. It was a lie that got us all here-"

"Sleepy, they were all so sleepy," She glared into each pair of eyes that focused on the task at hand: shovel, lift, relocate, burn—burn—burn.

"*A Vessel can only ask for such warm slumber whilst pretending to be mortal,* lorala sisa," the goddess whispered through Anara's lips.

She observed them, too worn to shut their eyes for more than a minute at a time, "It is Death's Cradle for them. Who knows who will stare out of their eyes when they wake?"

Their lips parted with the same rhythmic vibrations, "Water, they pray not for God, but for water. Where is the great flood when you need it?"

"They are taunted by the screaming of young women being ravaged or tortured as dark entertainment for the primitive needs of the newly released Nexum prisoners," Anara stood with her back straight to glare over the land before her, "As if there aren't enough whores to share their seeds willingly."

The human slaves hovered over the corpses and bloodied mud; half searching for the past, the other half searching for hope or a quick end, "Thirst, a soul thirst."

"They feast off the weak of souls: insecure, virgin and innocence. Where do we fall in? I mean, look at you, you're not terribly ugly nor are you a young virgin. No, I smell sin on your sweat. A mother once I do believe, not skinny or plump—neither you be old and weak, and myself, well—I'm sitting here among a pile of rotting corpses and all I can think about are the faces of forgotten souls! Goddess, give me strength to forget and stop the beating of a dead heart."

The woman nearest to her shucked a lump of bloodied mud up at Anara to gain her attention. The Ahzai blinked her eyes at the woman struggling to recognize her face. It had become thinner than last she had seen this face, huge bruises encircled large, brown eyes and sweat matted dark, wavy hair to her forehead. Still, her commanding voice triggered Anara's memory: *'It was never about the love of the man. Anara, it was about the love of the child.'*

"Anara! Shut up, they will hear you!" A woman hissed, "If you die today, all hopes of getting out of this wretched dome are gone!"

Anara silenced herself at the thought of losing everything to her miscalculations. She needed to begin placing new players and pawns, start a new strategy, "Hope, it still grows in such shadow, Carrier. What was your name—yes, it was…Bioni," when dealing with mortals, one must seek doubt for truth, "We dwindle away in slavery and serving the Darken. Their winged beast has supped on more meals than you or I could ever dream of. Why should this mortal body continue in the darkness of this creation?"

"If not for me, than for the hope of the children who still remain in here," Bioni covered her trusted friend's mouth with a crusted hand, "Those things eat the dead, if you want to eat the rotting flesh from the dead corpse, chow down. I don't need you preaching to me. You sound insane with your blathering!"

"You there!" Anara shouted and stood up staring directly at the fat contorted guard with a fat nose that stormed her way. She snapped her eyes at Bioni, "I think I might just do that!" She shouted and stomped her foot like a child throwing a tantrum.

Anara lifted the arm of a decayed body from the ground biting a chunk of flesh from the bone, coagulated blood oozed from her chapped lips. The guard stopped and stared dumbfounded at Anara as other guards surrounded her just as she spit the flesh from her mouth at them and attacked them with the shrunken arm of a lost Soldier; even in death the Soldier would continue to fight and serve.

It took one thrust from a copper staff to bring the raging woman down.

Giggling, Anara dropped the arm staring up at the guard with a grin stretching across her pale face, "Must be nice beating the weak and weary. Tell me, is that all you've got?"

The world around her faded into the sound of Bioni crying out, it felt as though a ton of bricks had fallen over her body to form some kind of shelter. Then there was only darkness in her world of chaos, a swirling of painless ecstasy that only a condemned soul could dream of in the depths of a scorching hell. Such times merit such obtuse actions when there is no hope for the weak and the weary. Here in the dark prisons of hell where only death and decay haunt the souls of both innocent and guilty, Anara found answers to questions asked.

"You know the power gathered from Death," she hadn't expected a response to her blatant accusations.

"Death is great. Death is our sister in the darkness and fires, Anara. Time will come to our aid with Life at her side like a sword blade thrust into evolution. My promises to you remain there."

Anara chuckled at the voice in her head, "They have come to fear decay over death, a night full of rotting flesh and cysts, puss and boils out-weigh any torture given by the Breach's trinity of power starved hypocrites."

"Anara, I ate a finger for you. The least you can do is shut up with the broken narration and let me do all the telling," Bioni leaned beaten against the cold iron bars of the prison cell taking what comfort from the slimy chill the metal offered, "By the way, what in all the hells were you thinking!"

Anara stared contently at the burning scones on a moist wall, "Air conditioning, a heaven in the faces of—well I can't imagine a world without a few sweet memories."

They sat there in silence at the thought of all the joy that had faded as if never to have existed. Life was simple in the eyes of what they faced now. A scale being weighed and neither of the women were sure who would outweigh the odds of surviving. Anara needed Bioni safe to play her role as Carrier until the real Carrier return, her firstborn daughter Mercy. With the virus released within the dome, Kamenah needed Bioni to absorb its pollution before the shield dropped and infected the entire population.

The longer Bioni remained in the corporeal world, the lesser chance of planetary contamination. There was also the possibility that Bioni would be able to control the virus if she lived long enough to consume all of it. That alone was a weapon worth surviving for: not everyone can control a beast from the Nexum.

A voice muttered from the adjacent cell, "So you heard the rumor, too?"

"It can't be just a rumor, we have lived in this dome for far too many clammy nights to revert back to rumors and gossip," Anara forced herself to sit up and stare bluntly at the old woman who stared back with a full face of pity yet still she shown a rare beauty behind sarcastically arrogant eyes. Was she of the Breach or of one of the Slaving Colonies imported here by the Darken?

The woman looked familiar to her but she couldn't place the aged features against the dull light of spit and dust. She only shrugged and return to the constant etching of words and symbols on the muddy floor. Whenever she focused on all that had happened before the Breach, things became muddled and she could hardly hold a thought that linked to the years long ago when she began working with Owen.

"You do not recognize me," the old woman frowned at Anara, "You cannot see passed all these wrinkles and weather."

Bioni curled up into a ball as though searching for a peaceful dream of the past, "At least we aren't shoveling corpses anymore."

177

Anara studied the face of the old woman whose eyes glittered between the bars, "Starla?"

"Yes, your trusted informant," the once beautiful young receptionist exhaled, "Dame left me to Lukan and Lukan left me to Tarel, who fed me to the wolves. Tarel let one of his *Obryn* drain me in the depths of this tower. Who would have thought Owen would have such terrors beneath the surface?"

"You have more to worry about now," another old woman laughed mocking their lack of suffering. She could have suffered the same blasphemy as Starla had—nothing in the darkness was as it seemed, "They take you out of the fields for reasons. Truth is, you're safer out there, unnoticed. Nexum's buffet is in here, darkest realms of Hell it is, a banquet of the living."

The elder woman spoke with an accent that was not of the Breach. She wore a six pointed star tattooed upon her right cheek and a moon between her eyebrows and a sun upon her left cheek: her families were Drillers. They first arrived before the Score in search of a rare metal known as the Irinoi Core. They introduced the power of the Irinoi to the Breach's civilization creating a shift in the evolution of the planet, bringing forth the Score. The Ahzai avoided the Drillers because of their undying belief in the One God. The influences of a goddess did not affect them and the Ahzai was forbidden entrance into their domain within the great Mountains of Aerwane.

"Aye, we weren't always so aged and fruitless, no, we were young likes you girls," another woman echoed with the second.

Anara stared blankly at the old woman listening to the cries of a human girl echoing through the soggy floor, "You are lost to the Hierarchy who has sent Darken to ravage this land. Without the spirit of hope we live on in deception and the utterly sinful desires of forgotten bliss."

Bioni choked back an exhausted laughter waiting for another moment of insanity from Anara, "What dwells beneath?"

"The torture chambers are down below. When the master has guests, he sends their personal servants down there to pick out a new toy or a tender appetizer," a young woman who may have been a young teenager whispered from scarred lips. Her drained body dangled limp through the corner of a suspended cage, "I was down there once, in the cold darkness with not but that oily stench to keep me sane. I play the strings of melody, a violin and human harp that *he* commands me to enchant. They use me to sooth the ears of the human bodies they infect so that their screams will drown in my sad symphonies. Anara? That is you name, yes? It is a beautiful name not of this land, I am sure you'll meet the Darken soon, you smell of power and defiance. You have an unmistakable taint about you, like a forbidden melody. I will soon play you a melody."

"Maestro," Anara smirked at the child thinking of the days that had taken place on the Prison Island. "*Maestro*," she muttered once again under her breath.

If the Hierarchy could corrupt the girl's innocence, the Darken would and could Summon darker and more powerful beasts to the surface and out of the Nexum. There were infinite evils out there and a skilled maestro could control those evils. A maestro could ruin the Ahzai in her. The girl twitched her lip envisioning the last breaths of their past victims. She stood up frowning, her hair short and curled to reveal a collar around her neck. Blood drizzled down from the thorns that constantly nicked at her flesh.

The girl's humanity was almost spent, her body almost ready for a new host, "They will have a banquet to welcome slavers from Karone. Tonight they will feast on live flesh, an arm, leg, breast or thigh—hopefully not the poor soul of a newborn child as they once did in Karone. I survived to be sold on the first line of maestros, as a gift to Master Tarel for his triumph."

"A tyrant always hungers, starving for more. Always more," Anara pressed her body against the molded bars, "Karone? When last were you on their vibrant shores?"

She looked away shaking her head, "Karone seems so far away. They took me as a child, before this invasion here. Time is endless there, beneath the clouds of dusk. It was slow some days and rapid through the nights, I care not to remember. Perhaps with all the chaos of this world, it has dried up and slaves will soon be needed no more. I had brothers who sought me. I do not know where they might be or if they have gone to Death's Cradle."

This girl was useful and so were her brothers if they still searched for the girl. Anara shook the bars only to fall back at the sound of the dungeon door cracking open. A burning tingle singed through her heart as she watched Bioni stand up clasping her forehead feigning a headache. The Carrier hidden within Bioni had been activated, and Anara knew Bioni was suffering from a fever at the moment.

The guards were both decaying and suspended in decomposition. They would either continue as a walking sack of rot or they would evolve into something more disgusting and deadly. When a mortal was possessed by souls from Death's Cradle or the Nexum, their bodies must be prepared in order for it to be preserved. Much like a Vessel's body must be prepared and strong enough to host the extra energy of a second entity, and the entity must be willing to give energy to its host…the Nexum disease would not make such sacrifice, mortality meant nothing to them. These fallen Soldiers weren't prepared for what squirmed in their bodies, and from the amount of decomposition that had set in; they had already been dead when they were taken.

The shortest of the guards began selecting the appetizers, quickly pausing when his eyes fell upon Anara and Bioni, "They are the whores from the field, let them be flayed and served to the Darken masters."

Anara's mind lapsed forgetting where she was and to whom she yelled at: an Ahzai will always be Ahzai as the Vessel will always serve the link, "*Sao tome met ome lao!*"

The guard held his hand in the air ready to strike but was stopped by another guard, "Do you like your fruit bruised you dumb bastard?"

Bioni stared confused at Anara, an expression and state-of-mind that she always found herself jeering in when Anara surfaced in her life. She knew Anara was slowly relinquishing grasp on reality; she was losing control over her mortality. The glow in her eyes burned with a chaos and a hunger for destruction that would level this planet before the next evolution. Deep down, Bioni knew that what was to come would have nothing on the Score. She could feel the dark silence creeping into their existence.

Anara was just a box of Hell waiting to spill over for them to sweep up and bury before the rest of the world could see the truth. She had been switching between three different languages since the moment she had returned to rescue the mortals from the dome. The Reaper's Curse had finally caught up to its untouched mark. It was only a matter of time before Anara would seek Death out.

They formed a line between the guards to be ushered up a long flight of slimy stone stairs: frequently pulling away from the nasty hands of the deformed and defaced guards who were the epitome of a walking-dead-man. One stood especially tall with singed hair and crusted lips that looked like a fish had been over cooked and stranded far out of water. Scales curled around its neck revealing gills that had been stitched up and replaced with tiny, puss-filled holes that let a torturous small amount of desired oxygen to be received. Anara studied the ocean dweller, trying to remember the name of his people and why he was so far from home.

Bioni watched the Ahzai study the guard and smirked, whispering the name, "Naoplatin."

Anara muttered at the complications that continued to surface, "If the water is compromised than the Nexum is everywhere, not just within this dome—evolution is everywhere."

Blood stained the walls with a decaying stench lingering in the soil and air. Mold grew on the vomit left behind from past slaves as they were dragged back to their cells: thin as bones and soullessly drained. The scones were made from skulls and were half lit, casting a light on the stairs, twinkling in and out of existence as they ascended up the sewage the Darken used as a dungeon.

"I knew the Dame Towers was built to create a Hell away from Hell," Anara muttered to herself, "Who would have thought it capable of becoming the Nexum."

Young servants waited at the entrance with long robes and sponges. It was as if they were decontaminating a contagion, they quickly tore the tattered clothing from the slave's bodies and commenced in bathing them hastily. Scrubbing with a bristled brush, they ripped at the human flesh trying to find the meat beneath it.

Bioni winced at the odor of sulfuric acids mixed with lilac and lavender. She jerked each time they found a tender wound, fighting the need to plant her fist in the young girl's faces. She kept the thought of her daughter far from her mind as they prestigiously cleansed her body of contaminates. Anara looked down at her hands and body with a sigh. Her flesh shimmered brighter than the other women who stood at her side. Her hair glistened with a radiance only meant for a queen.

She glared at her dear friend and whispered with an ironic melody sadly seeping from her bruised lips, "I could have prevented this."

Bioni continued to stare confused at Anara who stared ignorantly through space and time, "What does it matter? If not this world, the next would suffer as well. The gods cannot expect you to save us all."

"It's not about *His* sacrifice, it's about mine," Anara chuckled at the limited knowledge of her mortal friend, "and it is time I began to play the offense of this game, I grow weary with so much defense."

She closed her eyes and made her first strike in the confinements of Celeston: *"Send unto a jester to awaken a Devourer."*

17

Celeston

Akisma exhaled at the irony of Divine Intervention. *He* sends help but the mortals of the Daeviti, specifically the Breach, cannot receive it until a chosen time because it is at the mercy of the goddess. Even then, it is unknown whether this Divine Champion will be ready and willing to fight in their defense. It would be left to the current defenders of the Breach to convince this champion that the planet and the realm of Daeviti, was worth saving. All the great players of this game will rise to place wages, Entities of immense power will surface to do the bidding of one god or another—havoc and chaos will reap the land: Folly would reign with frolicking havoc.

...

The Game Room stirs with commotion. Hands are being dealt without second calculations. Bids are being made without history uncovered. Folly spreads throughout Celeston with complete mischievousness. Akisma yields a tender grin at the cause-and-effect the Wise Men receive from their previous plays.

Malice twined his nervous fingers together, seeing the intervention no one saw because of how small and unseen it was. Yes, they knew a god had joined the game, but they knew not what this higher power had done to interfere. Where one intervention lay, greater ones lay in wait to engulf the land with light, or deliver it unto the darkness. That was the way miracles and condemnation worked: balance must be met.

Malice stretched his fingers across his chin with thought gleaming from his eyes, "They can interfere with our play but can't join our table. What sort of mockery is that?"

Sams the Silent shrugged at the beauty of being over-thrown by an unknown divinity, "Divine mockery I would assume."

"Watch out my little pustules, gods are at play now," Saul's chuckle vibrated every roll of fat he had to offer. Pink from laughter and red with flush, Saul hid his hand for the embarrassment of the new loss which currently held him at a stale mate.

Akisma watched the men within Celeston, wondering when the Bluff would grace their table. Folly had made her pact with Kamenah long ago when she arrived in the form of Anara. From one Vessel to the other, they swore to do what they must to delay the complete enactment of Control. Now the day has come that Control would destroy what innocence was left in the Daeviti realm.

'Sisters are made from souls—not blood and flesh,' Akisma closed her eyes with the sweetest of smirks gracing her pale face.

The goddess she occasionally hosted has served Kamenah from before the Great Freeze of Anara's home world. Unfortunately, the Vessels of their rank had obligation, therefore, none assigned to the Breach could be freed until their mission was complete. Akisma could not leave Celeston until Kamenah was no longer needed as the iron fist of God—not just god, but God: He who is great, he who was the first and the last.

And then the Breeders were born, Akisma could hear the voice chuckle in her mind. It was a tender voice, a child's voice. Her goddess was younger than most attending this realm. Itarah was frozen in Time, but more clever than many other entities. She also allowed Akisma more freedom than most Vessels received.

She had originally arrived in the clouds of Celeston on command of Kamenah to scout for Anara, the *exiled* Ahzai. It was to be Anara's punishment to give the life of her first born child to *Him* as retribution of disobeying the Law. What was the importance of one mortal woman, a single Ahzai? Akisma often contemplated such thoughts. It hadn't occurred to her that the Ahzai's disobedience would bring an entire realm crumbling to its galactic stellar feet.

"Forbidden is she to this man, the Ahzai must take his life or give the life of her first born to Him," Akisma winced, remembering the words of the Oracles and Prophets. Both the Oracles and Prophets agreed that a mere mortal held the fate of the Daeviti in her hands. If she was not capable of completing her mission, Divine Intervention would activate and the planet of the Breach would be the price.

Akisma glared down at the universe through thunderous clouds and knew there was little hope in saving the last innocence of the Breach, "He doesn't appreciate disobedience…He is a wrathful God…"

She didn't care too much for the God, she wasn't born of *His* kind. Her existence took breath upon *His* existence and she was the only one who knew *His* true origin and the truth of *His* beginning. Time has her secrets as did *He*…Itarah respected that. She was the only goddess who did.

…

Crows circled the impaled corpses of the tortured and tormented men who fell to the claws of long forgotten beast. The frozen night's chill competed with the unrelenting heat of day, whispered Death's endearments in the ears of men with the sun's blistering rays filtering intensely through the reddening shield. If the mortals knew that the source of the shield lay fifty feet beneath the bloodstained dirt they suffered over—they would bury their bodies in hopes of finding the power switch.

Damu had appointed two overlords to the dome's territory to oversee the search for Owen's Prophet's Eyes and Traveler's Scrolls. Tarel, who was Damu and Lukan's half-brother, controlled the infected Nexum population. They were the only ones capable of overthrowing the Darken within the dome because they were an evil that would corrupt, consume and convert the weakness of humans. It was their commander Zelbue's responsibility to oversee the slave's obedience: a slave rebellion would not be good in such tight quarters.

"Keep picking at it and you'll bleed to death," a young man chiseled deeper into a sediment boulder searching for the last grains of Irinoi fragments.

The man who was clearly older than the young Karonan slave exhaled with fever, "You make it sound like the bastards won't spit on another wound once this one heals."

They shrugged, chiseling another shard out of the boulder as another man from behind chuckled mischievously, "Don't worry, Roan, he can use the vinegar they call water to wash it out and the salt we sleep on every night to dry it up. Ain't that right, Jest?"

"You damned Breach-born," Roan spit down at the shovel he kicked into the gravel, "Vinegar my arse, more like piss-water."

Jest paused, hearing the whisper of a woman calling to him in a language he had never heard before. He shook his head assuming the heat of the irinoi mine was beginning to affect him and returned to the work at hand: pang…pang…pang, he pounded the mallet deep into the rock—and sent the iron head flying behind him into the head of a Nexum foot-guard.

They froze looking around for the other four guards who stood watch with the line guard, to charge in and administer their punishment for murdering one of theirs. None were around to witness the unfortunate fortune. Jest shook his head at the lifeless corpse with his misplaced mallet head fixed between his eyes. It should have taken more than just a wedged mallet to kill that which was already dead: they required decapitation or blazing fires.

Jest didn't care, "Grab weapons," he muttered at the timely blessing.

He saw an opportunity that could not be passed up, and so he took it. Freedom is more intoxicating on the lips of an ambitious slave than the succulent drops of fresh rain water. Jest had no intentions on questioning the soft voice in the back of his mind bidding him, 'come hither.' Escape was a reasonable feat in the current event that a group of strong, fit slaves stood scrambling for weapons, in the mines of their prison. Jest was not a leader, nor a Soldier, but by all the gods that existed on this planet and beyond, he had every intention on leading this small group of men out of the hell they sweat under. Little did he know that he was being Summoned by more than luck: a goddess called him to the game.

To ignore your Summoning was to invite insanity, and insanity always welcomed the kiss of Death. A journey no mortal cared to travel knowing that the Cradle would dine on their souls while picking their teeth with their bones. The Cradle would make of them slaves for eternity.

18

Fresh air whispered through the windows of a dimly lit chamber as silence echoed endlessly through the halls. Tattered paintings dangled dangerously against the irinoi walls of Dame's cafeteria facilities. The Darken, out of what seemed to be humor, added pieces of their culture to the décor. Exotic and mysterious darkness violently polluted the once diverse equity of Dame's great Towers.

The slaves stood bound at the sides of each chair awaiting their Darken host. The delicacies of one man, does not always entice the intrigues of another. Whether be it foul, beast or fish, there was always a mortal human to fit the equivalent of each gluttonous supper. They now dined with the souls of the Nexum; entities which require a darker sustenance than that of a vegetarian meal.

Anara glared blankly down at the table, counting the empty black china and shimmering black goblets, and noting that light would not befall the crystals. They cast their own shadows and infected the light with disarray. She could almost see the light run from their embrace, fleeing a dark poison that boiled within the core of each umbra.

Her ears burned with the sound of the harps bloody strings striking its first delicate notes. The young maestro from the dungeon glided her thin fingers painlessly across the stained strings feeling nothing of the self mutilation she endured. Aged pieces of flesh flaked from caked blood as she plucked each silken string.

The guests filed in with their noses high and their eyes glaring with abnormality. Anara could taste the possession of each corpse that would be dining in this chamber. She could sense that they were no longer human or Darken, or even Naoplatin—their genetic markers had began to evolve if not decompose under the strain the Nexum creatures placed on their stolen bodies. Only faint flames of the drained souls echoed in the glistening pupils of those possessed.

The thought was discouraging to know that once the Darken had finished their invasion they would leave the land to the beast of the Nexum to conquer.

"How long has the Darken been host to such evil," Anara thought to Kamenah as she watched Bioni grind her teeth fighting the urge to flee or strike, *"or is this another effect of my disobedience?"*

A young woman with hollowed eyes walked calmly around the table pouring foreign liquor which had the likeness of blood. Anara studied Bioni as she watched the liquor ooze from a deep silver pitcher into the goblets of the guests. Younger women silently entered the room with plates that seemed larger than their own bodies were, held high over their heads so as not to see the meal until it had been set upon the table. On each platter lay raw meat and a fruit Anara could not place. The Breach was vast and home to billions of unknown life.

The teenager from the pit continued with the harp as though she were trapped in a subdued trance. Her delicate eyes glistened in a distant stare, gazing upon a fantasy world she would never know of as she delivered this world through the music she composed. For such a young maestro, this girl vibrated power with every string her tormented fingers stroked. A Maestro would gladly serve the symphony of her strings without force. Anara could already see fresh blood moistening the strings with a pale pink sheen.

She listened to the masters speak in the tongue of out-worlders and Nexum-lex. To Anara—each sounded like they were choking while coughing up phlegm. Their human lips struggling with the dark language the Nexum offered to bodiless souls. They struggled now because the lips of humans didn't mutate and shift like the ever-changing forms of whatever creature or beast they had once been before.

The plates were garnished with whatever the guests desired and once emptied they were removed and replaced with a steaming stew. Bioni helplessly focused on Anara who only stared aimlessly into the dark boiling liquid—Bioni glared disgusted and gagging from the stench.

Anara's eyebrows lowered as she watched a Darken take the arm of a slave and commence to peel back a thin slice of her flesh to garnish the stew, lapping it's tongue over the wound as though to close it. The slave's eyes were unfocused and in a daze, she had been subdued by the Darken's link. There would be no freedom for that slave, for once a link is made it remains there until the master is dead. Even when the slave's body passes on, the soul would remain linked with the master.

It was in that moment that the Ahzai knew the Nexum had released some of the most dangerous of its prisoners. Contenders that had the power to over-throw dynasties and possess the simple minds of the Supremacy: and if they could possess the Government of the Breach, they could take on the Hierarchy…leaving the heavens unguarded.

A chill ran down Anara's back making her feel exposed and entrapped. If the Nexum attained the rights of traveling the heavens, they would trigger a universal evolution sending Life and Death into war and giving Time her undesired crown.

The goddess in her stirred, *"The Resistance of Time."*

The Ahzai had figured out who the high bidders were and who Kamenah needed to imprison: her own sisters.

They bowed their head as the Host entered motioning for his guest to continue with their feast. Three seats from Bioni a slave swooned, she would have hit the floor but her captor held her wrist tight in the air. With a swift motion, Anara heard the body thump to the floor, the beast holding the severed hand to his nose to lavish in the scent of fresh blood.

Bioni's eyes widened significantly at what just happened. Anara watched as Bioni began to shake and hyperventilate once the female Darken took her wrist firmly into one hand and placed a sharp bronze blade upon her forearm. Resting it on her flesh to tease fear from Bioni, feeding from not only the human's flesh but from what fed her soul: emotion. This beast was an empath before she had been cast into the Nexum for whatever crime. That woman was what her own daughter could become if she didn't protect her.

"Is that why you were sent to take my Ana? So the daughter of the most powerful Ahzai and Darken wouldn't become a tool for the Nexum?" Anara grit her teeth needing to desperately find her daughter. Most Entities never think of the spirit, they protect the life and the soul, but neglect the most important part of the Triad. The spirit is what a mortal lives for, without it the soul starves and life drains from the vessel. A walking corpse with no meaning, only hunger is left.

Kamenah sighed at the Ahzai, *"If you fail... what do you think will become of Ana? All the inheritance will fall to her... your energies will go to her... even if I preserve your soul... it will take time to heal your body. In that time... a girl of her temperament can level a universe."*

Anara forced herself to stand still as her Nexum master began to unravel her bondage. He paused, taking in the scent of her flesh. Had he noticed the difference in the scent of her evolution? Anara steadied her breathing.

If he knew what he feasted on…what if?

Anara would snap his neck and send his evil soul back to the Nexum with the poor impudent bloke he possessed.

It was her turn to pause, wondering if it would be wise to unleash such power before her current company. She didn't truly know all that lay hidden beneath the fleshy corpses that lined the table, feasting as if they never tasted human meat before.

Where did such strong actions invade her reaction to her current situation?

"Kings and queens of the Nexum, the time has come," the Darken host muttered with little interest to the guest, "Welcome to your reign."

"No!" Bioni squalled, jerking relentlessly against her captor's strength.

Anara tilted her head watching Bioni. An infernal fire churned in the Carriers eyes and Anara knew that if she were to evolve before their host, Hope would be lost. The Nexum would devour her soul before it grew into its prime and was able to defend and destroy.

The Darken stood up ready to strike, but before the blow could land Anara snatched the blade from her creature's cold hand as he readied himself for an attack. Her hair fell to her side as she took the flat carving blade down her arm and threw the flesh across the table. She would heal much quicker than a head wound to Bioni would. Bioni was human and sometimes it felt like she had a big head, but she would feel the scars of this war for ages to come. She was also vital to saving this planet from their self ignorance.

"Leave her be," Anara whispered, returning the knife back to her little glutton pet.

"It's not the same," she hissed, staring infuriated at Anara, "I will not share with a general of the Nexum. I am Darken."

Anara smirked at the female as she held her arm out for the demon to take his garnish without hesitation. She wasn't shocked to know that they were territorial and that power was an issue, "Isn't all human blood the same? Flesh of flesh…" She stopped herself from reciting the words written in the 'Dark Scrolls of the Ahzai'. Even her people saw humans as not more than animals to be herded along, "Besides, can you not smell the sweetness of my flesh?"

The Darken Master leaned back in his great chair watching his little slave smirk at the small battle she had won. Anara winced slightly as her blood drizzled down her arms mixing with the salty sweat that filled the pores of the missing top layer of flesh. She could already feel her body begin the slow healing it was writ to do. The scent from her blood filled the room with sweetness unlike any other human, the thought of 'delicacy' aroused in the senses of each captor, even the humans reacted to its perfume.

The essence of an Ahzai Breeder, any Ahzai, had always been intoxicating. It was the reason why her founding mothers gave their souls to Death in trade for the virtue of the Breeder. Only a Breeder has the right to choose who they bed and reproduce with. If a male tries to take from them what they do not give, Death would fall upon their existence and their soul would forever serve the Reapers.

"Take her flesh and blood as offered, Leera. I shan't share with any other from hence," the entranced Nexum at her side muttered at the taste of her flesh, "Truly a gift for gods."

The supper ended and the leftovers returned to the holding cells bellow. The young, talented girl would return with a high-ranked guest as a party favor to sooth a screaming mortal as she would offer up her life-force to a Nexum-lord and journey to Death's Cradle—in hopes to *arrive* at the Cradle and not in the belly of the tortuous Nexum.

The other slaves tended to their wounds with muddy bandages and acidic water that might have well been their own urine. Bioni was ushered into the cell with the old raving woman. Anara found herself at the end of the prison to occupy a dark empty cell, alone.

The guard threw her in laughing as she hit the wall, "Nice act you pulled up there! Those creatures love torturing the souls out of the likes of you. Congratulations slave, you've just bought your way through the *darker* reigns of hells."

The thought brought a tender laughter of irony to her pain. She winced as he spat at her, listening to the women moaning in their own circle of torment. The voice of Bioni yelled endlessly down the hall only to fade away into the darkness of her prison cell.

How much time had truly past?

Bioni watched them quit the room with a sloppy strut, "I thought they were all Darken. Why do the guards refer to them as more than what they themselves are?"

The red dawn of a new day melted through the walls of imagination with the servants pouring a brown mush into the filthy bowls for the slaves. The night was short lived for most, knowing their pain would only continue with the next meal. Anara could only stare at the shadows as they danced around the pale scones. She could feel the Reaper upon her, marking her with minutes and seconds. The sound of Sasha's voice echoed in her mind, laughing, mocking her of her sacrifice.

Would Death finally taste the flesh of an Immortal Ahzai?

Kamenah laughed now, amused at the soul that fluttered around her own soul in distress. The Reaper's curse was unavoidable by anything and everything, not even the gods could avoid Death's call. It is why the Immortals feed on such as they do; spirits, souls, blood, flesh, worship…it was the only way to mute the Reaper's curse: keep the Reaper busy and they won't be able to track the essence of an Immortal.

"Anara, talk to me!" Bioni shouted with a demand only a great friend and sister of soul would dare.

"There was but one *true* Darken in that room, the rest were half-blood and possessed by Nexum convicts. It is an arrangement that is given willingly, unfortunately. I am sure they do not know the truth of the contract they made with the evils of the Nexum. They are converted. The evil distorts and contorts them," Anara muttered answering the question that had been asked hours ago, "They have become consorts until no mortal soul remains. The soul of the beast will find a new host and devour that one slowly. Luckily, if you could say it is luck for a mortal, the demons of the Nexum can only remain corporeal for so long before the Gate Keeper finds them. Until then, which could be hundreds and hundreds of Ursan years from now, they will use up mortals. Depending on the power of the mortal soul, will decide how long a body will last for the beasts."

"That's why the monsters in the Blood Fields are like the walking dead," Bioni sighed into her hands, "Weak souls."

Anara didn't respond. It was true, the weakest slaved in the fields because they had already been drained and left as an open vessel for the lesser Entities of the Nexum that were lucky to find a way out. She could only sum up that the holes in the Gates leaked big, or there were so many of them that the Keeper couldn't keep up.

"You shouldn't have come back, Anara," Bioni muttered annoyingly to the air, "Are we just suppose to wait till they finish us off? Eat us alive? *You* must do something."

"I am," she muttered back with sarcasm, "*It* just hasn't gotten here yet."

Ignoring Anara's all too common babbling; Bioni continued the ritual over and over waiting for a response worth listening to from anyone or anything, "Anara, this is your fault. Eating that arm the way you did. You've made us brunch for the bastards, you shouldn't have come back."

"And you will be brunch!" a new guard strutted pass Bioni startling her. She had not heard him enter, nor did any of the other women, "What many meals you shall make for the lords. But for now, rest, he only desires one dish, one slave."

Bioni watched the guard prance his tall, puny body to the end of the hall and almost swearing that she saw bone moving in and out of his elbow. He paused to examine the specimen. Two, more built guards, flung the bars open and pulled Anara stumbling out. Her eyes were naught but empty shells of distant and shielded concentration.

"Gentle boys, he wants her as she is."

Bioni stared, struggling with what she could do to stop them. She noted every wound Anara had made that night to save her the loss of flesh. One arm had already begun healing. Bioni stepped back bowing her head, knowing she would be okay. That the Vessel had been wide awake the entire time they were out in those blooded fields amongst the corpses of mortals.

Anara's eyes went blank as rage quickly took over. She fought back uselessly and ended weak and limp in the arms of the soldiers like a good little human was suppose to do. A tender wave of energy cast back towards Bioni as Anara peered for a moment from the corner of her eyes.

"The little road with webs of white and grey is where you can rest, take ye that way," she hummed as her hair dangled knotted and dripping around her shoulders.

When they were first stationed in the Wastelands, Anara had assigned Bioni and Cara to exploring the Old World beneath Traverna. There were tunnels throughout this territory and only sixty percent had been revealed, each branching across the governed territories of the Breach.

Her amber eyes receded into an icy world far beyond the hell she was being dragged through. Bioni could only watch, knowing that in that shadowed world in the back of Anara's mind, no one could touch her. Bioni knew she would be safe, in that darkness only the Freeze may go: Anara hid from all who lived. She nodded understanding the Vessel's commands, spoken and unspoken.

Hope intermingled with exhausted whispers of a dying soul, "It's not the darkness she fears anymore, only the shadows within her light."

...

She lost consciousness somewhere between the 30th Floor and the 42nd Floor, she could remember passing a corridor that had once been lodging quarters for the Soldiers when they were summoned. Anara had begun to wander in these shady moments while the goddess subdued her as she withdrew to the dark, cold places of her past. The goddess had been meddling quite often now that Anara was suffering from Reaper Hysteria, babbling of knowledge and a future that would soon come to pass because of her own actions.

When she finally woke she found her body lying limp and lifeless in the center of an extremely large bed covered in black silk and fur sheets from an exotic world long forgotten. It was almost sinfully garish in the details that polluted this chamber. The room was cool against a fire that shimmered warmly in the center of a floor bath containing black water encircling the tall, narrow and glowing brimstone pyramid.

A double transport, Anara studied the pyramid, *the Fallen.*

Her eyes refocused on the dancing flames as her ears relaxed to the sound of a gentle harp—*a harp.*

Her voice vibrated in attempt to bring words from her lips, "Stop."

The Ahzai could feel her heart beat to the rhythm of the harp, submitting to its sweet melodies with unwanted pleasure. Even a god answers to the notes of a good *Maestro.*

Anara exhaled with a sigh, searching to find the energy to raise her voice, "Please, you can stop playing!"

Anara struggled trying to force her burning body up from the feather pillows and lace. When Death crept up on her in her dark spells, she would gain consciousness and find her entire body weak and tormented as if a mountain had just landed on her. The notes of the maestro did little to help her overcome her insanity.

She closed her eyes feeling her belly rumble, *that is what Death is for the likes of the disobedient: starvation, exhaustion—submission.*

The sweet symphony came from the young girl of Karone who had warned her about the appetites of their current masters. It was knowledge Anara had already known, and she wasn't surprised to find that Time would salivate in the extent of Gluttony. Time feeds Death, Death feeds Life and Life feeds Time: the sisters need one another to survive.

Kamenah knew this all too well, she could not exist without her own sisters; *Itarah feeds Opelya, Opelya feeds Kamenah, and Kamenah feeds Itarah… Itarah weakens as Opelya devours and swells and I devour and sit sated.*

With Kamenah refusing to yield the Breach, Anara and Ana, Time isn't completed and gluttons off of the leftovers Death leaves for her, for she has been overwhelmed.

We now resist Time. We are working in reverse to protect Ana from demise and keep you away from an ultimate punishment.

Anara sighed at the sacrifice the goddess was making to maintain Anara's mortal existence and her daughter's fate.

It will only be so for as long as I refuse to give you up. It will force His hand…

The Ahzai observed the maestro. There were no expressions on the girl's face as she plucked the blood-bleached strings. The pale shade of her dying soul trickled down each string, echoing through the talent of a true musician. Where once a maestro had left its brilliant mark in such a hopeless child—only a slave remained.

I could save her, Kamenah whispered the thought.

Anara tried leaping from the bed only to fall back realizing the burning of the cold chains jerking and tightening around her choked neck.

I could end this now, Kamenah echoed the temptation, *or you could—Ahzai.*

It was in the mortal's best interest that the goddess remained unknown to the Darken and Nexum alike. If they were clever enough to escape the Nexum, they were powerful enough to send her there as well. Even gods have Laws, His Law. Should she release the Vessel within her, more would surely die and to top it off, she would be the one *devouring* them.

I would do no such thing, Anara.

"But I would," Anara ignored the voice and examined the contents of the dark chamber finally focusing on the child, "You never told me your name, slave girl, what is your name?"

Truth was: Anara had encountered so many people, making thin links with so many souls: she could hardly remember the recent attributions.

Short-term memory—another side-effect from the Reaper's curse, Kamenah chided.

Anara crinkled her thin eyebrows debating if Kamenah was suffering from the accursed curse as well.

The young maestro rocked back and forth with the music that whispered enchantment through the walls. Her crusted hair fell long and stringy around her shoulders speaking of a long night, one in which most mortals would not have survived. She wasn't most mortals though. She was a maestro, gifted with that extra strength and energy only a Daeviti planet can supply and enhance. Like the Soldiers, she was not the average teenage girl…she was evolved.

Think of Ana, sisa, they are of the same age, the goddess chanted in Anara's mind.

Anara moistened her lips struggling for the proper words to speak, fragile, yet crossing, "Your melody is quite lovely. Where did you learn to create such perfect notes?"

It was unlike the notes played upon the Prison Islands, Anara was sure of that. Every maestro had their own signature, a mystery she desired to solve…with her hands gripping tight around the master maestro's neck. Anara exhaled a soft curse as she glared down at the blood on her arm. She dipped her finger into the wound and drew a symbol onto her palm.

A little energy wouldn't bring alert to the starved little beasts. Anara justified with Kamenah, *using the Ahzai would only alert the Darken of the Ahzai.*

She then placed her bloodied palm to her neck and began voicing her energy into her words, "You pluck those strings as though they were a part of you. Now, speak. I *command* you."

Hope fluttered as she watched the power absorb into the girls features while she shook her head in response to the message, "It is not my music that is so pleasing. I play the music of our master."

Anara forced a smile knowing that the amount of energy she was using would be enough to make the attempt in lifting the spell on the girl, "Did he tell you to play endlessly?"

"For you to wake, because only you will hear the melody within," she continued to strike heavily at the harp giving it life in the darkness of her own blood, "He said never to end the line."

What exactly was the demon trying to awaken, the goddess murmured with sarcasm, *know the spell within each note struck.*

Anara forced a stern face when all that she felt was fury and fire, "I have awakened. Therefore you may stop."

The melody within, Kamenah chuckled at her, *this Darken is the same master maestro who made the assault on you whilst you rescued the Krypt from the Cenilus Islands. You can't hear his signature for he commands the hands of another maestro through his mastery.*

"I need to learn how many overlords are here," Anara grit her teeth knowing the goddess was right, "Girl, how many masters do you serve? How many Generals are here?"

She lost her again.

It was as though something had interrupted the link. Anara wiped the symbol from her neck and hand knowing there was no more she could do without drawing more energy and attracting scavengers to the feast. She wanted to believe that she lost the girl somewhere in the physical pain that continued to drain the life from her body and the music that enchanted the fingers to continue to strike those deafening strings.

Anara was certain that she would remember this melody for the rest of her eternity.

She forced her fingers between her collar and collarbone feeling for a rusted bolt or weakened link to shatter with a jolt of energy her anger now offered. Anara had the desire to destroy something, to decimate the nearest abomination. Her thirst for vengeance was a putrid, if not alluring, scent that plagued the air around them. The maestro's head tilted up, catching the scent, her face paled even more so, with fear.

Her heart began to sink realizing there had been symbols etched into the collar much like the music the child strung away with.

Awake, Anara thought, *what are you suppose to awaken, child?*

The goddess refused to give the Ahzai all the answers. They evolved for a reason, Anara mustn't forget that reason. She was born for war.

When kindness failed her irritation began demanding an exit through mortal doubt, *humans always harbor self-doubt.*

"You will never amount to be his favorite," Anara could see a change in the girl's eyes, "One slave out of many and yet there are others more talented than you. It will only be a matter of moments before you are discarded for something fresh and more succulent."

The link between the Vessel and the girl was successful and Anara was shocked at the strength of the girl's spirit and soul, "If you have anger and jealousy you still have free will. Your Darken master is false to us with their peevish little games. You yearn to please a filthy servant of slaves? *You* are a mortal Human: superior to them. He ordered you to please me; a slave plucked straight from the Blood Fields. Is that all you have? Your music is disgusting, young maestro, for it is not your own. Sweet puppet."

Anara didn't realize she was speaking her home language as she stood in the center of the bed pulling on the chain only to slide with the silk sheets, "Did he give you a name, *desi*? I have a name, and it is known by none, which gives me power over you-"

"I see you have *awakened*," a dark voice chiseled the air with amusement, "and well rested."

Anara's head snapped in the direction of the Darken's voice that vibrated from the shadows. It was familiar, yet she could not recollect where she had heard his dark chime. Had he been there the whole time?

"Her name is Laura," he answered her question with a snide chuckle.

"Tell, Laura to quit. Do you not see the bones on her fingers? The blood on the floor," Anara hissed kneeling in his direction waving her hands at the droplets drizzling down Laura's pale knees and pooling at her feet.

He mocked her plea with a gentle click of his tongue, "Do you beg of me?"

Anara closed her eyes playing into his dominance.

"Will you serve me as she does? I can't release a good slave with no replacement," he waited for her to respond, "Will you die for her, *slave*?"

Anara tilted her head, forcing back the menacing grin that threatened as she struggled to control the wrath that flared in the back of her mind, "She is already dead! Let her soul be free!"

The Darken agreed, stepping into the light and revealing himself completely, "True, but free to go where?"

She watched the girl pluck the strings with ridged nails and bloodied bones, "To another."

"Would you die, for her to suffer no more?" He murmured with that evil amusement she yearned to rip from his throat.

Anara sat back tucking her head between her knees, hugging herself tightly.

It has always been my love of these mortals that have done me in, Anara.

"I will serve you as Ahzai until your rule of this territory is completed, so long as you give her unto me," *I fear I do not share the same affection, cold goddess,* "We both know who is more powerful."

The Darken blinked his eyes forcing his jaw to remain locked and his emotion tightly held around his mass form. He steadied his breathing, preparing for an attack from the creature kneeling on the bed before him. He knew not whether to kneel and worship her or to beg her for Breeding Rights, what knelt before him was a treasure amongst the universe.

Ahzai, he grit his teeth, he had found what his overlord had been searching for. They didn't need the Eyes of Prophets if they had a Prophet. If she was the woman Lukan longed for, *she is the last of the Ahzai children…*

Anara knew what sailed through his arrogant mind. The empty expression on his face spoke a million words, he knew who she was. What he didn't know, was she had long ago passed *that* particular gift on. He wouldn't gain the secrets of a Prophet, only the riddles of a goddess and paranoia of a seer.

"You know nothing of this girl and you would give yourself to save her from a little pain," he snapped his fingers, dismissing the girl, "It could be worse."

"She would be better off visiting the Cradle," Anara glared through empty eyes as she could feel her heart pound against every rib in her chest, "Know that Time *resists* and you will have but moments of my service."

If any at all, Kamenah's thought purred in silent knowledge.

A guard pounded on the chamber door, "Master Tarel. Prince Damu sends orders from the Traverna."

Tarel smiled at Anara, his eyes glistening with secret pools of diamond-ruby sin, "What of it?"

"A group of Karonan slaves have gained their freedom and have rebelled," the guard answered with his head bowed, frequently glancing up at the woman who knelt in the center of the master's bed, "Zelbue has been slain."

From the man's shredded uniform Anara knew he had once been a Soldier of the Breach and by the peeling patch on his torn sleeve, she knew he had been stationed at the Southrun Arkeon. It would seem that the Darken have been abducting, corrupting and converting for quite some time.

Tarel joined the guard, pausing to speak over his large right shoulder, "I will have your sup brought to you, slave. Rest. Be at ease. For your own comfort, call it a gift if you will. I will see to it that Laura is mended and returned to you in *mint* condition."

Anara smirked at the Darken while he faded into the shadows of the stairway, "Is that all I'll receive for my talents, Tarel? You should owe me a kingdom for my services."

He only chuckled at the sneer in her voice. There was sin in his eyes as he glared hungrily at her. His desire for her power would spread like a disease throughout his senses. Her sarcasm was a plague, a challenge and invitation for those powerful enough to dare pursue control over her.

The chamber door whispered shut and the locks snapped into place as if they were strong enough to keep her contained in such confinements while he was away hunting for rogue slaves. The locks were the sound of mockery for the walls echoed with enchantment and barriers that would take energy and time to shatter and break through. They were an enticement left to draw out her true strengths and to exhaust her while they sat and watched what she was capable of, to know what it would take to control an Ahzai. She had no doubt that she was being watched.

"Only one man had succeeded in such ambition," the Ahzai could feel the chill of the faded memory invade her flesh with goose-bumps and cold-sweat.

"And vengeance will be succulent," the goddess whispered.

Anara could feel the comfort Kamenah offered and realized her submission to the one man had disheveled her more then she would ever willingly admit. Her eyes opened, really opened, at the truth she now accepted. She loved him, but never believed that her beloved king returned the same love. She was a possession, and now that the goddess shared her body and soul, he could no longer influence her. Anara could taste the freedom that had been opened to her, now that she truly saw her error. She was in control of her own fate with the power of a god to dispose of.

19

Perfection came so simply in the sheets of darkness. The ominous shadow would waver or stiffen, always watching and never permanent among men. Truth came so sinfully and bit with as many sharp teeth shone by the black beast that circled the night sky with poison falling from its great wings. Observation is all that rested in the eyes of a trapped slave, a prisoner chained in the cold sweat of secret conspiracies and compromised words. Day became unknown, stealing time from every second spent within the chambers of a Darken.

Anara could sleep endlessly in the silence of solitude and the shear delusional honesty of being alone. Her meals were delivered while she slept or as she silently paced across the bed with a blink of her delicate eyes. The Ahzai puzzled over the foreign fruit that tasted so delicate and ripe. She occasionally noticed the wounds on her forearm fading and diminishing as though they never existed. She healed at a much faster rate than before, the Vessel was taking over her body and for the first time, Anara no longer cared. Her hair grew long and glistened to her every movement. The color of her flesh became rich and firm as the room she resided in.

Owen had succeeded. With this act of 'foreign' invasion, Control would consume the world. Dreams of a completed Project invaded her silence with dread and worry. Sacrifice surfaced in her reality. The Reaper would collect her bounty. The shield was incomplete judging by the holes that gave way to a sky of blue. Subtle and not seen by human eyes, but there none the less. With the superiority of the Darken technology, there were no reasons for the dome to be incomplete. The Darken were never sloppy in their creations.

A noise creaked through the chamber door and she watched the once still shadows rise. The scent of prey bringing her pleasure to her distaste in the world she occupied. Such interruptions were annoying in her meditation, she had much to contemplate and much more to plot. Kamenah was true when she warned Anara that Death always reaps the souls on her never ending list. She could sense her mortal existence was nearing the Cradle.

"Rested," Tarel smirked, approving at the beauty of the Vessel who sat meditating on his bed, "Rare, we thought all had abandoned this dome to its death."

"I have no idea what you speak of," she sat in the center of the bed looking away with implicit annoyance, "When you are done with me, will you hang me from your walls as a trophy to strike fear into all of the slaves?"

"Surely I would rape you over and over again first," Tarel lifted a surprised eyebrow strolling to the edge of the bed, "I smell a Breeder on you. I do not enjoy the company of these Nexum fools any more than you wish to ally with me. If I wanted you dead, I could have killed you a thousand times by now."

Awaken, the fury and defiance of the Vessel within her was poisoning her perception and she could no longer separate their thoughts. Her inability to overcome the Reaper's curse weakened her, as was its purpose, a device to force her to succumb to the accidents of Death. If a mortal cannot think straight, they grow sloppy, and they falter—then they fail.

Anara raised her arms from the sheets, "I have not seen day in such a long time. A measurement I am no longer sure exists. What do you want of me?"

Anara knew that to whine and divert the topic, as every mortal woman could do, may buy her time allowing her to learn more about the Darken Tarel and what his relations with Damu might be. Humanity offered plenty of maneuver and techniques on dissuading the male species.

He smiled, revealing sharp white teeth, while glaring mischievously down at Anara's tattered expression, "Nothing you have not done to yourself. The more you accept our ways the more you will become a tool in our scheme."

Anara threw a pillow to remove the smile from his arrogant face. She exhaled against a hoarse whisper that held back her desire to watch him bleed slowly as she inflicted as much pain that was allowed as she hummed to every drop of blood that hit the black floor, "You are desperate to poison me with your lies. I am a threat to you. I've only to learn how," *blah blah blah,* Kamenah sputtered at Anara.

"I am Darken, remember, cohort of the Death. It is expected of me," Tarel muttered with sarcasm as he lay back staring aimlessly through the ceiling, fearless and determined.

She thrust herself forward grabbing the sheets to pull him to her, "No, you abandoned what is expected of you a long time ago."

Anara froze at the ancient memory, with every death she had ever witnessed—it became more difficult for her to sort through her past and the past of the goddess. It was as if she were drawing her last breath and the Reaper who had come for her wanted her to remember all the deeds she had done, and remember the *one* deed she failed to do…

Tarel mused for but a small moment, "No?"

Anara sighed, letting her cool breath mingle with his.

Her face was a mask that seemed to beg for forgiveness as she looked to a sky she hadn't seen for so long. Her hands slipped under the sheets revealing a small knife she had snuck from a previous meal. She had finally surrendered to the goddess performing this Blood Summoning. It was Law for a Vessel to shed their precious life's essence to relinquish custody and possession of their body and temple.

Anara slammed the tip of the blade into her left wrist and smirked while the blood oozed out of her veins.

Tarel cursed in a language unknown as he threw her back against the bed. Taking the knife and pressing it to her neck ready to take the final blow that would prevent her from summoning the energies of this world to obey her commands.

She glared at him, waiting for the Darken to finish what she had begun. A Blood Summoning was as lethal as Soul Sacrifices. The blood is a powerful magnet for energy that could summon the greatest of entities with the proper symbols etched into the flesh or the mind's eye. She could not take her own life without forfeiting absolute control to the goddess.

The Darken only glared down at her with a calm heat flowing steadily from his body to hers. Anara tried to push him away. Tried to refuse the energy he poured into her body to make her wounds heal. She realized he was stronger and more talented then she had credited him and he now knew what she was capable of.

"Thoughtful," Tarel stared intensely into her eyes.

Her body tensed as the heat of his body began scorching her flesh. The Ahzai arched her back and turned her head to the side, parting her lips to suck in sweltering oxygen. He continued to glare down at her, concentrating on healing her body but ready to end her rise should he fail.

"A Vessel knows Death too intimately to be allowed that dark abyss humans go craven for," he exhaled upon her moist cheek. His breath labored from the amount of his life force he needed to heal the fatal wound she had created and no longer existed. There were no reminisces of a scar that remained in the center of drying blood.

Tarel studied her fondly admiring her frustrations, "The soul is dead but the body still struggles to live."

He brought his arm up to rest on his elbow and puzzled over the woman beneath him, "Have you met your Reaper?"

"I still drawl breath," she could feel his body tense against hers, "If the soul was dead, the body would feel nothing, a feast not worth devouring."

He pressed her farther into the bed with the knife still to her neck releasing a tiny dribble of blood that trickled down the edge of the blade. Tarel could feel his body yearn and plead to take what lay hot beneath him. The scent from the sweat that beaded upon her flesh enticed him, dared him to try. It dared him to give his life to the Cradle just to have one moment within her body.

She could sense his hunger and thirst mocking her sex with temptation. Anara moaned in the back of her mind as she watched through her own eyes, praying the goddess wouldn't give in to his lust. She was in need, but he was not what her body needed.

"A Breeder chooses her mate," he hissed rocking his hips back and forth between her legs.

"You must take me or I would either die or become a slave in taking you," he lowered his head to brush his lips to hers, "A Vessel's link."

She hissed pushing her neck hard against the blade, "Taint the *mortal* within you."

Tarel tilted his head so that his lips brushed across her ear, dangerously irritated, "Soul Sacrifice? I want that faint part of your mortal soul to whither so that I can make you into the Vessel I desire."

Anara, drowning in his words, fell silent as the oxygen that was being denied to her began to trace dull stars that glittered in circles throughout her mind. He lifted her hand to his lips to kiss her palm and make a trail to her bloodied wrist where he suckled at the sweetness left behind. She could feel his tongue lapping the wound as she faded slowly into her self-abyss with the dark images of an ancient soul wavering with mockery in her subconscious. The glimmers of light were dancing no more on the gray ceiling and darkness fell contently around her memories. If there was a reality in such a world that he, a Darken, could have such control over her—she had already lost this round in the game.

Darkness quickly became a shadow, and an image of a young servant dribbling cold drops of water on her forehead, became light. The beat of a drum striking loud shrills vibrated through her head with a cool irritating voice ringing beyond it. The scent of exhaustion and fear plagued the air with obedience. Anara exhaled knowing the little servant to be the girl from before, Laura, and she also prayed that the cold drips of water was truly water and not sweated blood from the girl's fingers.

"You wake. The master wants you to join him in the steam room to be bathed," Laura hummed against the melody in command.

A Maestro was born to comfort and enchant, her talents of muse were endless and always pleasing for whomever the bearer served. Even her voice whispered lovely notes of contentment, soothing her new mistress in her wake.

Anara laughed with a hint of humor in the back of her throat, "I am not bathing with him."

The slave girl frowned at Anara, "He knew you would say that, so he ordered three guards to escort you. 'Rip her clothes from her body if need be,' he did say, 'if that does not sway her, take her sister from the cells and *purify* her soul,' mistress, you do not wish such torture for your sister."

Anara refused the girl, placing a slender hand on her hip. The goddess held little affection for Bioni. She was unsubstantial and knew the process of rebirth. The Carrier within Bioni was not needed anytime soon. In the instance that the mortal fell deceased, Kamenah would simply send her soul crashing back into the womb of some random woman.

Anara, on the latter hand, held to the preservation of life when it came to those she had grown unwillingly attached too: Bioni being the soul in question. She had already triggered the Carrier within Bioni and Anara couldn't afford to forfeit another player in the game.

Laura gawked, hesitantly studying her new master, "Mistress, I do not wish to see you forced. He knows you are more than you are. Only one such as your self can recover from-" she paused and repeated, "-he knows of the woman Bioni. Have you no care of her? I will tend to her if that is the note, I will sing unto her a numbing accord."

Anara realized that Laura had delivered many mortal souls to Death's Cradle. The Maestro in her was too accustomed to the passing of one soul for her to be completely innocent of the ways of war. The girl who knelt before her in servitude showed complete loyalty to the Ahzai. The goddess could taste the worship that escaped Laura's spirit. Anara gave her hope, and in return, the Maestro gives her the rarest of energy offered a mortal: worship.

A soldier tapped at the chamber door anticipating the slave.

"Tarel is kinder than most. You should respect and honor him. Not all lords are as generous as he. Prince Damu is the beast of them all. He keeps no servants and kills with a single breath," she laid her hand on the strings to silent them.

Anara noted that the girl's fingers were healed almost completely and realized that Laura never once felt the pain of her master's pleasure. The evolved either accept their new founded powers or they defied the gift and felt the punishment of their true nature. A soul could no more deny their temple anymore than an evolved mortal could defy the natural function of their body.

She shook her head knowing that no matter what she could say nothing would influence the girl. She had been permanently brainwashed from an eternity of slavery and the lazy lifestyle of the creatures she served. Once a slave, always a slave: she would know only to serve. The mark of a child who was not raised of the Breach, a child abducted from her home and taken into another kind of Hell, a world where humans are cattle and slaves to the alien races. Sacrifice, was at what price?

Some science, Anara rolled her eyes at the irony of education, *Control-control-control.*

She staggered weak and exhausted, almost fainting at the great doors of the 'private spa.' Only a Dame would have a giant bathtub in his office-tower. Owen was a master of construction, how he could be so sloppy to underestimate the Darken he had been in league with, was absurd and ironic. He may have gained the act of Control, but he lost power over the dominion. It will take the Supremacy of Government years before they reestablished the claim over Traverna, Eere View and Woke Free Sectors.

Heat bellowed from beneath the door as it opened to a completely symmetric decor. Great alabaster pillars towered the edges of a long rectangular dark pool engraved into the center of a room made of obsidian marble and some other stone unknown to her. Shadows gently danced around the pillars as though to entice them to join in the flames; reaching out to share a warm, fatal embrace.

The thought of being wet became difficult knowing that the last time she had attempted to enter a large amount of water she had nearly been disintegrated. All doors lead to another in the house of Dame. The family hid transports throughout the Daeviti realm, and if they could, Anara was sure they would plant a device throughout the universe and all creation.

"One gene separate from the other," Owen had once said, *"Evolution can also be a flaw."*

She focused on the enormous bronze basins with brimstone and fire raging delicately from within, each set between the great pillars. The slave girl bowed her head and motioned for Anara to enter the pool. Technology made it hard for her to want to step foot in the water knowing that it could very well transport her to the raging inferno of Death's Cradle—or worse, the Nexum.

Death had been on her mind quite a bit as of lately. Every breath she forced into her lungs seemed to be plagued with the Reaper's invitation to insanity. Her fears and concerns threatened to surface but were quickly shoved back into the corridors of her mind by the goddess: it would appear that Kamenah needed her host, her Vessel to be somewhat sane. It was as though

213

they began a full merge and that their mind would eventually become one whole, and that their souls would function as one.

"Await for the master here," was all that escaped the girl's tender pink lips.

Anara turned looking for the girl, realizing she had been alone for a while. She took her first step into the hot water watching her ripples disturb the black surface. Stepping, cautiously farther into the pool she let the water wash calmly over her shoulders. She closed her eyes and let the heat comfort her. Her body gave no motion, allowing the water to settle as she listened silently for the Darken to return.

Anara fought the blur of memories that beat against her labyrinth of thoughts. She had seen many of Owen's constructions containing a master bath for his Soldiers to soak in. Such as on the Arkeon Barrier were it was frozen day and night and each shift was forced to withstand the Freeze.

Tarel leaned soundlessly against a pillar watching the reflection of every flame in the room dance yearning and hungrily around her submerged body. It was as though she belonged in such a world of power and war: A *Queen* hidden in the world of humans—a vessel between the living and the dead. He explicitly noted the sharpness of her hair claimed the territory of water around her shoulders, creating a shield of protection that threatened to devour the life around it. He studied her alertness and concern of thoughts unknown to him. There was a distant star that twinkled in her eyes as she waited fearlessly for what was to come.

He knew, while smiling, that she was here with purpose.

Tarel listened to soft murmurs escape her lips. He entered the water slowly, cutting through, leaving no ripples to announce his presence. Tarel was a warrior, a predator with shadow and darkness at his command.

Anara tilted her head back catching his broad chest. She paused keeping her eyes shut, wanting to be somewhere else. This was her reality, her punishment for disobedience and discord—this was what she was willing to sacrifice.

Tarel tilted his head slightly contemplating whether she knew he was there or the intimate movement was only by accident. Even her breathing was measured and relaxed against his body. He could feel an immediate response to her chemistry jolt throughout his bones, screaming for him to bond. He lifted his hand from the water drizzling warm droplets over her forehead as though baptizing an infant. He then placed his hand around her neck and turned her around to face him, wanting her body to respond in like to his.

She opened her eyes glaring confidently and defiantly up at him.

"Will you surrender?"

"No," Anara tilted her head, "it is you who must surrender."

He didn't blink nor move, only watched as the energy around her shifted and raged in an unknown turbulence. In this moment, the woman was Immortal and he would bet his last breath that if he were to attempt to draw blood that she would only bleed because she *chose* to. The appearance of a human was gone, only the presence of a goddess remained with the image of an Ahzai.

She glared distantly into the ever-changing eyes of a creature of evolution; one that had become more powerful than the humans of the Breach…perhaps even for a lesser Ahzai. A species which had no desire to conquer the turbulence the Breach breathed, so what was its purpose on the chaotic land of imprisonment and pursuit of perfection?

Tarel smirked faintly as he nudged her slowly into deeper water and held her above the surface to keep her face above the water, "We converted a secluded sector of the Naoplatin. It wasn't too hard to find this particularly small tribe. They had fled their kingdom deep beneath the water and colonized off the shores of the South Run Arkeon without knowledge that they sheltered so near to Darken Territory. The Chief of the Euoria told of the retreat of their kingdom; the Euoria choosing to stay behind. I wondered where they had traveled to, and it just so happens there is a rumor that Mr. Dame has a mirror which leads to the ocean Kingdom of Naomiah."

She watched his arrogance with a silent approval and suspicion. What was the need of alliance with the Naoplatin? Anara didn't blink as he pressed closer. His hand rose to brush a blade of hair behind her ear to whisper hints of riddle and future conquests.

He allowed a soft chuckle that vibrated over her flesh, "Sometimes there are things that make evil look good and good so good that it becomes the evil. Once we have found what the Hierarchy seeks, we will leave the land to the beast, who slumbered until now. The Nexum will roam freely and converge with the Breach, hindering those who seek to discover our path."

Her head tilted, smiling with a hint of secret, "Death will catch up to you. She always does."

Tarel stared down at the woman almost with confusion, "Why do you fight for these humans? Mortals who worship religions that were written in ink and not blood."

"It is written in soul," Anara closed her eyes impatiently, "Even if they do not remember their promise. These humans are stronger than you think. Do you honestly believe the One God would give them power over themselves if he did not think them capable? The *Humans* are his children, sinful and saintly. They are what make this planet so strong and resistant of Time's curse unlike several fallen Daeviti. They have not been stripped of evolution and they will continue to prosper when it would seem all hope has been lost. They will flourish like cockroaches even when *her* little box of treats has been opened. Some things remain universal. If a Carrier is Summoned; then a Box must be manifested, else Death walks freely without law. It is the Law of the God for he in this moment reigns over all others…for this moment."

"You speak of Law? Anara Starfallen of the shadowed Ahzai—child of the dark, frozen planet condemned by your own defiance," he studied the change in her face, "Yes, girl, I know of you."

Anara's eyes narrowed with a jesting playfulness, "You're not the only one with secrets, Tarel. *We* too have a game to play."

"Do you know of what is heading straight for this planet?" Tarel muttered smugly as though a devil were struggling to become a saint, "They will come once the mortals begin to give sacrament to the *shadow*. The Humans will—Supremacy demands Control now."

She leaned into his body purring at the reflection staring into the water, "They are not undefeated."

Tarel pushed her away so that he may see her face, "Are we to run for all eternity? Jumping soul to soul, devouring the innocence of others? Darkens do not scavenge."

A Darken knows little hope and plenty of survival. They are trained to destroy and conquer. Affection of hope was never taught, it was a sin and weakness for the Immortals and long-lived Darken breed. She now realized what they were seeking. The Darken sought unchained immortality, the final evolution to their species. The Darken desired worship and sacrifice and would Summon their slumbering ancestors to gain it.

"The Hierarchy comes," Anara exhaled at the complication she faced, the complication the Breach faced.

He cupped her cheeks pleading with a false endearment, "Join me so that I may be linked with you."

She pulled away, eyes burning with irritation, "Do you even know what your ancestors are? What they care capable of?"

Tarel glared down at the still water, "It is not for me to decide the course of this game. I have a role and I will tend to the fields as I am commanded."

Her eyes narrowed at the thought of giving him such power. Anara swayed knowing it was all her fault. This would not have happened if she had assassinated the Magna-King and not fallen in love with him. Once again, she was responsible for the deaths of billions of innocent souls. When would *He* intervene? These are his children who will suffer. Her jaw tightened knowing that it was the life of her daughter or the lives of the billions—a sacrifice she would not offer no matter what Law she had broken. Anara Starfallen would never yield her seed, innocent of all that rages around them. She would give no god their souls unless they, her children, chose to serve a single entity…even if the entity is the One, the All Mighty.

"The innocent should not be punished for my defiance," she exhaled to the distance fire, "I will not give *You* what *You* want."

Perhaps this was *His* way of intervening, his first move. Send in a Legion of his first children to deliver chaos out onto the land that sheltered the disobedient child and her offspring. Awaken the dungeons of the Breach's core prison and release the convicts and murderers of the Nexum to open the gateway for *His* Legion to pass through, summoning legitimately the ravens and seraphs of the Blessed world to feast on the corpses of fallen contenders.

What has she done? Could any one individual make a decision so bad that the consequence was the annihilation of an entire planet, the condemnation of the Daeviti realm? Disobedience was the seed for sin and a plague for the sinner. How could she repent and still keep her children in service of the living?

It was at this moment she wished all of these things were a dream. A nightmare she would wake up from, in her warm, lumpy bed with disarrayed pillows scattered everywhere; her children waking for morning breakfast and a race to Safrai Gardens to tend lessons in Traverna. Friends who would call her and ask of the children and tell of their children, they would call on a phone to just hear her voice. A Soldier who worked nightfall till day woke and still would leave on call to serve an employer who did all that was in his power to oft the man so that the Breach's prize possession was free to influence.

Anara frowned at the darker part of the peaceful memories: the empty bottles of whiskey and rum, the deleted phone numbers she pulled up on his record, the familiar voices on his messages he claimed belonged to fellow Soldiers, and it was rumored that 'Soldiers don't entertain Soldiers' and 'the mission comes first'.

She also frowned remembering her daughter consorting in Owen Dame for traded information on where Krypt disappeared to, on how to retrieve lost artifacts and save her mother the stress of saving a universe. It was a life so distant to the corruption she faced now. Was it truly a nightmare? Or is it a spell forcing her to see the unseen and hear the unheard…the Reaper's curse at its best.

Tarel roared throwing his hands in the air as though to invoke the wrath of the nearest higher Entity, "I am not what you need to fight! There are others who have become solid, who are walking through the gates as we squander!"

She refused to respond to him, staring through him as if he no longer existed in her delicate reality. If he knew his true origin, his home world so far outside the Daeviti, would he change his mind and join her side? Become a Knight in her game? Could such a permanent and vital piece belonging to an opposing force change sides? Change their true color?

He cursed reaching out and grabbing her shoulders to pull her closer, "We need hope, too. What gives you the right to delegate humans above those who are not? You are not God, you have no right."

Anara shook her head with a malevolent smirk crossing her face, power swirling chaotically in the center of fire swept eyes, "It is yours if you would take it. I've nothing to do with it."

Tarel brushed his lips upon her cheek and over her ear and hissed insanely, "I will take it."

She blinked her eyes and tilted her head to the side to study him like an animal. Had he kissed the Reaper, too? Was he resisting as she was, suffering the Reaper's curse?

"This calls for a celebration!" the Darken roared, pulling them both to the steps of the bath.

The slave's dreams became vivid and clearer with every hour he suffered sleep. The strands of the woman's hair felt silky and even sharp, so sharp and real that he would wake from the dream to find his fingers sliced opened and dripping blood. Her eyes glistened like amber stars with a black abyss blinking in and out every time she closed her eyes. The chill from her breath defined the deadliness of Freeze and tore at his face with frost and fire. He often woke only to moisten his face for it had grown chaffed during his slumber. Her flesh...

...her flesh shifted from solid to transparently alluring. Deadly and predatory, she demanded subservience. She demanded *control*. He fought her lure, but this last dream, the dream which woke with him screaming his sister's name—he knew he was running out of time to find Laura, to save her from the Waste. That was what the woman called the event to come, *Waste*. The carnage that is left, mortal souls who survived the disaster...the devastation's end...it was the blood that ran for the last time. The last Kiss, Death's Harvester would come to collect once the Reaper's take their final soul to their master in the Cradle.

Jest threw his hand out shaking his head, "Laura is still a slave serving Tarel. I can't just leave her to rot in the fields of blood and corpses."

He didn't want to share his nightmares with the other slaves who escaped with him. They would think he was insane and suffering from the Reaper's curse. A thought he conflicted with routinely ever since his mallet killed the guard and he led their escape. He suffered from the intoxicating dreams that lured him into their enemy's territory.

A fallen Soldier refused to believe it necessary to retrieve the girl. Before his enslavement, it was his mission to evacuate the Traverna sector of its politicians before the shield had been activated. He couldn't explain his mission to the Karonan slaves without exposing that he had knowledge of the coming invasion, "She may have already been shipped off this planet,

Jest. If she lives it would be certain death to waltz in and rescue her. Jest, I know you love her but she will have to wait."

They paused to the sound of three scouts entering the cave they hid in off the shores of Broken Bay.

"Mack," Jest slowly began to lose his control, becoming frustrated and annoyed with the Soldier, "You don't understand: we are so close to the tower. Laura is in arms reach."

Sweat rolled down the faces of the men as one man narrowed his eyes, "Laura?"

"The Darken's bitch," said the elder scout who poured water over his face and down his back, "She's the Maestro they use to enchant the slaves into submission."

"What?" Mack sent a jug of water in their direction, "you never said anything about her being a *Maestro.*"

Their clothes were covered in stale blood and dirt mixed with sweat. They had been tracking for a week while the Karonan's kept moving in a crescent around the shadow tower hiding from the sky beast and foot soldiers.

One man shook his exhausted head, "A woman in the Blood Fields said it was a good thing we escaped when we did because she thinks the invasion was in its final stage and the used up slaves were going to be executed before the court. We would have been dangling from the towers with the rest of the slaves."

The tracker coughed and took a large gulp from the jug, "Rumor has it that the Darken Tarel is keeping a woman in his chambers, a personal slave."

He paused to gulp water down a far too parched throat, "The witch woman is to mate the Darken for a mortal alliance."

Mack closed his eyes forcing his brain to think through the scenarios, "They're weeding out the souls who still have hope. Why haven't they hung the wench if she is a mere mortal? What makes her so special?"

Roan shrugged at the question while scratching his neck in thought, "Darken don't love. They breed: they aren't like mortal humans, they don't stick and run with whatever falls on its back."

"Hope can't be killed, it has to be given away," Jest laughed, shaking his head back and forth insanely, "He found a Breeder."

...

Damu traveled with an entourage of entertainers and more slaves for Tarel's new territory. Stolen from the Karonan shores and bartered onto slave ships, Damu's arrival was completely unannounced. He had no intentions of returning to the Breach until the intoxicating scent of a Breeder polluted the air, rousing his curiosity and interest to remain in the land of dirt and decay: where there is a Breeder, there is always an Entity.

Dianan had been well laid and ready to hatch. His commanders, Daeviti wide, now waited till the Gates were all opened to carry out their orders. The Breach was falling and no longer needed his encouragement for it was ripe with a new evolution ready to spill onto the lands: evolution meant a steady flow of unclaimed energy, pulsing for a place to go. His brother need only to surface to claim it.

Something has awakened, Damu glared up into the sky, *something waits for this energy to overflow and pulse straight to them.*

The tides of power had shifted with a spark of dark energy all too familiar to him, thus, his reasoning for making a detour back to the dirt-bowl and pestilence. He had a sixth sense when it came to the rise of new usurpers. He and his brother had planned much too hard and for far too long to allow anything to interfere with their sweet, juicy reward.

Owen had done his part, Damu glared across the horizon spotting shadows that did not belong, *his foolishness unleashed the virus... his obsession disposed of the one woman who could end their reign.*

...

The shadow in the distance had voices, low and urgent.

"There's a convoy of entertainers, we will easily blend in with the slaves," Jest let a mischievous grin escape his thin lips, "Let's not keep our lords waiting."

Roan tilted his head and pointed up to the sky to bid a blurred farewell to the Dianan moon, "We can infiltrate at the gates. There will be too much going on for them to care to count."

Mack noticed that Roan, along with all the Karonan were especially affectionate towards the Dianan moon. To ask why would be a waste of much needed breath in the dark times they shared.

'Why are you fixated on Dianan?' the question would begin and the answer would follow, *'Oh, because it doesn't have a dome with demons in it.'*

The tower rose high above them as they watched the master of the caravan enter and leave the slaves waiting outside the great barrier that surrounded the tower. They had traveled through a burnt down city, vacant of all life and existences. Only shadows lingered, caressing the barrier with a sad history. Blood stained the ground and painted the walls and tainted the air with a stagnant scent.

Mack followed as Jest walked silently with a solemn grimace on his face; head bowed and baring a false fear. He had grown to respect these men, even though he was a Soldier and they were slaves from another realm. They would have made excellent Soldiers, Jest and Roan had a way of looking at life as a fallen Soldier did: survive and kill or be killed.

Glaring over his shoulder beneath the cover of the wall's shadows, Damu watched the men infiltrate his entourage with a smirk for their attempt to fool him. He could have them slain with a single chuckled breath. He watched them blend in, adapt as an assassin might, intrigued with their lax ability to become the hunter and not the prey.

That wouldn't suit your purpose, a thought kissed his mind, *use the filthy mortals to clean up the mortal filth.*

If he had really been listening, he would have known that the voice was not his own.

At least he could give the mortal's the opportunity to slay Tarel from this realm. Lukan had no plans of keeping the traitor breathing, which included the spawn of Nexums that continued to sprout up like weeds within this dome. His young cousin had become too attached to the Breach, and this was Lukan's prize: it was time for young Tarel's departure and Damu was more than willing to assist in the deliverance.

...

Mortal suffering suffocated the souls within the dome. The new era had dawned and dreams of peace quickly faded into torturing night terrors. Control was a Heaven and a relief if ever the Darken left the Traverna and Eere View towers to crumble and be at a final rest. Running from something that they cannot see, yet when they wake, the touch of Reapers would be upon them with soured sweat and recent scars. These nightmares are what will force the hand on the Supremacy of Government and Control will take form in all owned territories while the Darken swoop in and seize control over the Supremacy.

What made the water so sweet to the lips of sinners? Succumb to the reality and the truth will surely fade away into a bloody abyss of what the mortals created. The Superiors had successfully conquered one planet and it wouldn't be too long before they disposed the entire galaxy to the Waste and wander they called Control.

"The prayers remained unheard and unanswered as the fantasies of God quickly faded into the open wounds of His diminishing worshipers," Anara returned the insane habit of talking to herself like a disturbed mortal, "Smite—I can hear the sentence throb in my ears. Once again, I have failed."

Her words spoken in her home language, none could understand the babblings of a lunatic. The Ahzai's blood-red lips parted with swift accuracy, muttering in a hushed whisper. Anara's flesh had grown pale and almost transparent from the drain of the Reaper's curse, her worries and paranoia sucking the life from her body. She knew her time was upon her and she wouldn't be able to run from it, not while remaining trapped in the confinements of the tower— nor the confinements of her own mortal body. She may heal faster than the average human body, but she wasn't human, she was mortal, she was an Ahzai—rumored to be invincible.

Tarel grinned darkly at his new prize as she stared defiantly beyond his grasp. He reached his hand out and caressed her shoulder with the backs of his fingers. She didn't wince and she didn't seem to even notice anyone was there.

Such a waste, the words echoed serenely in the back of her mind.

The servants and slaves led her to her new chambers. She would now have a mortal slave of her own. After all, she had been a good little silent Vessel for the past six-some-odd-weeks. Her rage quietly churned in her soul waiting for the right unwanted moment to lash out and curse all that she hid from. It was dyer for her to keep the energy under complete control so that the Nexum inhabitants would not know her true potential. Leverage was all she needed to gain access to the Darken's secrets and knowledge of the Hierarchy.

Her way out of this world was a breath away, *never mind that I will have to temporarily leave my body to acquire that information.*

226

Laura bowed her head deeply toward her mistress laying a sheer black gown over a large blood-stained chair. Black pearls and a large blue diamond had been set out on the marble table that stood next to the chair. Laura began undressing the new slave while another servant dressed her. Anara's hair had grown long and dark with a hint of fire blazing the bronze strands with light.

She lifted a hand ordering them to leave her side, seeking a moment of privacy that seemed to be scarce in the present condition she found herself in. It had become a comedy in such dark times to endure the parlor tricks and entertainment of the lesser reigns of the Darken. She had been given only one Breeding ceremony, and even then, she ran from it.

If only they truly knew what Hell really was, Anara paused to the thought of knowing what Hell could hold.

How would she know what lay beneath the Light?

When she glanced up she saw Sasha glaring at her through her reflection. The Reaper smiled sweetly at her victim, knowing what soon would befall the Ahzai. It was a real treat to escort an Ahzai to the Cradle for Death to devour. The amount of energy offered from her soul would impregnate the god with new purpose and reason for worship.

She was seated beneath an obsidian throne with a sheer indigo canopy to offer privacy. Anara lounged delicately on silks and furs, cushions and covers with the fictitious Darken arrogantly and possessively at her side. Scones glittered pale along the walls with great black-metallic basins lining the aisle for the guests to present themselves to the Master of the domain.

Her irritation grew every moment from the thought of the abomination she had become in order to find the right loop-hole to the Law. Knowledge was the key to her success and survival in this event's horizon. Sacrifice had always been her weapon of choice. There were none out there that could trump self-sacrifice. Aside from that there weren't very many souls willing to offer such gambits and intrigues to an ancient war of games that always hid a sleeping

227

contender. Anara had purpose, though that purpose seemed a mist of memories as she struggled to remember what that purpose should have been.

The evening dragged on forcing her to withdraw behind distant and dying eyes that no longer screamed of help or hope. The light of her soul had faded to a mere shadow of a dawning conspiracy she replayed intimately over and over in her mind. The longer she pretended to be weak, the more the shadows consumed her light.

A servant knelt at Tarel's side whispering as silence entered the room forcing her to look up to see what had graced the blackened floor. A tall man walked steadily to the throne sending chills down Anara's back. Tarel winced as he removed his hood revealing the silence that roared in the eyes of every Darken and Nexum possessed.

"He has been well missed," Tarel smirked sarcastically applauding the Karonan gypsies who parted the entertainment with a jester and dancing entourage.

The prince glared, smirking at his younger cousin while waiting to be addressed.

Tarel smirked back at him unafraid, "My brother, we were not expecting you so soon. Sit, and feast at my side."

The prince smiled as he positioned himself in front of Anara, "It has been a long time, Tarel. Such news as you breeding with a human slave has spread from realm to realm. I had to see what human could bare you strong offspring."

Anara forced herself not to look at the prince knowing he knew what she was and what she hid…he now had an opportunity to seek his master in her possession. Did Tarel even know Lukan had been…misplaced? Ever since Damu had melded with her mind it was as though whenever she thought of him or when he was near, she could hear the echoes of his thoughts and emotions.

Who would have thought a Darken had feelings? She allowed herself a slight smile at the thought.

Damu glanced fondly at Anara, "I do see why you would fall for this human though. She is exceptionally willful."

She refused to respond focusing on the jester that twirled a flaming hoop, hackling and babbling, "A fool's court is a dark court indeed, bah bah bah."

He is of Karone, she could see the glow on his flesh that all of the slaves who had been transported from Karone possessed.

"A magnificent sorceress if you train her right," Damu mocked searching for a response from Anara.

She gritted her teeth struggling not to roll her eyes; *Sorceress, really Damu? Am I so cold that you would compare me to a fable?*

Tarel bowed his head at the comment, "Perhaps you would share her tonight?"

Damu chuckled at the thought of sharing this particular woman with the knowledge of what irony rested behind the reality, "No, I would want to keep her for myself and I am not going to give you any of my sons to claim as your own."

Tarel winced at the amusement in the prince's voice, "If the prince orders it, she is yours tonight. Consider it a favor of the Darken tradition, brother. I shall slay the first born child she gives unto me so that we are for sure the second is *mine* alone."

The prince glared at Anara frowning at her shadowed eyes, "What does your *queen* want? She now has a voice being of your court."

Tarel looked to his queen for her answer, completely missing Damu addressing Anara as 'Queen.'

"To serve my master," Anara hadn't missed Damu's words while she muttered, looking past them, "I do as he bids."

Damu narrowed his ever-changing eyes at her yielding so easily. This was not like her to submit to anything of the male race. He smiled at her act and perfection in her role, she was an Ahzai and likely to castrate him the moment he placed a kiss upon her cheek. Anara may have forgotten the Game momentarily, but deep down: she didn't forget to *play* the Game.

Tarel smirked at his cousin, "The night is young, my *greatest* friend, let us enjoy the show these Karonans have to offer."

The new queen peered through the corner of her amber-bronze eyes. He smiled knowing she watched him, curiously wondering what he was doing there. Tarel reached his hand over to her shoulder to brush his fingers across her flesh; secrets seeping from his mischievous eyes. Anara chuckled under her breath at the sight of both Darken. Tarel sat uneasily and the prince fearless knowing that he could destroy the being next to him with a thought alone.

…

Fury trembled in her eyes as she glared down the balcony of her chambers. Stars twinkled in the stained sky with rapid flutters of tension and pain slithering within her intestines. She made so many sacrifices that she had forgotten the last one she had made. The contracts she had made or to whom she had made them to. Her heart beat against an empty airless lung that wanted nothing more than to dive down onto the white stone ground that glistened up at her like those twinkling stars that blurred in and out above her, suffocating the life from her limbs and giving her *freedom*.

Anara glared farther beyond what the dome held within, "I wonder what I could accomplish on this planet once the transformation has completed."

A tender voice whispered from behind her, "It is cold. Do you wish to be ill, mortal?"

He exhaled wrapping long, masculine arms around her thin body. She was expecting Tarel but the scent of Damu's sweet breath was what caressed her neck and chin.

She continued to stare blankly over the horizon letting him know his place at her side.

Damu chuckled, gently smelling her hair, "Will you not talk to the man who once looked through a man's eyes just to envision you upon your bed beneath him?"

Anara shook from the cold closing her eyes at his touch, biting down on her lip, "Take me from here, Damu. Take me to the clouds."

"You have never been mine to take, Breeder," Damu turned her to see the reaction, knowing that she may belong to someone.

She rested her head against his chest letting his scent intoxicate her for the first time, "Where is the King?"

He lifted her chin to kiss her cheeks and proceeded to lap his tongue over her lips, "Are you so blind that you cannot see?"

Anara stared into his raging eyes defying his demands. She knew where the King was, she had been the one to send him there. He needn't know of such *follies.*

Damu twined his fingers through her hair remembering the strength and taste of it against his lips. The scent lingered in his palm the day she fell from his grasp. He had created a link with her in hopes of her submitting to his will.

"What have I done?" she demanded struggling to remember those blissful falling moments.

He lifted her from the floor sitting her on the balcony rail, "You are not the only one who has made sacrifices," his face became serious and brutal, "A King he is no longer. He has evolved. Is that not what you wanted?"

"Named?" Anara whispered, almost whining.

He laughed at the irony in her voice, "Stripped."

This was new information. She had only the intentions of Sending him to aid Akisma in her deeds or for Akisma to baby-sit her threat. When an Entity is Stripped they are removed from mortality and given a new purpose to start a game anew.

Damu froze at the pain in her eyes realizing she did not remember the word that slipped her lips long ago, "Your short term memory is amazing, Anara."

She blinked fighting away visions of a past that may have been fabricated throughout the dark games, "I-"

He shook his head pitifully at the woman who struggled with an identity that she couldn't nearly comprehend, *or pretended not to comprehend.*

Anara still remained confused glaring somberly at Damu, "Fallen?"

"He has not fallen," Damu pressed his lips gently to her ear, whispering her name, "Anara, my beloved soul who is loved by so many and loved by so few. You hold the key to giving hope to this planet and yet you still deprive it of its claim."

"A claim is earned, not bred," *love* was the ultimate sin in her life, the part of her soul that had been locked away by God himself.

She let his fingers journey across her body, "I will take what love I can from you. Love can't be hidden, only misplaced. Anara, my love will never hurt you: you who hold a piece of *darkness.*"

Anara narrowed her eyes at his submission to her, so faint that he didn't realize what he had just done. She had triumphed in taming the beast: at least one of them.

Tarel watched them from the center of the chamber curiously pondering on the power this mortal may have to win the passion of his prince, "You have met before?"

Damu paused to the sound of his voice, "As if you didn't know, as if you didn't know she belonged to another. You take what was never yours."

"Let him come here and smite me," Tarel snarled with a shrug, as though he had already known her identity and yet hesitated on estimating her true power, "He never took her, he had been forbidden from her soul."

"Foolish," Damu tilted her head back kissing her long neck, "You have not bound her."

Tarel sat down crossing his legs lazily, "Why should I? I have Bioni rotting down in the cellar like a good Carrier."

"You know not what you attempt to conjure, Tarel," Damu exhaled a gentle word letting her body fall limp in his arms, hypnotized into a subconscious dream only she could read. Her submissive role had weakened, or so it would seem. Damu knew better than to let his guard down. He had nearly lost his sanity in the attempt to control her: unbound, Anara could Travel with a simple slumbering thought.

"Of course I do. Somewhere in that damned delicious body is the key to our success and somewhere in her thick forgetful head is every answer I need to destroy *Him.* I grow tired of the visions the Eyes relay and the bastard riddles we must answer because we are not of *His* brood. Anara, maker of Shadows and lover of Death is the *Vessel* for us to sail unscathed to freedom," Tarel pointed to the horizon that split the blinding sky of the Breach waiting for Death to take the wretched lives of what remained tormented within the broken dome, "They are already here, do you think the humans know? Do you think they know what they tamper with? If they are not careful, they will become a Darken as well, or worse, they will sell their souls to a devil. Most don't even know what a true Darken is."

"We infiltrate and invade, that is all that they need know of," Damu chuckled hysterically bordering insanity, "Do they ever know anything? I highly doubt it, Owen knows even less and he is half a Darken—meddling long lost cousin of ours on your father's side if I might remind you."

Tarel watched Damu brush his hand over Anara's face, caressing her flesh with intimate delicacy.

"I hope she hasn't caused you to grow weak, our woman has that affect. Beware of her, she contracts with many beings we do not know of. The memory has been taken away from her," Damu smiled at her face, "Her allegiance belongs to her world, *always* remember that."

"Her soul belongs to her children," Tarel lay down next to his prize, "The eldest beloved niece of ours, have you found her yet? Does she remember that the child is truly yours? Lukan should have bedded her while she was a child sneaking into his chamber at night. Take her to the clouds like he loves to do with all the others."

Damu tested his conniving cousin, "He was warned to not touch her, now, I fear he grows tired of following the Laws. Not all of us are as devious as you."

He nodded thoughtfully staring down at the peacefully sleeping Vessel who lay much like a girl, "The power which is forbidden."

"The passion between them would fool God himself into believing they had been together for an eternity, and I believe it has cursed her from the moment they first met. I remember being there when she followed my essence to his kingdom and found Lukan instead. Even as a child Ahzai her power was wild and uncontrolled. She laughed at the King on his first visit to her world. Even as a child her mind was way beyond her years like all Ahzai born. He couldn't hide his heart and she immediately attached to it," Damu brushed his hand through her hair, "I saw her first, watched her as she slept searching for Lukan and our King blocked her dreams. She still fought to see him, I *comforted* her when she was confused about the world and wanting nothing but to end it—she had the power to end it then."

"Ironic how we bumped back into yours and Lukan's love affair," Tarel whistled between his teeth like a human might, "Stuffing her into that evac-pod was a huge mistake on your part."

Damu laughed at the sarcasm knowing that Tarel didn't know the half of the reason they shoved her into the pod and sent her catapulting into space, "It was a mistake to tamper with her memory and shove an unwilling soul into a pod for safe-keeping only for it to drop in the bare waste of the Arkeon. What are the odds of it changing destinations in mid warp and entering this realm?"

"What, no Travelers?" Tarel chuckled at his warning, this was all information he knew all too well.

"No, a Traveler will always side with the higher powers," Damu laid a kiss upon her forehead, "*Ka-vel or-da, lorala.*"

Tarel puzzled at the prince hearing those intimate words escape his lips, 'I claim you, beloved.' He knew that in the end, they were only a whisper on the wind—dead words.

Celeston

A Vessel can link with any soul of familiar acquaintance. Should a soul shake the hands of one with such power as a Vessel, they would forfeit their free will in the name of the Law. Any Entity with the power to join possession of a corporeal temple had the ability to leap from one soul to the next, so long as they have previously met with the host.

Akisma's letter of Summons began with a distant formality:

"Time has never been a human's friend. It gives life, than takes life back. So is the proof of a new born child that had taken first breath only too frail and faltered returning to the arms of Death with the stroke of a Reaper's regretful command. Time is our enemy but it is not the evil we fight for all eternity. Don't believe the darkest Demon could touch ground with the Shadows the way this Game bounces from one Realm to the next. If I hadn't known better, hadn't been trained better, I might have mistaken Time with the Game and the Unseen for a Satan. I, Akisma Royale, Summon you in the name of our goddess and holy queen—*Kamenah*."

She grinned sheepishly at the note in her hand, folding it delicately, letting it morph into the form of a legless crane and placed it intimately over a blue flame that quickly devoured the essence of the parchment leaving the scent of roses in its memory as it traveled to its destination.

Akisma tilted her head at the reflection in her bronze window and smiled at the foreign Immortal that awaited her command, "For your head I give thus bid the sorrow of such or pass on. You must answer me this, would you, too, last?"

"For the queen," the Immortal nodded letting her thick hair wisp serpent-wild in the reflection given, "Young Folly, I will send thee knowing that I will once again be free of mine own world, make me free of your Nexum."

Akisma pursed her plump lips letting her starry yellow eyes glisten for a moment at the Immortal she had just breathed life into, "Go, do as I asked and be careful not to turn to stone all that I have let known. I bless thee with control over thine eyes."

The Immortal bowed her head and wavered out of the Realm that hid between all worlds. Akisma waited and then finally rose from her perch exhaling mournfully at the job ahead.

Akisma paused biting down on her lower lip, "If *she* had faith in the Ahzai queen she would not have gave unto me a list of trustworthy Ahzai operatives. Trick the trickster. How easy the Angels mock a job they could not even do," she spat letting the moisture fade into smoke, "Better have beginner's luck."

...

Stale Mate, true Masters of equal power will always in the end, middle and before the beginning, find their selves trapped in a world called Stale Mate. Where can one go once a drawl has been made? Start back from the beginning, this time pick new players to add into the equation and hope that the siege will be lifted and the game will move forward to the contender's benefit. Patience must be practiced above all. The life of a Vessel knows little patience and nothing of compromise. How would they? Sacrifice comes so easily knowing that your soul will live on forever, whether it is bouncing from one host to the next or collected into a Master Collector filled with many.

In all her years Akisma Royale never had an ordinary conquest and always dealt a handful of confusion to the nearest victim who tested her worth in whatever game that sparked her interest. Her origin was founded among a dying race overlooking every galaxy in the Daeviti's Shadow Realm. She shared the soul of the goddess' youngest sister, the most mischievous of the girls—Itarah. Though her sister was the goddess of the cold world, Itarah had no world and demanded no worship.

Akisma was born a Whisperer. Taken at an early age, her breed was forced to train and serve the humans in the battle against good and evil. Why not? Their world had already faded out from a dying star, what other noble way than to serve for a purpose that a child does not yet comprehend. Kamenah housed many Vessels that evolved into the positions and ranks they carried secretly throughout the universe. She had always been a link between good and evil, touched by the One God and kissed by *His* Angels: coveted by demons and respected by Celestials.

"Energy is energy and it is meant to be worked," Kamenah would always remind her sisters.

When it was known that the goddess had found her final Vessel, an Ahzai, Akisma had all intentions of learning the history of the girl who had numbed out her past. Anara was born of a tormented world. Her temperament, defiance and pride, bled through her youth as an uncontrolled rage that no one, not even the first Angel sent to their world, could control. Anara was what she was and the only thing that ever slowed her down was when God stripped her of immortality. Even with her immortality lost, the queen continued to play the game.

"Guess no matter what you do, you can't ignore what swims through your veins and to your heart. She had seen in visions, Death walking arm-in-arm with the suffering and chaos of wars, forever at her heel," Akisma muttered as she glared into her own past trying to recollect her first brush with the Ahzai.

She shook her head at the girl who knocked on her glass door with a face of pure condemnation, "You can only run so much before your responsibilities catch up to you."

Akisma had been ordered to activate a Collector, Sera Demeska, and send her to Antila even though she nestled deep within the Traveler's home on Dianan. It didn't matter how much power you had, nothing could move a Collector—who did not want to answer a Summons. Time refused to work with her, not with the new player sitting across from her in the Game Room of Celeston. Her own goddess was refusing to collaborate with Kamenah out of spite for Bluff's position at the table.

Summoning Sera would be ever so—difficult. She who seems to be unknowingly innocent and most would believe her innocence while she opens the gateways for Death to proceed in collecting its souls; *she always had their best interest in mind.* She was host to their sister *Death*, Opelya. Opelya was the only one who accepted what she was but denied the rules that had been given the Vessel. She refused to take body, but refused to let loose her hold. Sera didn't even know what lurked within her flesh.   Time is non-existent for the Vessels. A universe of universes cannot control such a luxury as Time. Humans like to think they can manipulate the universal code, but in the end they are not mentally capable of keeping up with every code that makes a code. Even the Collector has difficulty keeping up with every minute collected and borrowed or given but surely knows how it is used.

Akisma glanced at the Folly at hand, her companions of four male Entities with foul names to compete with: all witty, all conniving against her and her purpose for their own gain. After all, every world has their contender. Three of which she has come to call the Wise Men and the fourth her sworn enemy of the shadow games, Lukan the Bluff otherwise known as the Dark King. Lukan, who is in love with Kamenah's host, Anara.

Akisma closed her eyes at the odds weighing in the palm of her hands, "I wonder if the goddess already knew of their affair before she linked with the exiled Ahzai queen…"

Akisma is certain that deep down in the flesh and soul of Lukan the Bluff is still a beating heart belonging to Anara and Anara alone. Another problem: Lukan's brother, the Prince Damu; he who spies on the Collector Sera whom has been Summoned several times by the queen in their desperation to gain control of their own Charges. Unfortunately, Lukan's soul has gone missing from his shell of a corpse that now housed a link with the Devourer of Souls.

All of this is information which Akisma cannot afford to reveal with the Blunt, the Silent and the Trump. Akisma must keep her position as the Folly of the Game. There is always one last Folly that ends every game, and Akisma will be the one to deliver it to them.

Or so she would hope.

Akisma glared blindly through her glistening starlit eyes, yellow orbs of twinkling energy that only her breed shared upon each evolution. Lukan had proven to be a worthy opponent and advanced devilishly through the secrets of all the Realms. Saul had even cursed him for his cleverness, stating that Bluff was his perfect calling: for lies was all the king Lukan had to offer. That was all a Devourer had to offer: lies and deception to lure a naïve soul onto its dinner plate.

She shook her head at the obstacles that lay before her. Darken or no, he would prove to be a powerful player. If she could bring the soul of Lukan back to his body, then she could rid herself of the damned Devourer. Kamenah had sent Lukan's soul away and Akisma failed to understand why she would risk such an exchange. Who perched in the king's body?

She froze to the raspy, burnt chuckle of a familiar voice, "Hello Sams."

Sams stepped into the light of her imagined chambers, humbled and thirsting for knowledge, "Hello Akisma."

Akisma turned to him motioning for him to join her at her side, grinning all the while, "You have much to speak, say pray you play me a piece."

His crispy, handsome face crinkled and cracked with the sharp curve of his blood red lips, "I was an empath before I found my turn here, as are the rest of my kind."

Akisma raised her thin honey kissed eyebrows at the card she had just been offered, "Does the gift follow you within these chambers of Celeston?"

Sams shrugged, still grinning at her as she leaned back against her thick ebony window seal, "I can taste your well baked worries as though poison to my lips."

Akisma couldn't help but to laugh, "That is one way of putting it, Sams."

"Silence is best when trying to sort through the emotions of evolution," he then frowned letting ash fall from his manifested cheek.

"And what is your opinion on my feelings when our Bluff arrived?" She pressed letting him lean over her with his charred arm resting on the window seal above her head.

Sams only stared into her always glistening eyes, "A man can burn in those stars you keep captive in your eyes."

Akisma looked away letting him sigh at the gesture, "That does not answer my question, Sams."

"I was less interested in your feelings and more enticed by his," Sams lifted his glowing fingertips to her chin to return her gaze to him, "And I did answer your question. You would burn him if you could benefit from it."

Akisma smirked at his clarification stepping away from his heated touch, "Very well, what do you want in return?"

He drew a choking breath and sat down on the floor placing his arms over his knees, "That you will share with me a truth of you and that you will listen to a truth of mine."

Akisma knew that sharing truth was a step to intimacy in this Realm. It was a note of allegiance even if it only stood for one round in any game. She studied him and finally joined him at his side, "When I was a child-"

"No, I have come here so I will share first in this game of trust," Sams stopped her to allow courtesy, "I choose this form because it is of my own world. I am of a burning land and fire is all I know. I was formed from molten lava and carved into this ash and ember you see next to you. Though you see me wearing a human body, because that is what I want you to see me as. Something you could relate to that perhaps I can win a friendship with you. My true form is quite terrifying for the eyes of humans, for purity is feared by *sinners*. I can journey from star to star and live peacefully off the power of the heat and energy that my twinkling friends are made of, even *you*, a Vessel. When I come of age, for I am still a boy to my kind. I am fond of your eyes for they do remind me of home."

She blinked her eyes realizing he could feed off her at his own will and because she was a Vessel, the goddess would offer him as much nutrition as he desired. Akisma tilted her head studying him and smiling at what Sams had chosen to share with her. The reason why he was in this game, it was his responsibility to make sure Shadow never wins. Therefore, she had allegiance with him.

Akisma pulled her honey glazed hair back behind her shoulders so that she could allow Sams the comfort of her starlit eyes, "I was plucked from the Daeviti's Shadow Realm. I am of the Second breed of Whisperers and I am assigned to this Realm of Celeston to save the mortal race. I am not Human, no more than I am mortal. When their souls burn out, I will live on and will never know rebirth. Through another host of my people I will reside until my service is summoned once again. *We* control energy: give, take and manipulate, *we* provide a conduit for its passage. *We* are linked between good and evil," she finished letting him glare at her in a hidden amazement then revealed another secret, "I too can summon the power to read emotion but have been trained not to feel it."

Sams frowned, feeling the numbness she expelled, "That is false, Akisma, you feel emotion."

With a swift motion he leaned forward tilting her head back and placing his lips to hers. She gasped at the hand knowing it would not be able to burn her. Why was she not pulling away? He let her go and stared into her eyes as she studied his, pleasure: burning pools of hot blue-white pleasure.

Akisma pulled back confused and thirsty for more, "What was that?"

"Call it a token from me to you," Sams shrugged grinning at his performance with a male pride, "Or simply me marking my territory."

He nodded as he pushed himself from her embrace and made his way out of her temporary chambers. She only watched as he left her blinking two yellow stars in and out of existence. The tables had turned if indeed she made a true partner in this chaotic little game. Akisma returned her glare to her little blue flame that began to remind her of Sams' burning blue-white eyes.

Something deep within her began to flutter, *the Breeder.* Akisma ignored the feelings and returned to the game at hand. *Breeding wasn't safe in these dark times,* she reminded the butterflies tickling her soul's need of companionship. It would be near impossible to breed.

She had been *forbidden* this act upon entering Celeston…

"His words are dead to my needs," Akisma spoke aloud with a sigh and frown trying to convince herself to become numb to his passion, "…they are only dead words…"

…without flesh…

Damu paced from one end of Tarel's chamber to the next. Anara slept still and lifeless, yet constantly dreaming. Tarel's head on a platter would be sufficient to his cause: that was a sure assessment. Treachery is known among their kind…blood was not thicker than water. It had come to a point where Damu could only see everyone around him with a dagger dangling out of their backs waiting for him to shove the metal back in its rightful place.

There had been a time he embedded a dagger into the shoulders of Karonan slaves just to watch them suffer as a lesson so that they would know that if they should betray him, they would not be killed but tortured. They would suffer and pay for their actions with agony.

I had intentions to begin with the youngest of one's family and work my way up to the slave himself, he reminisced on the past. Unlike the majority of his people, Damu had spent little time among the Darken and the Obryn. He had bigger fish to fry, a greater game to play.

"What do you plan?" Tarel's voice echoed through his concentration, "Ravage her in her sleep?"

Damu grinned at the thought but shrugged the offer away, "Tell me, have you heard from Dianan?"

"I believe Lukan takes care of that domain," Tarel curved his lip to form a mischievous smile, "Oh yes, and I've been forbidden to tamper with Dianan."

"Does she have any clue of the endeavors our King now pursues?" Damu tilted his head in Anara's frail direction.

Tarel allowed a short laugh escape his plump lips, "Give a bitch a bone? Not likely, here's a dangerous little Ahzai we got before us."

Damu stared emotionless down at the woman who manipulated a game of her own, "Keep it that way. She'll only get in the way if she learns the truth of Lukan."

Tarel nodded waving his hand to her, "Have her, slumber or no, pleasing I've been told. Won't even know which hole you've jabbed at. Breed her. She'll believe it's the King's. He was the last, yes?"

Damu pondered on the offer and thought, "He was the last, yes, and if I *take* her, I want her to remember it."

Tarel chuckled, flopping back onto a silk chair, "You never felt in control until they screamed your name. You haven't changed much, brother."

"Haven't I," Damu traced his hands up her body embracing her breast. Her heart began to race as though it knew it was being touched without permission. For a moment, he could have sworn she welcomed it. If that thought could be true, the bliss he could create with her, "No, I'll wait. Time will resist for only so long."

…

Slave quarters, was a prison shy of being in the bloody 'dungeon' below. The stench was bitter but the walls weren't covered with piss and blood. The screaming torture of poor souls who could very well have been a slave mate on the ship they too were aboard on their transport to Traverna from Karone echoed throughout the halls. Nothing would ever be accommodating so long as they remained slaves to the Darken Court.

We've been stuck in worse places, Jest reminded himself staring through the only window that showed the hallway across from their own cell.

"We could break out of this," Roan pointed out the rotten hinges that held the door together.

They glared at Mack who had a keen sense of whether to act or flee; wait or strike. He had been a Soldier before the shield lifted—strategy was familiar to him and most important: he had been trained to infiltrate. The Karonans had been trained to entertain, serve and succumb; few had been trained to fight.

Jest shook his head in a definite no, "Laura is first. Need to locate her."

"Did you see the eyes of the queen? It was as though it were only a body sitting at the side of that Darken," Jest stared up at the ceiling as if he searched for the deep storm-blue skies of his home, "Laura could be just the same."

Roan laughed at the thought of Laura being a walking corpse, she had always been a survivor, cunning, clever and adapted to whatever may come to task: Laura was a *Maestro*, "You see the dress she was wearing?"

They all smiled at the vision that tainted their minds, "Lack-there-of."

Jest grinned at his younger brother, "The Darken always had taste in Breeders."

Mack wrinkled his brows unsure what they spoke of, "Breeder?"

Roan licked his lips, "A Breeder is a female of power, a Queen. She picks her mates and will produce for no other. There's a chance that this Tarel will receive nothing from her. That is why he must-needs wed and bed the bitch to force the Game's Laws upon her. Gods, you could even smell the sweetness of her scent in the air."

They silenced at the opening of the rear chamber door where a girl was being escorted up from the dungeon. She turned her head to face the illusive gypsies and forced herself to look away. The girl knew that she could not afford to reveal a familiar face to the Darken for fear of having them beheaded or worse.

Jest stared tormented at the girl, "Laura," he exhaled noting every scar on her body.

He had last seen her when she was eight-Isosalan-moon-turns. The Isosalan moon takes one-human-year to orbit the Breach. Laura was now what seemed to be an estimate of four-and-ten-Isosalan. It had been so long since last they were safe on Karone in the house of their deceased father.

"Bring them, too," a silky, dark voice vibrated the air with stench and control, "They too can entertain the master's whore."

Jest looked at Mack forcing back a grin—it would appear they weren't the only ones out to kill the queen and the rest of the Darken.

"Are you ready, jester?" The disfigured guard questioned the slaves.

The jester let out a wailing laughter that hid the faintest hint of hope, "As ready as a whore's mother! Blah-blah-blah!"

Laura sat at her blood stained harp in a trance letting the music take her away into a reality that she had never known. Her hair lay with a tender whisper damping away the dried blood that left the memory of the night before. Torturing visions of what could have turned Laura into the slave that dwindle before them blurred his vision as they entered the queen's chambers. Yet, her fingers had never changed as they struck each string creating the greatest music of all the Daeviti worlds.

Jest watched as the guards left them alone in the chamber. He gawked at how much they trusted them to not kill the bitch-queen. While Jest knelt at Laura's side trying to get her attention, Roan took short, slow steps to the slumbering woman. She lay there lifeless and drained, dead to the living that circled her body like crows over carrion. Her hair lay wild across silk pillows devouring the covers her dreaming head slumbered on. Roan drew his hand up to brush her hair from her face just as Mack pulled him away.

"What are you doing?" Mack growled, "Just kill her and get done with it."

Roan pulled a dull knife from his sleeve and held it to her neck.

"No!" Laura screamed, "Roan, don't kill her, please."

"She's one of them now," Roan growled back at her.

Laura continued to pluck the strings of her harp, "No, she is something else."

They turned to Jest for answers, permission to dismiss their brainwashed and delusional sister.

"My music will wake her from his spell," Laura shook her head and pushed him away, "She has hope."

They stared at her enlightened.

Roan bowed his head to Laura with gritted teeth, "Let her majesty sleep that she will feel no pain."

"Don't you think she's felt enough pain already? You are still as stubborn as always, Roan. She's the only reason why I'm still alive," Laura snapped at Roan as though he were a child.

Anara opened her eyes feeling the knife at her neck, "Kill me or get off."

Laura yelled once again, "No, Mistress, he is my blooded family. I want neither of you to die."

Roan turned to face the queen at her sudden awakening, "My goddess, your eyes are like stars."

"Yes, if you stare at them long enough you will forget you are in the Hell called Traverna," Anara rolled her eyes at the man who held the knife to her neck.

Laura got up and ran to her mistress' side, "Forgive them, they are dumb."

"They respond well enough," she choked on a laugh that struggled to escape her mouth, "How long have I slumbered?"

Laura looked away pursing her lips, "Six days."

Anara lay back against her pillows with her hair scattered like wild blades of short-swords, staring at the endless ceiling, "He has right to breed tonight."

Laura shook her head, "He will not return until the morrow, Master Tarel and Prince Damu has gone to a port for the new shipment of slaves."

Anara leapt out of the bed, shocked with hope smeared across her face, "They have left me here, alone?"

Laura nodded, watching her eyes light up like a child's. The hope that seeped from her mistress was infections and made her yearn for that same feeling. A freedom unknown to her blossomed within her soul, and now she craved for more.

Roan stared enchanted by the natural glow that seeped out from the woman's soul. He found it glistening yet dark and mysterious and burning, yet deadlier than the Freeze. The Karonan have seen some interesting creatures, but none compared to the deity before them.

"Figures they would leave me here to die," Anara glared irritated at the men who only stood staring dazed and confused at her as she paced back and forth on the feathered bed with the chains that imprisoned her clinking and clanking as she held it gripped tightly in her fist, "What's so important about this shipment?"

"I am not so sure," Laura frowned trying to remember what had taken place while she slept, "They watched you the entire time, but I believe it to be more than just slaves—for Tarel."

Anara wrinkled her nose with the new found knowledge, "What does the master Tarel retrieve…"

...

Twenty shaggy and worn children began its trip into a caged wagon. Tarel smiled at the precious cargo they escorted home, each morsel fresh and vibrant with the energy and essence of innocence: all except for one.

A girl stuck her face through the rusted bars glaring only at the Prince. Her eyes were of pure innocence and complete neglect with a dark bruise encircling her mysterious diamond-chiseled stare. Purpose and ambition tainted every strand of energy that escaped her slender, but far from delicate form.

Damu glared back at her curious of why she focused her complete attention on him, "Speak child. The words burn at your lips."

She grinned devilishly and laughed, "You haven't seen me since last I was suckling away at your mother's teats."

Damu studied her face, her perfect eyes that matched the shape of Lukan's. He opened his mouth to speak, but only stopped.

The girl had plenty to say in his place, "They know you plot against their desires, Damu. I am here in rags such as a slave would wear and our mother is no longer in this plain of existence because of your folly. I would have been shipped to the Nexum if not for my royal blood on father's side. Nomede unintentionally saves his brood once again."

He raised his eyebrow disbelieving what the child spoke, "Dimonah? What have they done to your father?"

The girl looked to the sky forcing back an irritated smirk, "He was protecting me, Damu. They stripped him of his title and cast him to the stars, the Nexum I do believe."

Damu growled with humor watching Tarel stare wide-eyed and annoyed at the girl, "Nomede is in the Nexum."

…

Anara forced her fingers between her collar and collarbone, "Do you have keys to this stupid thing?"

"We could cut your head from your shoulders, should that help?" Mack muttered to the queen that fingered away at the leash which held her to the bed.

She sighed at the man knowing his hatred seeped freely from his body, "Tell me jester, do you know of a woman named Bioni?"

Anara froze glaring at Laura as chill bumps rose from her flesh, "They have returned, stay as Laura's personal slaves. Keep your heads bowed and eyes to the floor. Which means you must behave, now, can you do this? Can you keep from attacking the prince and Tarel?"

They shrugged at her request and began positioning their selves around the room pretending to entertain, "Fine."

"Mack," she waited for a nod, "I want you and Laura to find a woman named Bioni. Escape to the Old World and find the chambers that will lead you into Antila, you must fight."

"Old World," Roan shook his head, "We are not from your world."

Mack nodded once more, "Beneath the ruins, I know."

"Bioni will take you," Anara blinked her eyes from a blurring pain which began churning in the back of her head, she rubbed her temples trying to speak, "Damu-"

Her body fell limp as the room spun uncontrollably away from her sight. She only had the sadistic chuckle of some dark voice to guide her from a bright light—a voice that was as powerful if not more powerful than Kamenah, a voice that was ancient in evil and seeped of Hell.

Oh God, not yet, Anara thought frantically as her flesh began to tingle.

"*God has nothing to do with this blasphemous soul that Summons you*," the voice mocked arrogantly against the fire burning from within her flesh, scorching her soul. It was then that she realized she was alone. She could no longer feel the presence of Kamenah…the goddess was out of reach. Anara was out of reach.

…

Damu puzzled over the sleeping woman in his bastard-brother's bed. Anara only lay there with a pale face and a furious look etched into her curves, her fist balled up and ready for battle. Her eyes moved rapidly with silent visions racing to keep up, words barely forming. Her soul hunted for something or someone and he had a good idea it was of absolute importance to the Ahzai—he just didn't know it wasn't the Ahzai who searched.

Laura stammered to the Darken who massaged his chin irritated and half blind-sighted, "She's been like that for some time, my prince. She just fell over."

Tarel stood with his arms crossed and cursing constantly under his breath. It was rare to see the Darken so humanly expressing their emotions with slaves so close at hand. His eyes grew completely solid and black as he struggled to control his anger.

Jest watched him, confused at their interest in this human woman, a mortal. Their utter concern for the slave who slept before them made them more mortal than any Human in existence. This woman held more bafflement in one snore than any Prophet's Eye they had ever sought for.

Tarel growled at the slaves, blaming them for her slumber as if a Human could muddle a Darken spell, "I cannot wake her."

Dimonah only giggled under her deceptive breath at the Ahzai woman the Darken feared the most. She puzzled over the mortal that snored and growled incomprehensible words and mockeries in an unknown language—a language that was not Ahzai. She was the Vessel who brought the Darken race to their Immortal knees.

"Mayhap she barters with more than just the likes of you," Dimonah taunted the men in the room, challenging them to contradict her when it was clear that the woman laying upon the bed muttered whispers of a language none of them ever heard before.

Damu narrowed his eyes at his naïve little sister forcing his entire self not to shake with fury, "Darken can break Darken. So what has she bartered with, sister?"

Dimonah blinked her eyes at him addressing her as 'sister' as she watched Anara with a distant stare that could only mean she was hiding more than she was willing to share with her brothers. She hid the hatred that churned in her deceiving Darken heart. This woman had turned their own King against them. A slither of a voice chanted in the back of her mind waiting for a response and action, 'Kill her, Dimonah.'

Dimonah glared at Tarel through the corner of her eyes, smirking, recollecting the list of names she could have chosen from, "Hells if I know, perhaps one of the colony's deities or demons, a Satan or Lucifer. I heard that Lucifer packs a powerful punch."

Damu swung around narrowing his eyes to his sister, "Lucifer? Some devil of what the Colony calls Divinity World? Be serious, Dimi."

"She just got here, Prince Damu. She could not possibly know what is happening with the Ahzai," Tarel defended the girl who was much older than a girl.

"Funny how this didn't happen until she arrived, Tarel," Damu snapped at the man without a noble title, without acknowledging his rank.

"It is logical," she stepped back as though dodging a blow from her brother's fury, "Lucifer and his realm are the only things strong enough to challenge you on this planet. He is of the evil below, and we both know that darkness begets darkness and evil is linked in *all* worlds. The colony that settled on the other side of this irritating planet of our Kings could easily open a door for their devils. Are we not linked with the dark things of this world?"

"We would be able to sense its presence!" Damu growled as he crouched ready to attack the girl who spun tales like a spider weaving her web to capture prey.

"Insanity," Tarel forced out a hiss as he marched from the chambers; infuriated at the assumption of Hell's gate being opened.

If this foreign demon had breached the core of their universe than his and Lukan's mission was near compromised. It would be time for them to leave evil to fight evil and let Divine Intervention wipe Hell's gate out if necessary. The battle was not his nor the Darken's to wage war with, and the God responsible for this Lucifer would be Summoned and have little to no choice to answer because the Breach had no defenses against another Realm's demons.

What he did not know is that this play had been well laid—by someone. Dimonah could be right with her lies and not know it while she stood there innocently lying to hide another move made by her masters. It was a trump card easily bluffed if the players at the table did not know that it takes a long list of sacrifices in order to open the *land* to Hell's realm. With the

Breach undergoing Control and in the predicament it was in: it was a task that could easily be achieved within moments of engagement. Laws did not change from Realm to Realm, only more Laws are added to the contender at board. Darken were only Immortal with the mix of dark bloodlines and mortality. They were once people who believed that Darkness could not be without Light.

"I should have kept you close to me," Damu cursed under his breath.

...

It had been several days and the queen still slept at constant war with whatever Summoned her—weakened her, left her in such a vulnerable state…unable to protect herself from physical attacks. They had tried everything within Darken powers just short of drugging her with adrenaline and injecting her with Nanytes to animate her body and let her be a walking corpse like those who were possessed by escaped Nexum souls, except Damu knew that nothing short of a god could possess her body.

She remained defiantly under the spell of the Entity that Summoned her. It is rare for a Summons to last so long—especially with danger peeking through the chamber doors.

Dimonah bowed her head entering Tarel's private chambers to peek in on the sleeping beauty in her brother's great bed, "Be silent, *desi*," the Darken took measured steps puzzling over the slumbering body of the Queen, "Thou accursed plague," she gritted her teeth reciting a verse from a Prophet she had beheaded upon her exile to the Breach where she *lived* among the Colony, "Consume within thyself thine own pain."

She had enjoyed her freedom among the foreign colony. They came from a world with many evils to feed the starving soul and billions who were more than willing to create religions to offer their worship. And with their worship, they would spill an abundance of energy for her to manipulate.

"What a sleeping beauty you make for the royal family," she smirked at Anara's unguarded human body, a fragile jest of mortality that mocked the power the Ahzai was capable of.

"Pity *they* want you freed and the males don't want to humor the Hierarchy," she ran her fingers through Anara's long hair, "Allow me to let down thy hair, says the young witch."

Dimonah chuckled at the irony of the world Anara had unfortunately fallen to, "Zale would be pleased to have done this himself."

She pulled a dagger from her dress and began laughing hysterically.

With one clean stroke she drove the dagger through Anara's neck letting her head roll to the side, "With Anara's death the Pact is complete. Let all the Gates be opened!"

From the chamber door came the most sinister growl ever heard, followed by Damu pouncing towards his sister sending her crashing into the wall, "What have you done!"

Tarel gasped, forcing a dumbfounded expression towards what lay lifeless upon his bed with blood quickly pooling around it.

Everyone has a role to play.

Dimonah gurgled back the blood that flooded her mouth, "You will thank me for this, brother. Trust that you will thank me."

"And so will she," she exhaled running to the balcony, the young Darken leaped from the ledge and landed only to take off once again.

Damu ran his fingers through his hair confused and broken, "Lukan will not be pleased."

~Epilogue~

Naval Star, Breach Orbit

Neither the Soldiers nor did Owen Dame and the children transport with the great ease they desired, nor were they all intact at a single destination as they should have been.

A complete miscalculation on Owen's part, or was it? Perhaps it was interference.

The Soldiers transported to the *Naval Star,* and yet, the children had gone elsewhere. He hadn't the time to dig deeper on the whereabouts of the children. No, he was fighting the currents of solar military and the Alliance, who without a doubt, would seize over command and add all the pieces together and know that he held a huge hand in the ongoing invasion.

The Alliance had evolved races who served them, ones who can pry out the thoughts of anything that had a brain or a soul to dig into. Even with the growling and barking of the Commanding General of the *Naval Star*, Owen found it impossible to follow through with the Protocol as was his responsibility.

"Enter those codes!" a furious General barked at Owen Dame from his command chair in the control room.

Owen shouted up from his small seat in front of a starry screen that showed their set destination, "General Gray, has the jettison pods even escaped soil? Not so much as one!"

Of course there would not be any escape pods jetting out of the Traverna and Eere View Towers, not with the Darken shields preventing anything from entering or exiting. It was much like the Domes they use on the Sektra Moon, and if they were alike, than no one was penetrating the shield without Darken authorization or absolute divine intervention. Owen knew better, it was only a matter of time before they would drop their shields and leave the lands for the Superiors to fix.

"They are lost Owen, the most honorable thing we can do now is to end their suffering. I understand what you are feeling. I have family down there, not prize possessions, but family—flesh and blood. That is why we must follow Protocol. That is why we have a Protocol," the General frowned knowing the pods wouldn't be able to jettison from the ground with the Darken shields, even if there weren't any pods prepped for evacuation.

Owen closed his eyes with the vision of *her* smirking sarcastically at him. He began entering the codes and before he punched in the last segment he turned and glanced over his shoulder at the General. Dramatically exhaling with too much frustration, he groaned and began deleting the codes and proceeded to enter a new itinerary.

The General began barking out curses and orders, "You are the most-"

A man entered the control room, dark and foreign to the ship. He grinned profusely at Owen and smirked arrogantly at the General, "No, he is exact. Protocol will resume soon, several of our allies have been compromised. You have orders to surrender command of the *Naval Star* to the Alliance."

"Who the hell are you?" General Gray shouted, irritated and red at the man who smugly ordered his men to stand down. He wanted to leap over the consol and strangle the nearest man, Owen Dame.

"I am the envoy for the Alliance. You have failed to launch Protocol relinquishing your command to us," the man stripped the General of his ranks, unceremoniously, "Never trust a *half-breed* to do a job right."

Owen threw his hands in the air marching out of the command room to leave the General to his rampage. If this man knew what he was than his position had been compromised. There was nothing they could do now that the Alliance had received word of the invasion.

That is why you keep Protocol, arrogant bastards.

Yet again, the voice of the Ahzai mocked him in his failure.

"Anara was right to keep the secrets she had. If God only knew about the little demons running this project-" Owen muttered as he marched in his fit of fury.

"Which would include you, right?" Leaning against the irinoi wall in the hall staring out the little circular windows was Krypt, shaking his head, "How well do you know my Anara Kamen?"

Owen chuckled under his breath and rolled his eyes, motioning Krypt to follow, "Enough to know she isn't your wife and is well capable of taking care of her own flesh. I'm the one who arranged your *marriage* as I last recalled, just because you knocked her up with a son doesn't make her *yours*. We have other predicaments to discuss now. Walk with me."

Krypt replayed his words over making sure he had heard him right, "I have a son?"

Owen pursed his lips into a smirk as they walked down the hallway, "Ah, she didn't tell you. That does not shock me. Our Ms. Kamen has many secrets it would appear. Enough for Lukan to burn a treaty and invade Traverna and apparently enough for Damu and Zende to abduct her for whatever purpose that was meant for."

"Indeed," Krypt growled at the secrets and illusions. Not that he had been completely faithful to a false marriage, nor was he suppose to be allowed such a title being a Soldier, but damned if he felt that Anara was a possession and only he had right to keep her. That he deserved to know all things that involved the Ahzai woman. Right now, he cared for little more than a fifth of anything that would set his throat afire and drown his irritations—perhaps an easy lay would deal with the rest of his frustrations.

After Leigh had been… eaten, Krypt began to see the severed arm dangling from a thorny rope, *no, must not think of her now.*

They arrived in front of Owen's quarters and Krypt stopped at his door waiting for him to begin to speak, "When the operation Eyes of Prophets had been launched, the Supremacy of Government thought of a bright ideal to ally with the Alliance. If Protocol wasn't followed in instance of, oh, say an invasion, the *'space patrol'* would come and fix the leak. They want the Breach to be dust or as close to it as possible. They have this theory, 'Control at all cost.' We don't want that, now do we, Krypt?"

His words were like a snake and slithered like a worm through mud. Everything Owen said was thickly coated with assurance, and Krypt knew there was more to his ideals than mere matters of Control. Dame had wanted Control from the moment he first took breath and he was the reason the Soldiers journeyed to every Hell on the planet to find the Eyes.

No, they want Control over the planet, not for it to be dust, Krypt thought as he narrowed his eyes at the thought of Anara being on both their minds, "No, you don't want them to have Control over *her* dominion. Remember? Why couldn't she transport? Owen?"

"I would assume Damu did something to her to keep her from the leap," Owen sneered, "Back to my insinuations, the Alliance will use all means necessary," he closed his door when Krypt finally entered, "See, now that the Darken has given the Breach to the Hierarchy, bigger players will come out and play. The bid is far higher than before."

"How is it that your office is so well furnished? Planning on living here ahead of time?" Krypt took a seat on a velvet lounge chair and began shaking his head at the luxury of his suite, "Bigger players?"

Owen puzzled at Krypt's ignorance to what the universe held, "She really didn't tell you much, did she: evils and evil goods that fight in the name of good, half of that plus much more evolution and creation—who is the greater god? Which Hell will suit you best?"

Krypt placed his head in his palm listening to the reality of the world in the voice of a half-breed traitor, "I never believed in a god. Why should I believe in a Hell?"

Owen finally shook his head at the senseless conversation he was having. Either Krypt was playing dumb or the mortal truly was ignorant to reality, "If we blow up the Breach now, we lose the war."

...

The stars twinkled against such darkness that the sun dimmed as though it too was being drained of life. Some would believe that the only humans existing were only in this small cluster of stars and planets. Science knows better than to let such selfishness invade its strategic mind. Evolution wouldn't allow the living to rest without a sacrifice for Death.

The Naval Star only hovered over its native home with a sad glimmer of energy racing through its veins. Life scurried in and out of shielded windows with mechanical devices fluttering across its exterior armor. It wouldn't be long before all the movement would be silenced and the solar vessel would make for the nearest safe-haven for orders.

They would choose other sites to begin the process of evolution and create a new Eden. The crew of the Naval Star watched the red dome over Traverna, Eere View and Woke Free Base helplessly for six tormenting months. Hope faded away into a world of myth and dreams as the green and blues turned to black and red. There was a fog that filled the lucid sky within the dome blanketing the planet from the onlookers of space. No need to worry, they were not alone in such dark times. Closer and closer the black ships of a distant world neared their galaxy watching as shadows that light could not pass through: Watching the progress of their infection.

General Gray leaned against the table in the cafeteria considering what Krypt proposed, "Take back command of the Naval Star by murdering Eureof Grened?"

Kai Thareck made sure to remind them of the fact that not everything was lost, "The atom cannons didn't work because something controls the Old World's energy projection fields. The Darken are using our own technology against us. If we can get to the generators we can use the Waterhole to transport the surviving humans."

Krypt pretended that he hadn't heard Kai's optimism, "We could detain him until we know for sure that the Sector is not lost."

Kai intertwined his fingers in thought, staring unconsciously at the black coffee that sat still in a black cup with stars decorating the nearest Daeviti worlds.

"We don't have that luxury," Nathus leaned back against his metal chair locking his hands behind his head, "Our only hope would be that Bioni is alive to hit the kill switch or that Anara found a way into the dome."

Krypt smirked in considerable agreement, "There's always a luxury tax, that's what Anara always said. Isn't that right General Gray?"

"I need your crew on this ship," Gray rubbed his forehead as if the pressure would dissolve the pain, "Let's give him a chance to prove he's capable of carrying out the mission. Learn his intention."

"Assuming his mission is *just*," Kai narrowed his eyes at the old man, "He remains loyal to his own world, keep that in mind."

"We remain loyal to ours," Krypt narrowed his eyes at each Soldier who sat near them.

Nathus grunted with a small fragrance of anger, "That's a decision easy for you all to make, sit back, idol, while your own race is slaved and sent to other hells out of our reach. We should act now, not later."

Krypt agreed knowing what Nathus risked every day: they were all close friends, even brothers. Every one of them had family beneath the shield suffering if not dead. Their mission may have been a success but it failed in too many unpredictable ways. Like every war, both sides suffer casualties so much so that he was finding it hard to decide who was a terrorist and who was not.

The rules of the game, Anara had always told him, *they never change, only shift to the beat of new rules and loopholes.*

Krypt never understood why she was so cautious about every decision they had made together, even now he hesitated without her ghostly input.

"Time will only give the enemy the break they need to build a better defense or make a great escape. It won't be long before they take the war to the skies, the Breach left behind many defenses that if discovered by the Darken, can and will be used against us," Krypt summarized speaking into his made-graced hands as if praying for help from whoever would listen.

The General knew that was truth and he wouldn't and couldn't stop a mutiny if one should occur, "One week."

Krypt nodded staring at Nathus and the other men whose families weren't tucked away on the ever-reflecting sister ship *Isosa Merayne* waiting for transport to Dianan or Sektra. His own children were missing when they should have been transported to the holding ship with Owen and the rest of his crew. Kai had said that Mercy, Ana and Jon were right next to him when a light consumed both of them before they hit water.

Owen leaned against his chair relaxed and dazed from the long night that would haunt him over and over, until sleep no longer existed for his human half. Control had shifted from the humans to something worse, and it was not in his favor.

Mr. Dame rolled his pencil over a worn notebook with words unknown to the human language carved into the foreign, cerulean leather, "How much is the soul of one woman worth in this battle?"

Anara made sure to keep *His* origin silent—what was the importance of a single *Entity?*

Owen had always known that there was something she kept from him. Every time he was near her, his hair would stand leaving him shriveled and in need of either raping her or slitting her throat. Wisdom had always seemed to find itself stuck to her hips like a nursing child.

Read the Signs and the symbols will follow, she had snickered at him when he was stupid enough to ask. He rolled his eyes at the obvious grace of God and curse of gods.

Owen drew in a deep breath stretching his fingers over the spine of the notebook, "If God did not name you, what Entity did?" He opened a drawer and let the book drop into it in punishment for holding too many riddles and not sharing enough of its secrets with him, "Off to politic."

His cozy room echoed in mockery offering no rest for the wicked. A ship was meant to be his home whether by sea or by space, it held no love for him. The world seemed to dim as he walked through the corridors to the receiving quarters to welcome the Naval Star's new guests.

Grened smiled in appreciation for the conspiring beauty of his colleagues. Three women and a young servant boy entered the flight deck with only two guards dressed in black uniform. Beauty would be the last thing the male cared for, it was the powers underlying the flawless flesh. These were without a doubt the Kiinak of the Ahzai, "crowd control." The Breach

264

had not only been compromised to the Darken but they now surrendered to the Alliance and the humans didn't even see their enlisted enslavement.

"Attention crew! The Alliance has graciously joined us in the battle to regain control over the Breach. They have Summoned the most revered of the Daeviti universe to aid us in this battle. I would like to present the Kiinak Ahzai: Tarace Gruen, Estavve Fariale, and Stama Ureale," General Gray cleared his throat forcing as much respect as possible out, "Welcome to the Naval Star."

Krypt glared at Gray with his eyebrow raised at the formality the General expressed. Insidious, was the only word that echoed in his mind.

The bastard brings more bastards on board while the men and women of this ship live lives broken of their own kind, Krypt watched the women stand tall and alien before them all, *at least they are women, I will enjoy corrupting them. Mind controlling wenches or not, they are still wenches.*

Eureof decided to have a banquet with hopes of raising the moral of the crew: or rather to allow the Kiinak the opportunity to weed out the deceivers and threats to the Alliance. How a foreigner was supposed to excite them after taking over, was beyond Krypt's comprehension. He may have been human but he was still not one of them. Eureof was not born of the Breach.

Tarace smiled warmly at the men focusing on Krypt's table as he glared off pondering the next step to every day. Thought was all he knew since the moment he awoke in this world: everything was a calculation.

This world's on fire, it will burn you if you let it, Anara would remind him every time he forgot to send the taxes in or passed out drunk beneath the stars.

How could you blame me? The Night's sky is intoxicating out in the Wastelands.

"We are not so different," Tarace had whispered at him almost with enchantment.

Krypt exhaled calmly trying not to snap as he felt the Kiinak probe his mind like Anara had done so many times. Unlike the rest of the men on this ship that were not a part of his crew, Krypt had been trained to build the walls that would lock out assaults and invasions like the ones the Kiinak specialized in. He lived with the greatest Ahzai mentor in the universe: she taught him well.

"No, you are very different," he muttered with his eyes focused on his coffee.

The dark coffee began swirling and glistening the reflection of the Kiinak who spoke to him. Her reflection winked up at him with her rosy lips, blackened and parted in a smirk. Krypt grit his jaw forcing his mind to regain control over her tampering, if she toyed with his mind any longer, he wouldn't be able to tell a dream from reality.

Tarace smiled with a stern glitter in her eyes; forced and completely detached, "Come, Stama, let us refresh."

He drew a deep swallow of his black coffee watching them turn their narrow backs and waltz off to find their own people. He hated the Kiinak Ahzai as much as he respected the one Ahzai he trusted with his life. Krypt had always hated *unexpected* visitors.

Kai chuckled under his breath, shaking his head while swallowing his last swig of coffee, "Felt that too, man, felt that too."

...

Krypt glared out of the nearest window as their ship attempted to take to hyper-drive once again, "If space had a mountain, we would have leapt from Hell and back again by now."

Ever since the Alliance had seized control over the *Naval Star*, the space craft had become an unnerving nightmare. Even the rotors were ticking the wrong way, not to mention every Mechanic had been activated and forced to work every inch of the hull before they could even so much as attempt a hyper-drive. First signs of failure appeared right after the codes to unlock all drives were entered and then the destination coordinates refused to unlock for travel. The *Naval Star* tripped and stumbled, feeling like they had just jumped straight into a mountain.

Krypt watched as the stars refused to glitter into the telltale light-year travel passing by in seconds, "No, they twinkle sadistically, if not sarcastically, back at the entire ship, and soon, an entire fleet."

The more allies arrived to their aid, the more victims the numbing static entrapped. Entire fleets Summoned by the Alliance were snared into the orbit of the Breach. Nothing escaped, all transportation had been denied and none knew who controlled the block.

Space was once heaven in his mind. His body agreed on every level. His joints sang merriment as the arthritis became history and his migraines mellowed to a mere occasional ringing in his ears. The urge to strangle his ranking officers died down to the frequent daydream whenever he passed them by in the labyrinth of halls and during chow. Daeviti Laws could easily be forgotten in the silence of the darkness beyond the Breach's radiant clouds.

His only problem now was dealing with Owen Dame and the Alliance's very own Eureof Grened. Who was in many likenesses an older Owen Dame. It would appear that both Owen and Grened agree that it was in their best interest to save *Dame's* territory because the loss of it would affect the production of Control in the Antila provinces. That was far more important because they were far more ahead in the Project and Krypt knew that deep down it was just a ploy to jump-start the drive in the Soldiers: make them thirst for blood and they will believe anything the proper Superior whispered.

Krypt is a Soldier and fight was in his blood, so the battle for the Ursan Sun seemed theoretically logical considering the vengeance he, a Soldier, could reap.

That was before Grened became a commando, suicidal, genocidal alien. At this point in the game, Krypt wasn't even sure if the man was even considered human. He could bet his

Irinoi blade that the captain of this ship could change his appearance from typical human to serpentine demonic in the blink of an eye.

Krypt began working overtime with Owen; therefore he hadn't seen his own bunks in weeks. Owen lost his resolve when one fine day—or was it night? He woke shouting and cursing because he was—or wasn't dreaming about Anara.

General Gray rationalized that it was space dementia; "It is apparent that everyone is getting space dementia."

Then, the great General began seeing what he called 'angels' on the ship and they were telling him that; "It is time to water the gardens."

"On another note," he contradicted the man's insanity remembering, *vividly* remembering Anara's daughter waking to nightmares, screaming those same exact words; "*It's time to water the gardens!*"

Irony should be sin.

"Attention all crew: Order seventy-two-fifty-seven, shutters will be opened for eight hours. All report to stations and commence safety precautions; Data-log seven dash eight dash twenty-final."

Krypt rolled his eyes still refusing to comprehend the computer's need to mention the Data-log and what 'seven-eight-twenty-final' actually meant. He had never heard a data-log that sounded remotely like the ones he had to suffer through since first launch.

"A penny for your thoughts," a woman's voice sang out from behind him as he walked.

This was a voice that tickled his groin and purred through his mouth when he spoke back through memories of warm bunks and too much Black whiskey, "Kristun."

He couldn't place why he had become so formal with her, it was just sex.

Then, she held out a fifth of Black Starlyte with a grin, "Devil Juice?"

There were a few things he wanted to say in response to her enticement, "You're dorm is closer."

She grinned sheepishly and led him down the hall, turning right three times, and then a left. The next left turn lead them straight into, "Oliver."

Oliver Tommad Thisland was Kristun's ex-steady who was also one of Nathus' many seedlings. He stood about a half-foot shorter than Krypt and was about fifteen years younger, the same age as Kristun. It wasn't a secret that his ex was running from bunker to bunker, dorm to dorm, warming the beds of several, definitely more than a few Soldiers. It would only be a matter of time before Kristun and her friend, Jessika, made their way down to the Mechanic's halls. With so much time in such a confined space and nowhere to go: Sex was sex.

Oliver tipped his head and said not a word. In the beginning, he would roar and threaten a fight, the boy had spunk…that or balls of steel. Now, he just didn't try to acknowledge the girls. Sex was sex.

Krypt found respect for the boy, he was also a part of the few who wanted to get back to the Breach and destroy the Supremacy of Governments. He was a young Soldier.

They finally made it to Kristun's dorm (guys have bunks and ladies had dorms), she didn't waste any time pulling her shirt off and Krypt didn't waste any time ripping the cap off the Black Starlyte thinking: *gods save good whiskey and smite those who'd waste it—every drop counts.*

He watched as her breast, spilled out of the rim of her shirt and bounce on her ribs like balloons. Even now, he couldn't decide whether they were real or fake. Didn't matter, they tasted all the same when they're dipped in his demon juice. Krypt took a deep swig of the Black and begged for Dead Words. That was, not only his favorite but also the strongest brew—Dead Words. Got to give the girls attention, they knew what it took to get a bottle of Starlyte on this ship. It wasn't like they had a local brewery on board, and with Traverna fallen and encased beneath a shield, they wouldn't see the name brands for a very long time. Antila would be his last hope of drowning.

Whiskey was whiskey, damned the sex.

He pulled her into his arms—she was a good foot and a half shorter than him so he had to bend down to take her salty mouth into his. At least there was a spicy-pepper Black taste on the other side of those lips, the tongue tasted even sweeter. She nursed the kiss trailing her small hands down his chest to pull his shirt up over his head. Her lips following her hand's path down as she got to his buckle and pants, popping the button open and pulling them down just enough to let his 'dominate brain' breathe.

Salty lips, begets salty flavors. Krypt tilted his head back praising whatever gods there may be for creating evil and allowing whores to be born Soldiers and enlist.

Write your voice away to the Supremacy of Governments, replace it with my, Krypt started his Company's old motto and stopped to let the girl finish her good deeds. He came and still wasn't done. Where did the extra hard-on come from?

The door to the dorm opened as Jessika entered, pausing just long enough to let the sound of the door shutting echo in his ears. She grinned much like her friend, except she had a tooth that was crooked and yellowing from smoking Stardust, which was okay because he couldn't see much between the blur of the whiskey and the dim lights.

Yep, that's where that came from, Krypt thought as he watched her strip her shirt off and eyeball him like carrion for crows. All that was left for him to do was get plastered drunk and smell like woman with an ultra-hangover when he woke up.

Bastard, Krypt crinkled his eyebrows, waking with Kristun and Jessika entangled around him. Jessika still had her hand wrapped around his favorite tool.

"Was it good? Did that satisfy you?" Okay, it wasn't him hearing things. It was an odd voice made from the voice of every female he had ever met.

This is where the good Doc Bell diagnoses him with that space dementia, "What the-"

Jessika's hand began moving again, up and down, up and down. He blinked his eyes trying to sober up, and what do you know, he was ready to go another round.

"It wasn't even legit," Krypt went to push up as Jessika shifted and wrapped her lips around the tool again. The warmth of her mouth drowned out the voice invading his mind and he fell back against the pillow, for a moment, muttering "One more, just one last drop."

"Will you rip their hearts out like you have done to so many others?"

"Gods," Krypt whispered as Jessika quickened her movements, "She doesn't have a heart to give me anyways."

With that mutter, Kristun stirred and took his lips to her mouth. They tasted like woman, the salty, cream-filled kind. He relaxed back against the bed, and let them do their thing as the voice finally left him to his climax. Just as he would have finished, Jessika lifted from his side and straddled him. He growled with an agonizing moan.

Krypt sighed wondering if it was too good to be true, *what's a man suppose to do... open wide his mouth and let breakfast be served.*

"You should listen to her voice."

Shut up, Krypt thought to the voice.

It was silent inside his head while moaning and screaming entered his ears, but that was too good to be permanent.

"Dine with the Dead that ye shall know an eternity of sin."

...

Owen Dame stared annoyingly into the window of the ship's infirmary where the once wounded Nick Ansel stared hungrily back at him. Owen was nearly amazed at the species the man had molded into after being poisoned by a cannibal's dart on the Prison Islands. Every infection seemed to have resulted in a different species. Of course, Owen had the poison tested and retested on several other unwilling humans in search of not only a cure, but a reason. Dame assumed it was because the poison was meant to return the human form to its true form: primitive, determined and infinitely hungry. He also summed that it was created by a scientist that had gone off the grid on the Prison Islands long ago, one who might have created the native tribe there today.

Every man has a different ancestor, some ascended from beast of land, of water and that of air. The gods had a crude way of conceiving the race of man. That was the way of gods, to have an unsolvable riddle in the end. There had been many times where Owen concluded that the secret to becoming a god was to have a riddle that no one could solve. A secret unknown to anyone other than one's self. The thought of a tribe being capable of replicating a genetic decoder was baffling in his eyes. How could they create such a poison and put it to use on the tip of an arrow? Who had given them the technology to such a biological weapon?

His thought came to a simple resolution, "Evolution with a prick."

"Evolution has nothing to do with what has happened to my brother. How do we change him back into his human form?" Krypt tapped his knuckle on the glass window towards another victim fell to the Breach.

Owen shrugged scratching his neck as a cat would an irritating flea, "I would assume the same way a demon changes from beast to man. Since I am no demon and I've not mastered the way of man, we will just have to leave it in the capable hands of our genetics and research team."

"Make him a rat for that is all he is to them. Why does his eyes glow when he watches everyone pass this window?" Krypt cursed at this science with true hatred and conviction.

"He's hungry," Owen exhaled with a simple uncaring shrug, "I will assume that his true origin evolved from a predator. When he sees a meal, it excites him."

He turned and began walking away wanting Krypt to turn and retreat in the other direction: like fleas in his fur, the mortal followed itchingly. Krypt stuck to the half-breed's side knowing that this man had as many answers as the Alliance General Grened. Krypt knew he had a better chance at squeezing information out of Dame than the Alliance.

So nipping up to the bastard Owen Dame was what he would continue to do, "You should tell me something I don't know, save a breath of purified air or two."

Owen paused at the evolution of this human's curiosity, "Many Saviors have walked our planet, by-the-way. Daeviti worlds are like honey, all the bees and insects want in on it. Like a hive, in the center is its queen. Kill the queen and the hive will die, but let the queen live and the drones will strike you down with their own life."

"Are you a drone, Owen," the mortal raked his fingers through the white hair on his chin, "why does it feel like you speak of Anara?"

"Krypt, you must let her go, she leads a war that you can't hardly hope to keep up with. We can only hope that she chooses to return to the bright side of the universe when the lines have been laid—when the honey overflows the battlefields," Owen added in as an afterthought and walked away reassessing the board he currently meddled with.

Owen knew that once hope was drained and humanity lost, all that would remain is an Ahzai warrior overflowing and unclotted, seeking her source which slumbered in the heart of a planet that would wake with a hunger unlike anything breathing in this existence. She would become a shell for the will of Vessels…if he had read the journal right. It was only a matter of whether that world still slumbered with all the wandering souls being delivered from their corporeal temples and flung confusingly into the world of Nexum and Purgatory—praying for Death's Cradle.

"Why would a Reaper even try to keep up with the chaos of fleeting souls when the game advanced undefeated as it was?" Owen closed his eyes trying to imagine a world filled with peace, "Damned boring it would be."

...

Staring through a broken mirror of foreign eyes, the world crumbled at her pain. She clawed at her neck struggling to release the thought of choke and chain. Glistening bronze hair with tainted strands of burning red danced quietly around her exhausted body while her flesh burned from hellfire and scarred with torture. Her eyes held no emotion, only a furious hunger unknown to mortal existence. Dry lips split as to wait for their death, a satisfied expression accepting *Death* to her side. Anara had tasted the singe of the dark realm once before and the addiction remained intoxicating.

Anara tried pulling away with a hissing growl escaping her thin esophagus. The world around her blackened as her body turned cold, falling swiftly. She hit hard into boiling water as fire began to rage around her. Pain ripped through her flesh like dull daggers nicking quickly into her soul. Light, pure black light glowed in her eyes as a roar of rage chuckled out of her lips. Her skin peeled back as new flesh revealed with the glisten bondage of her temple. She screamed as power engulfed her body and an evil presence touched her soul. Her head tilted back savoring the touch of the fire, every lick that lusted to taste the glyph of her being.

The dark presence began caressing her tiny form and memorizing every new curve. Sniffing her metallic bladed hair and feeling its razor silkiness. It pulled her body closer to its own with a sadistic interest. She opened her eyes, pure golden pools of sin and power unknown glistened above a mocking smirk that wrapped ecstasy around her curling lips, devouring its toxic evil and tainting it with her own seductive freeze.

Then his blasphemous image cut through her pleasure as she pulled away from him, shaking her head in fury and disgust. The energy he offered willingly would consume her if she continued to manipulate it.

"Don't touch me! Where am I and what are you?" Anara's voice demanded the dark spirit before her, feeling the blasphemy that its evil expelled.

He chuckled at her absence of thought, "Now that was unthinkable, you have lost your memory in all that pain."

She looked around tilting her head as images of a little girl twinkled in the back of her head, a little girl with a young woman's voice and rusty-red hair flowing straight, down a slender back. Her eyes whispered of a coming storm on a dawning horizon.

"What is it that you see?" the dark beast whispered seductively.

Anara smirked at his curiosity, finding footing in all the chaos that swam through and around her, "I haven't forgotten who you are, foreigner. How does it feel to not be the only evil on a planet? They thought you posed a threat... ironic."

He shrugged and took a solid form of pure temptation. He wore no clothes bearing a solid body ripped with perfectly formed humanistic muscles. His eyes burned brimstone and desire with sin curving delicately demanding reddened lips.

She forced his image out of her sight listening only to his slithering seduction echo in the air.

He purred while admiring the specimen entrapped before him, "They have returned what was yours to begin with, I see. I see everything Anara. I saw you coming, I saw you *change*, I saw your birth, your death and rebirth. I saw you making love, I saw you being ripped to pieces. Literally ripped to pieces; completely soul shattering. I saw your heart break and crumble: your *mortal* heart that is."

He knows of the goddess, Anara fell silent, the world around her fell silent already willingly beating to her command, "How can you be so sure that you have seen all that there is to be seen, you who is imprisoned beneath fire and earth?"

"I saw you tap into my realm and fall, I saw you lust and sin, and I saw you become the worst enemy mortals and Immortals could have dreamt into being. I offered you a contract," he reminded with coy temptation.

The link between Heaven and Hell sounding so familiar to a deafening pound in her mind, "Perhaps that was all an illusion, and perhaps you are but an illusion. What business do you have with me?"

He disappeared leaving her in the dark fiery hell that pained her no more. He reappeared behind her. Nearly touching her, letting the energy he expelled caress her flesh leaving a trace of his essence on the surface of her image. She could feel his evil polluting her thought and emotion, seducing her primitive wants and desires.

"I want you to remember. I want you to rule. I want you to regain your powers and feed upon the Eden our *Father* has been creating. I want you to give birth to the ultimate war," a voice that echoed a mere whisper of authority, "I want you to *Control.*"

She mused, realizing what he had planned. Her voice was annoyed and tattered, "I can no more provide you with a Vessel anymore than I would give you ultimate havoc," a host for higher Entities could not house two Vessels in one temple at a time without destroying the fabrics of existence, "You seek the impossible. If you cannot do it for yourself, why should I offer the universe to you on a burning platter? What with the Others competing for the throne, those I am more loyal to that are not…not *you, a foreigner.*"

She peered deep into his eyes searching for the memory that would explain her contract with this conniving Fallen. The most loved and eternally shunned by the most Holy of Entities, Deities, the greatest of Creators that breathed upon a planet, that gave not only his first born, but sent his beloved Angels to save a condemned piece of rock and dirt. Why was this foul creature coming to her now when he could wreak infinite havoc on his own? He had no influence over the dark energies of the Breach or what was of the Daeviti Realm. She had opened the gate and it was up to him to face the demons of this world. What else was on her Contract?

His eyes began to form dark pools of ashen coal, deceptively giving off the impression of cool and content, but Anara knew better—he would burn your soul if you got too close, "You chose my realm. In doing so, I want you to Summon my freedom—it is but a simple task only a foreigner can do. All you need to do is kill a few demons of the Daeviti."

She narrowed her eyes and spoke in her home language, "Bai-et faed morda daeni-vae?"

Anara chuckled watching him fade into the raging fires. She knew that nothing could kill a true Demon. You could only hope to send it to the Nexum and pray it never broke free.

"What's a few dead demons to you?" The great evil mocked her words.

She already knew the answer to her question. Anara would act as a distraction while this condemned son of the most powerful and spiteful God in existence gathered his Legion and marched through the gates of his Hell onto the lands of man once again. He was predictable; all Demons are predictable when it comes to cruel intentions. There was a suffocating feeling plaguing her chest and spreading throughout her body. She could feel her nerves quiver at the thought of this demon walking amongst the living of the Daeviti Territory.

His voice became a sinful charm, "An *intervention.*"

Anara growled at what he asked for, the only way to distract the Holy of all the light and darkness so that he could plant his seeds of infection throughout the land, "You ask for Divine Intervention. Is there not enough evil on the land?"

"Enough of this, you must wake now," his mocking voice vibrating in already foreign eardrums, "I would suggest building a new body for the one you had before is…without head."

Anara's mouth dropped suddenly feeling the humorous truth to his words. Her body had been without a soul for some time now and she finally felt the disconnection. The blood in her veins began the slow stages of clotting and healing, the power of the goddess and her bloodline consumed her. Anara Starfallen laughed uncontrollably at the irony of this game. The insanity of her curse no longer existed for she had kissed death and journeyed to a Hell unknown to her hungry sister. Even more interesting and well played by this foreign devil was that…the Ahzai now had her Immortality back.

"Thou fallen the soul Discord in all her glory," Anara sang from the Book of Travelers, "Let me in, for I have come."

Anara was cast out from Hell and awaited patiently in labyrinths of Limbo while her body prepared her temple for her return.

32332558R00157

Made in the USA
Lexington, KY
16 May 2014